TITUS: A Comrade of the Cross.

A TALE OF THE CHRIST FOR THE CHRISTMAS-TIDE.

(REVISED EDITION.)

BY FLORENCE M. KINGSLEY.

David C. Cook Publishing Company, Elgin, Ill., and 36 Washington St., Chicago.

CHAPTER I.

ABOUT seventeen years before this story begins there was mourning in one of the most beautiful of the homes of Jerusalem. In the court of the household the servants were gathered about the great central fountain, some weeping loudly, some talking and gesticulating.

"We shall never, never see him again!" said an elderly woman, wringing her hands.

"He was such a darling—so sweet!" sobbed another, "and so beautiful, with his lovely eyes, and his cheeks red as a pomegranate."

"Oh, my David, my David!" wailed a fourth, sitting flat upon the ground, with her head upon the edge of the fountain, and her tears mingling with its waters—"who could have the heart to take thee from thy mother!"

"Thou knowest not everything," said an old woman.

"His mother will die!" said the woman who had spoken first. "I have it from Reba, her waiting-woman, that she hath gone from one fainting fit into another since she was told the child had been stolen."

"And Prisca gone too; dost think she stole the little one?"

"Nay, woman! Prisca loved the lad as her own life; she would never harm a hair of his head."

"I know that she loved him, but I fancy that she loved that beggarly Greek better. Dost think the Greek carried them both off?"

"How could he?" broke in another. "There was no way, had he been so minded."

"Thou knowest not everything," said an old woman, who had not spoken before. "I have it from master's own body-servant, Malchus, that the master caught the Greek talking to Prisca in the gateway once, and bade him begone. The man answered something in an unknown tongue, but with a bold look withal; the master gave command to have him seized and scourged, which was done forthwith. And a heavy scourging it was too, for he was a Gentile. That was ten days since, and now Prisca and the little David have both disappeared."

Here all the women broke out afresh into loud wailing and lamenting.

In the meantime a far more painful scene was passing in the interior of the palace. The sunshine was filtering through the branches of the trees, making wavering spots of brightness on the velvet sward. Roses, lilies and oleanders glowed in rich masses around the basins of marble fountains. Birds singing sweetly flitted here and there. Yet everything seemed sad and forsaken, for the mistress of all this beauty and splendor lay, white and grief-exhausted, on her couch in a shaded chamber. Near her, his face buried in his hands, sat her husband.

"No, Anna," he groaned, "I can get no trace of him. I have sent the servants in every direction; Malchus hath searched the city since early dawn; I myself sought all night. Yet will I find him!" he continued fiercely, springing up and pacing the chamber hurriedly. "It were too horrible a thing to endure patiently. May the God of Abraham witness that I will be avenged of this wrong! And yet who can be my enemy? Who would dare to steal David, the only son of Caiaphas? 'Tis some plot to make me pay moneys for his redemption. Yet would I pay—to the whole of my fortune. Oh, my son, my son!" And the unhappy father rent his garments, and lifting up his voice wept bitterly.

"Nay, my husband, do not despair," spoke the soft voice of Anna. "There is yet hope; he hath only been gone since yester-eve."

Yet as she spoke, the vision of her three-year-old darling rose before her, and she fancied him wailing for his mother; perhaps sick and lonely in some dark den of the city; perhaps dead. And her courage failed her, and she too wept bitterly, smothering her sobs, woman-like, lest she add to her husband's anguish.

And so the hours, heavy with sorrow, lengthened into days; and no tidings of the lost child. The days became weeks; still no word of hope. So passed away months; and the months, leaden-footed, became in their turn years. The wailing in the servants' quarters ceased; the symbols of mourning were laid aside; and nothing but the anguished look in the eyes of the mother told of the hidden sorrow—a sorrow more bitter than death.

No more children came to fill the house with play and laughter; and while the gentle Anna became sad indeed, and silent, Caiaphas, the master, grew by degrees gloomy, taciturn and of a temper not to be trifled with. Over the home once so gay and happy, lay a pall which could never be lifted.

Once at feast time, Anna fancied that she caught a glimpse of the missing Prisca. The woman held by the hand a boy of about ten years, dark-eyed, dark-haired, and with the color of a ripe pomegranate in his lips and cheeks. But before she could call a servant, the two had disappeared in the crowd, and could never be found, though Jerusalem was searched from wall to wall; and outside the walls also, among the pilgrims encamped there.

"Perhaps after all it was not Prisca," said Anna sadly to Caiaphas, as they sat in the garden at twilight. "I did not see her face, by reason of her veil. But the boy! Oh, my husband, he was so beautiful!" And bursting into tears, she hid her face on his arm.

"Nay, my brave wife, weep not. Am I not better to thee than many sons?" And so he strove to comfort her sore heart.

And again the empty years rolled on.

Sea of Galilee.

CHAPTER II.

THE day was closing; and night, doubly welcome in an almost tropical climate, was close at hand. Over the waters of the lake glowed a thousand tender colors, constantly shifting and melting the one into the other—gold, crimson, rose, and rare purples in the sky above, and again in the glassy water beneath, which reflected also the distant shores embowered in trees; while here and there the early lights in a white-walled villa, or distant village, twinkled starlike through the dark masses of foliage.

The surface of the water was alive with

craft of various kinds; some, standing out at a distance from the land with white and parti-colored sails, seemed endeavoring to catch the light breeze, which as yet scarcely ruffled the surface of the water; others, propelled by the oar, skimmed lightly about nearer the land. One standing on the shore could catch melodious snatches of song floating over the water, and the calls of the fishermen as they prepared to set forth for their night's work. In truth it was a fair spot, this lake of Gennesaret. And a fair city was Capernaum. Standing as it did near the head of this miniature sea, it carried on a busy trade with its neighbors. Ample warehouses, with wharves and clustered shipping, occupied the waterfront; while behind lay the town with its great synagogue, built of white and rose-tinted marble, its public buildings, squares and streets, stretching up to the base of a high range of mountainous hills, which swept like an amphitheatre about the lake.

On this particular evening a solitary fisherman was engaged in fastening his

He walked quickly away.

craft to the bank of a little creek, which emptied into the lake about half a mile from the city. The scene was a familiar one to him, and even the flashing glories of the sunset, now dying into a dim twilight, scarcely awakened more than an undefined sense of happiness. He was thinking chiefly of the fact that he was hungry. Stooping, he hastily shook the rude fastening to see that it was secure, then took from the bottom of the boat his net, and a number of fine fish, which he proceeded to string upon a twig plucked from a convenient tree.

As he walked quickly away, carrying his net over his shoulder, the fish swinging from his hand, he seemed rather more than a boy—a well-grown lad of perhaps nineteen years, well built, strong and muscular. A skin browned by exposure, black eyes under level black brows, jetty hair slightly curling, a nose curved like the beak of an eagle, and well-cut lips, made up a countenance of unusual strength and beauty. He was clothed in a single sleeveless garment of coarse white linen reaching to the knee; this was bound about at the waist with a girdle of some scarlet stuff, and from the girdle depended a primitive kind of pouch or wallet.

Ten minutes of brisk walking brought the lad to the outer wall of the city, where he found the watchman about to close the gates for the night. As he passed hurriedly through, one of the men hailed him:

" Ho, lad! Thou wert like to pass thy night outside the walls."

" And that were no matter," shouted the boy in return. " Many a night have I passed on the lake, as thou knowest; and mayhap I know another way to get in save through thy gate here." And he darted laughing away, as one of the men made a motion as though to seize him.

" Dost know the lad?" said one of the men to his comrade, who had joined in the boy's laugh with a low chuckle.

" Yes, I know him. His name is Titus—a bold fellow. He dwells near to the fish market with his father Dumachus. They call themselves fishers—" Here the man stopped and shrugged his shoulders.

" What meanest thou?" said the other idly.

But the gate-keeper was fastening the huge locks—with much puffing and straining, and many a smothered groan—and did not hear him; at least he did not answer; and his companion presently forgot that he had asked the question.

Meanwhile the lad was threading his way through the narrow streets, quite dark now by reason of the lofty walls on either side. Occasionally he would come out into a paved square or open space, where numerous small booths, lighted by flaming torches, proclaimed a market-place. At one of these booths he paused a moment and looked at its wares, which were displayed in flat baskets; there were cakes made with honey, dried figs and dates, small cheeses of goat's-milk, and various sweetmeats, together with nuts and fresh fruits of many kinds. After a moment's deliberation, he selected some delicate little cakes, which—wrapped in fresh green leaves by the obliging huckster —he bestowed in his wallet, paying for his purchase with a copper coin taken from a corner of the same receptacle. Then turn-

ing and making his way through the crowd which nearly filled the square, he plunged into a labyrinth of streets leading apparently into the meaner portion of the city, for the open spaces became smaller and less frequent, and the walls lower and more closely

The lad at the gate.

crowded together. Finally pausing before what dimly appeared as a doorway in the rough wall, he entered, and carefully closed the door behind him.

"Is that you, mother?" asked a feeble voice from the gloom within.

"No, Stephen boy; it is I. Where is the mother?"

"Nay, I know not," answered the voice querulously. "She went to the fountain for water, a long time ago, it seemeth to me, and I am parched with thirst and so hungry! Canst thou bring me out into the court, Titus?"

"Aye, lad, that can I, and give thee to drink also." And laying his fish and nets

upon the ground, he crossed the court, now plainly revealed by the moonlight which flooded the heavens.

At one side of the little yard appeared a dark opening from which was looped back a leathern curtain. Stooping a little, Titus entered, and immediately came out again bearing in his arms a figure, which he tenderly deposited on a pile of nets.

"There, Stephen boy, see the moon, how bright it is; and here is water, albeit not so fresh and cool as the mother will fetch thee presently." And Titus poured out, from a small skin bottle or gurglet, water into a cup, which he handed to the lad on the nets.

The latter seemed scarcely more than a child, so small and shrunken was his figure; and as he moved painfully to take the water, it appeared that he was cruelly deformed and misshapen. But his face, as the bright moonlight fell upon it, was, despite its pallor and emaciation, beautiful, for the features were delicately shapen, while the light golden hair, fine and curling, made an aureole about the brow, from beneath which shone wonderful dark eyes.

"Truly the water hath a foul taste, but it hath wet my tongue and moistened my throat, and that is a blessing. I am glad that thou art come, Titus, for now I can go upon the roof. This day hath been a heavy one, and my back hath hurt me cruelly."

While the sick boy was speaking in his weak, fretful voice, Titus had been busily engaged in building a small fire; and presently the fish hanging from a stick began to splutter in the heat, while an appetizing odor stole out upon the air.

"Cheer up, Stephen lad!" Titus was saying, as he made his preparations for the simple meal. "I have a fine treat for thee in my wallet here."

Stephen's eyes brightened, as he lay quietly watching the flickering flames. "Is it something that I can give to the baby?" he asked presently.

"It will suit the baby rarely," said Titus, laughing. "I had him in mind when I picked out this particular dainty at the good Justin's stall. But thou must not give it all to the baby; thou must thyself eat."

"Yes, I will eat," replied Stephen contentedly. "But, Titus, I love to see the little one when I give him a cake. He is sweeter than the sweetest of Justin's dainties. Hark! I think I hear him now!" And raising himself on one elbow, the lad listened intently.

Titus likewise paused a moment in his culinary operations, and the sound of a baby's gurgling laughter, and sweet broken talk, floated down from a neighboring housetop.

"Ah, the young rascal!" said Titus. "He waxeth a bold fellow."

"Yes, truly," said Stephen eagerly. "Last night he clambered over the parapet between our two roofs, and came running quite alone to me. He loves me," he added in a tone expressive of deep conviction.

"He loves sweets, that is certain," answered Titus, laughing. "But here is the mother at last," he added, looking toward the doorway.

A tall figure, heavily draped, and bearing on her head a water-pot, at this moment entered the courtyard.

"Where hast thou been, mother?" demanded Stephen. "Thou did leave me at sunset, and I had been dead of thirst by this time, but for my Titus, who gave me a sorry draught indeed—but better than none at all —from the gurglet."

The woman let down the jar from off her head, and hastily poured a cup of water for the child, saying in a soothing tone as she did so:

"Nay, thou shouldst not chide thy mother, child; 'tis unseemly. But the time at the fountain did pass swiftly enough, by reason of the marvelous things which I heard. There was a great crowd there, and I had to wait my turn. The good Jocunda, our neighbor, had the tale from her husband; he heard it in the market-place. All Capernaum is ringing with the wonder of—"

"Let us have supper first," interrupted Titus, "for the child is faint with hunger, and I am well-nigh starving. We will have that marvelous tale of thine later."

So saying, he took the fish from the fire, while Prisca—for such was the woman's name—hastened to bring the thin cakes of bread, which served the treble use of dishes, napkins and food. For tearing the tough, thin cake into large fragments, she gave to each a liberal portion, while Titus broke up and distributed the broiled fish in the same way. Laying the fish on the piece of bread, each of the humble party proceeded to break and eat alternately from the fish and the bread, finishing by wiping their fingers upon the bread, and tossing the fragments to the dog, which made short work of the clearing up.

Titus ate heartily, with appetite sharpened by youth and long abstinence, finishing his meal with a draught of water from the jar which stood close at hand.

"Now, Stephen lad," he exclaimed, "I feel like a new man. Would that thou couldst

"Here he is!"

eat more than a bird; but thou shalt have the cakes now."

"Nay, Titus, carry me up first. I will have my cakes on the roof."

"Wait, lad, till I take up thy bed; thou'lt sleep better up there in the cool air." Saying which, Titus disappeared again into the dark interior of the house, emerging presently therefrom, bearing on his shoulder a small roll.

"I will fetch thee when I have spread down thy rug," he said, as he rapidly ascended a rude ladder-like stairway, which led from the courtyard up the outside of the house to the roof.

Down again he came quickly, whistling gayly, and lifting the helpless Stephen carefully from the pile of nets, on which he still lay, bore him steadily up the stairs on to the flat top of the roof. Here in the shelter of the rude parapet which surrounded the edge, he laid his burden down on the little pallet.

The boy drew a long breath as he gazed into the glorious sky now fully spread out above him. The moon was sailing high in the heavens, while here and there glowed dimly certain bright stars which even its full-orbed splendor could not quench. A light breeze from the lake blew gently over the city. Behind loomed up the dark masses of the hills.

"Ah, my Titus!" sighed the boy, "I could not live were it not for the nights. I loathe the days, down there behind that hateful curtain, with nothing to do, and often no one to talk to. And when father is here—" The boy stopped and shuddered slightly. Then another thought struck him. Raising himself on one elbow, he called in a gentle voice, "Gogo, here's Stephen! Gogo!"

A little gurgle of delighted laughter, and a woman's voice from the adjoining roof said,—

"Here he is!" lifting, as she spoke, over the low parapet which divided the two buildings, a small naked figure, which toddled unsteadily on its tiny dimpled feet, to the spot where Stephen was lying, watching his approach with delighted smiles.

"See, Titus, how well he walks! The darling! Come here to Stephen, Gogo; I have some cakes for thee."

At this magic word, the baby broke into a staggering run, which would have ended disastrously had not Titus, who was watching the scene, caught him up and conveyed him with a single stride to the would-be haven. There he nestled down beside Stephen with cooing, unintelligible words, which seemed to afford the lad the greatest satisfaction.

"The little beggar!" said Titus. "He is thinking of cakes."

Opening his wallet, he produced the dainties in question, somewhat damaged by the heat, it is true, but received with tokens of a lively joy by the two on the rug.

"Is thy mother with thee?" again spoke the woman from the adjoining roof.

"Not yet, good neighbor," said Titus. "But she will come soon, when she hath put things to rights below."

Even as he spoke the tall figure of Prisca was seen coming up the stairway.

"Good-evening to thee, neighbor," she said, spying the figure of the other woman. "Come over and I will tell thee the tale which I heard at the fountain."

"Meanest thou of the wonder-working stranger who hath come to our city? I too have heard of him," replied the other, stepping over the low boundary between the roofs.

Then the two, seating themselves with their backs against the parapet, prepared for a comfortable gossip.

CHAPTER III.

WHEN I went to the fountain to-night at sunset to fetch water," began Prisca, "many were there before me, and I was forced to wait; so I sat me down on one of the stone benches to rest; for in truth the heat to-day hath been burdensome. Then said one of the women, 'And what sayest thou, good Prisca, to these marvels?' 'What marvels?' I answered, for I had heard nothing of note. 'Concerning the man from Judea,' she answered. 'Hast thou not heard? Thou art a keeper at home and therefore to be praised; but know that a great worker of miracles, the like of which hath never before been heard of since the days of the gods on Parnassus—or, as the Jewish women say, since the days of their Moses, who brought them out of the land of Egypt.'"

"What is the nation of the man?" interrupted the other woman.

"Said I not that he was a Jew?" answered Prisca.

"Nay, nay," replied the other; "but that he came from Judea."

"Well, now that I bethink me," said Prisca, "Jocunda said that he had always lived in Nazareth near by; but I had Judea in my mind, because he hath just come from there, and at Jerusalem hath worked many wonders of late."

" What wonders worked he in Jerusalem, mother?" asked Stephen, who had hitherto been too much occupied with the fascinating Gogo to pay much attention to the conversation of the women.

" Great miracles of healing wrought he," replied his mother. " They do say that he hath opened the eyes of the blind, healed sick folk of all manner of evil diseases, and even cured cripples like to thee, my poor Stephen!"

Stephen clutched the baby, who lay half asleep in his arms, close in his excitement, but he only said:

" Go on, mother; tell it all."

" Now, mother, believest thou this idle talk? Thou art forever hearing of wonders from the gossips at the fountain," said Titus, who had observed Stephen's suppressed excitement, and guessed its cause.

" 'Tis not idle talk," said Prisca indignantly. " Knowest thou the worshipful Asa, who lives in the great house near to the lake?"

" Yes," said Titus briefly; " he serves Herod Antipas."

" Well," went on Prisca, " know, then, that his only son lay grievously ill of the fever; all the doctors had given him up to die, and his mother and father were wellnigh distracted with grief. His father had heard these idle tales, as thou callest them, and he believed them; insomuch that he set forth himself to see Jesus—for so is the Nazarene called—and meeting him at Cana, he besought him for his son. The Nazarene told him to depart in peace, that his son would live. And, lo! as he returned, he met servants coming to meet him, who told him that the lad was recovering, and that he began to mend at the very hour when the Healer promised it to his father."

" 'Tis true," said the other woman. " For one of the servants who went to meet the father is of kin to my husband; and we had the tale from him."

" Well, then," said Titus stubbornly, " 'tis likely that he would have recovered anyway. Thou knowest that not all die who have fever. I had it myself, and lived."

" Nay, lad," replied the woman, who was called Adah; " but this young man could not have lived; he had the black spots on his body, which come only when death is certain. Our kinsman helped care for him; he saw it with his own eyes. And at an hour when all thought him breathing his last, he suddenly opened his eyes and asked for water; and when he had drunken deeply of it, he turned and slept—slept like my baby here—and wakened wholly restored. 'Tis a true miracle."

" It hath a wonderful sound," said Titus. " What else hath he done?"

" There was a tale from Cana last year, which my husband heard in the marketplace, but I know not whether it be true," said Adah cautiously. " But 'tis reported that at a wedding party there, of one of his own kinsfolk, the wine ran short; and when his mother spoke to him of it, he caused them to fill many great water-pots with water, and at a word changed the water into the best wine. The man who told my husband said that he knew the people, and that they gave him a gurglet of the wine. As I say, I know not whether this tale be true; but about the son of Asa, I do know."

" How worketh he the cures?" asked Stephen.

" Nay, I know not; 'tis magic," replied the woman. " They say that he teacheth strange things also. 'Tis whispered among the Jews that he is one of their great prophets come to life again."

" Is he here now, in this city?" asked Stephen, his voice trembling slightly.

" I know not," answered his mother. " But the women at the fountain said that he was coming."

" Do you suppose, mother," said the boy in a low, faltering voice, " that if he comes, he could heal me?"

" Nay, lad, think not of it; 'twill only bring thee fresh misery," broke in Titus harshly. " If these tales be true, 'tis likely that he would heal only the rich and the great, like young Judah, Asa's son; or at any rate, being a Jew, he would only despise heathen Greeks, like us. All the Jews hate us," he continued, grinding his teeth. " One spat on me yesterday when I drew my net too near him in landing. I could have killed him! Aye, and I will kill him, if he dares to do it again."

" I hate the Jews, too!" observed Adah. " But 'tis certain that this Jew doth not mind the rich only, for of the cures at Jerusalem they say that the greater part were of mere beggars; and thou knowest many of the beggars of Jerusalem are foreign-born."

" When he comes, if he doth come, my Stephen, I will see him for thee. There is nothing I would not do, to see thee well and strong, my son," exclaimed Prisca with a passionate sob.

"Hark!" exclaimed Titus. "I hear some one coming!"

All were silent for a moment, and the sound of harsh voices and loud laughter was heard in the street below. Then the door of the little courtyard was thrown wide open, and ten or a dozen men entered the enclosure.

"'Tis Dumachus!" said Titus briefly.

"I must go home," said Adah, rising hastily; and catching up her sleeping babe from his snug resting-place on Stephen's arm, she wrapped him in a fold of her ample garment, and stepping over the parapet, was quickly lost to view.

"Ho, Prisca, woman! Where art thou?" called one of the men from the court.

"I am here, my husband," meekly answered Prisca, beginning to descend the stairway as she spoke.

"Come along then. Get us food and drink quickly; we are famished and not disposed to wait patiently," answered the man roughly.

"Keep thou quiet," whispered Titus to Stephen, who had shrunk into a frightened heap on his bed at the first sound of the man's voice, "and I will go and help the mother. Nay,"—as the boy held a fold of his garment in a nervous grasp—"he shall not touch thee. They will eat and drink, then sleep, or go away again for a fresh carouse in the town. Let me go, lad."

Then he too hurried down into the yard below, leaving the trembling Stephen alone.

"So thou'rt here, boy?" said Dumachus, as he spied Titus on the stair. "Hurry thy stupid feet, and fetch us some wine quickly!"

Titus obeyed, bringing a skin of wine and filling the cups which the men held out.

"'Tis a vile draught!" roared one of the men, spitting on the ground.

"Thou hast the flavor of the wine-skin we took yesterday from that portly merchant in Samaria still lurking in thy gullet," said another, chuckling.

"A pretty fellow he was; and how lustily he roared for help, when we overhauled his belongings!"

"He'll make no more disturbance in those parts, nor elsewhere, I'll warrant!" growled another.

"Aye, we quieted him, as we have many a better one," said the man Dumachus, with a great laugh. "Titus, lad, thou didst miss some rare sport, when thou didst choose to stay at home this time."

"Nay, I did not choose!" answered Titus hotly. "I was on the lake fishing, at thy command; when I came back, thou hadst gone, I knew not where."

"'Tis true, boy," answered Dumachus good-humoredly. "We gave thee the slip; we had business on hand that thou shalt know anon. Thou'rt quite a lad, and shalt have thy fill of booty before long."

"I care not for the booty," said Titus, his great black eyes flashing fiercely, "but I love the fighting, especially when we fight the Jews."

This speech was received with a great burst of laughter from all the men.

"Thou hast a rare pupil in that boy," said one of them, nudging Dumachus.

At this juncture, Prisca interrupted the conversation with the announcement that supper was ready. Immediately all fell to eating ravenously, and little was heard in the place save an occasional hoarse request for drink from one and another of the brutal group. Presently, the edge of their hunger being blunted, the wine began to circulate freely.

"Thou sayest that the man is here?" said one, between great gulps from the cup.

"He is here. And multitudes followed him into the city. To-morrow we shall have rare doings in Capernaum."

"Rare doings, indeed!" put in another.

"I had it from Blastus himself, that at feast time, when he was in Jerusalem, people ran out into the streets to see him pass, and followed after him, leaving their doors wide open. No end of booty was secured. The people seemed stark mad."

"Let them be mad," said Dumachus with a chuckle. "The madder the better for us. In truth, I saw a wonder there, myself. A beggar who had lain for years near the corner of the market—half blind, lame, and covered with loathly sores—when he heard the man was coming his way, shrieked out, 'Jesus, thou son of David! have mercy on me!' and the man touched him, and, lo! the beggar sprang up and walked."

"If he doeth such wonders here," quoth another, "we shall see the city in an uproar."

"True, my Gestas," replied Dumachus. "May Jove help him! But what think you of the man? Some say he is Elias,—though, truth to tell, I know him not; others say one of the prophets of the Jews. But no one knows of a certainty. He hath followers enough to raise an insurrection already."

"Let it come, say I!" shouted another. "War will break up the rule of these Romans; dost remember how they caught and crucified some of our best men last year? I hate the law!"

These words were greeted with a wild cheer, which Dumachus sternly repressed. "Fools!" he said. "If we be caught here, we are like rats in a trap!"

It was now close upon midnight; and gradually the talk died away, as one after another fell off to sleep, announcing the fact with loud snores.

About one o'clock, Prisca crept wearily up the little stairway to the roof, where she found Stephen wide awake, his eyes shining like stars.

"Oh, mother," he whispered, "I heard what they said about him. He is here!"

"Yes, my Stephen, he is here, and thou shalt see him." Then bidding the child sleep, she lay down near him, and composed herself also.

But long after Stephen's regular breathing told the mother that her darling slept, she lay open-eyed, thinking of the time when he was strong and beautiful, and of the awful blow on his delicate spine which had made him the shapeless cripple that he was. And in her heart she hated the brute called Dumachus.

CHAPTER IV.

HE next morning Stephen awoke to find himself in the room behind the hated leathern curtain. He had slept heavily and late; and as he rubbed his eyes sleepily, and looked about him in the semi-darkness, he became aware that he was alone.

"Father and the men are gone, and I am glad," he said to himself. "Titus is fishing—at least, I hope he is—and mother is at the fountain."

The room in which he lay was very much like those of the humbler sort in the East to-day. It was, in fact, the house—there being only the one apartment. The walls of rough stone, plastered with clay, were windowless, and over the one door hung the aforementioned flap of leather. This was torn in several places, and admitted here and there two or three dazzling sunbeams, which afforded Stephen some faint satisfaction, for by means of them he could guess a little at the time, which at best dragged heavily enough. When the yellow shafts of light rested on the wall opposite the door, lighting up the shapeless, smoke-blackened wineskins which hung there, then it was three hours before noon. As the sun climbed higher in the heavens, the sunbeams descended from the wall and lay upon the floor —yellow pools of light, and cheerful to behold, though they rested upon a wretched floor of dried mud. When they disappeared towards noon, Stephen felt a daily sense of loss, which nevertheless always gave way to a lively satisfaction, when he reflected that presently night would come. Night brought Titus, and the long, cool hours on the house-top, and best of all an hour of play with Gogo.

He fell to thinking of Gogo now, as he lay idly watching the motes which danced in the yellow shaft of sunlight. How smooth and dimpled his little hands were—like rose-leaves, Stephen thought; how straight and strong and rounded his little limbs. And then his beautiful eyes—golden-brown, with such long, curling lashes—and the rings of golden hair, half covering the tiny pink ears. And was not his voice sweeter than any bird's, and his teeth like little pearls!

"Nay," said Stephen aloud, as he finished cataloguing these varied charms, "there is no baby in the world like Gogo!"

At this point in his meditations some one raised the leathern flap and entered the room. It was Prisca.

"Hast thou fetched the water, mother?" said Stephen, half raising himself.

"Nay, child, I have not been to the fountain yet." And turning her back hastily, Prisca made a suspicious sound as if she were choking down a sob.

"What ails thee, mother?" queried Stephen, too much accustomed to see his mother in tears to be especially alarmed. "Hath father been beating thee again?"

"No, no, child! Father and all the rest went away before daybreak, and Titus with them. It is not that; but oh, how can I tell thee!" And here Prisca broke down completely and sobbed aloud.

"What is it? Do tell me, mother!" said Stephen, now thoroughly frightened.

"Well—I suppose I must tell thee," said Prisca reluctantly. "But I fain would spare thee, my poor boy, thou hast so much to bear. Our neighbor came early this morning to call me—the baby—" And here the woman wept again, covering her eyes with her hands, as if to shut out some painful sight.

"The baby!" exclaimed Stephen in an agony of impatience. "Oh, tell me, is he dead?"

"No, no! I only wish that he was, for then he were out of his pain. This morning, Adah told me, she wakened suddenly—she was sleeping on the roof and the baby with her—by the sound of a heavy fall in the courtyard below; in a moment she saw that the baby was gone, and running to the edge of the parapet, she saw—" and again Prisca covered her eyes with her hands. "Yes," she went on, in a broken voice, "the little fellow had wakened up early, as all babies do, and had crawled to the edge of the roof; in one place the ledge is broken away and he had fallen on to the stones below. He is frightfully hurt. He cannot live the day out. Thank the gods for that! But I must go back and stay with her, though 'tis little I can do to help."

Stephen had heard this frightful tale in silence. But now as his mother looked at him, she saw his face white and drawn.

"I cannot bear it, mother!" he gasped huskily.

His mother was frightened by his look and words. "Oh, Stephen!" she cried, "thou'lt break my heart! Thou art my baby and all I have! Thou must bear it, lad, for my sake. I will not go back; I will stay with thee."

"No, no!" wailed Stephen, "go back; thou mightest do something to ease him. Go quickly!"

Prisca hastily placed some bread and dried fruit, with a small gurglet of water, near the lad, and went quickly away, saying, as she left the room:

"I will come back soon, if there be a change."

For a few moments after she had gone, Stephen lay as if stunned. His baby! His Gogo—crushed and bleeding! Could he never see him again? Oh, those little hands! —never again would he feel them like rose-leaves on his cheek! Those little feet—never to walk again!

"I cannot bear it!" he cried, and again and again, "I cannot bear it!"

Presently into his brain, half-crazed with suffering, flashed the remembrance of the Nazarene. "He is here—not far away. He could heal him. Oh, if mother would only come back! She could find him. But she is not here! She will not come! Perhaps he is dying even now! If only I could walk! I can crawl—a little. I will try. I must try. I must do something to help! Oh, my Gogo! my Gogo!"

The boy had taken a desperate resolution. It was true that he could crawl a little; but of late the exertion had caused such an aggravation of his malady, that his mother had forbidden it.

Slowly he let himself down from the raised platform—which occupied one end of the room and on which the family slept—to the earthen floor beneath, every movement causing the most exquisite anguish in his injured back; but he persevered, and at length reached the door. Then came the painful journey across the courtyard. Suppose that he could not open the door that led to the street! It was a terrible thought. Great drops started out on the boy's forehead.

A few feet more and the door was reached. It was unlatched. Prisca in her sorrowful haste had forgotten to close it after her. Stephen pushed it boldly open, and in another moment was in the street. Here he paused to reflect; at the end of the street was a market-place.

"I must go there," he thought. "I must find him before long, or it will be too late."

The street in which he lay was so narrow, that one standing in the middle of it, could touch the walls on either side. There were no windows. No one was visible. Which way was the market? He did not know. It surely must be toward the lake.

"I will go this way," he said aloud; and nerving himself for the effort, he crept painfully down the street. The stifling yellow dust almost strangled him; the small, flinty stones cut his limbs, and the burning sun beat down fiercely on his uncovered head.

Presently he stopped. His heart beat thick and painfully; black spots floated before his eyes; but he could see that the market-place was not far off. Already he could catch the hum of voices—or was it but the roaring in his ears? Another effort—an agonizing one this time—and the lad found himself at the corner of the street. He had succeeded in reaching the market-place. There were the booths with many things—principally fish—spread out thereon, just as he remembered it when Titus had once carried him to see it, a long time ago. There were many people there, buying and selling, but no one who looked like the wonderful Nazarene. No one noticed the poor little figure, lying there in the dust. One man, it is true, nearly stepped on him, as he hurried along with a huge basket of fish on his head; but he only muttered something in an angry tone about beggar brats, and passed on.

Stephen's misery increased with every passing moment. The pain in his back was well-nigh unbearable; he was burning up with thirst, and faint with hunger. Still he strained his gaze eagerly after every passer-by, with a hope which ever grew dimmer. Presently, he saw with terror that two or three of the fierce, half-wild dogs of the town were sniffing about him. He shrieked aloud, and covering his eyes with his arm, screamed frantically:

" Mother! Mother!"

In the midst of his agony, he became aware that some one was speaking to him. He looked up, and saw, standing between him and the blinding glare of the sun, a man. To Stephen, lying prone in the dust, he looked very tall. This the boy saw; yet it was something else which hushed his sobs, and caused him to look upon this man with breathless awe—that face of mysterious beauty; those wonderful eyes—deep, tender, unfathomable. It could be no other than Jesus! Gogo was saved!

With a cry of joy, Stephen raised himself, and with hands clasped and eyes still fastened on the stranger, half whispered:

" Thou art Jesus—he that healeth! I know it! Thou canst save my baby! He fell from the roof and is crushed and dying."

A beautiful smile dawned in the stranger's eyes, and lifting his face towards heaven, he said:

" I thank thee, O my Father, that thou hast hid these things from the wise and prudent, and hast revealed them unto babes." Then looking again upon Stephen with a tender, compassionate gaze, which comprehended all his weakness and deformity, he laid his hand gently on the boy's head.

" According to thy faith, be it unto thee. Go in peace."

And, lo! under that blessed touch the boy felt all weariness, all pain, all weakness, pass away; and with a cry of exceeding great joy, he arose from the ground perfectly healed.

" Blessed," indeed, " are the merciful; for they shall obtain mercy."

CHAPTER V.

HE short summer night was almost past. The moon had set an hour ago; the stars were melting away into dimness; while in the east a faint, rosy glimmer showed that dawn was at hand. Over the surface of the water a cool wind was blowing, which caused two fishing-boats well out from the land to roll heavily. The occupants of one of these boats were busily engaged in hauling in and examining their fishing nets; yard after yard of the net came in dripping and glittering, with but here and there a little fish caught in the meshes.

" We may as well stop for to-night," exclaimed one of the men impatiently, throwing the last fish overboard.

" I told thee," said his companion, " that with the wind in this quarter we might as well bide at home. Hail the other boat, Simon. It may be that they have something."

The last yard of the net having been hauled in by this time, Simon stood up in the bow of the boat and called, making a trumpet of his two hands. Presently came back a faint answer.

" Hast caught anything?" shouted Simon, with all the strength of his strong lungs.

" No," came back the reply.

" 'Tis as I said," observed the other, who was named Andrew. " Let us hoist sail and make for home. We can cast again in the bay near the city; we sometimes get a good haul there, when not a fin is to be seen anywhere else."

In less time than it takes to tell it, the anchor was hauled aboard, and the great wing-like sail raised. As it caught the fresh breeze, and the somewhat clumsy craft began to move smoothly through the water, the two sat down in the stern, Simon grasping the tiller.

" Canst see what the others are doing, Andrew?" he inquired.

" They are raising their sail," he answered.

" They also are weary," said Simon, in a somewhat absent tone. Then he continued: " Dost know what has been in my mind as we toiled in the night?"

" How could I?" replied Andrew. " Thou hast hardly spoken, and that were a marvel

there be whispers against him of late? He is not of the Pharisees, nor yet of the Scribes. And in truth, he doth strangely set aside many of their laws and customs."

" I know," said Andrew solemnly, " what John said of him. He said it twice in my hearing, before the baptism in the Jordan, and again afterward; 'twas this: ' Behold the Lamb of God.' John believeth him to be the Christ. Perhaps thou art right, Simon, about the fishing. If what John Baptist saith be true, and he is indeed the Christ, we ought to be with him where he is. And now John lieth in prison, and we cannot tell what may befall him there. May Jehovah grant that Herod cast not his evil eye upon the Master."

" Amen!" said Simon fervently.

After t h i s a little silence fell between the two, broken only by the sound of the green water as it swirled away behind the rudder in a long, f r o t h y wake. The dawn was brightening momently now, and all the solemn pomp of sunrise

Ruins of Tel-Hum, site of Capernaum.

for thee, who art somewhat free of speech."

" I have been thinking of the Nazarene all the night through," said Simon. " I care not for the fishing now, whether our catch be good or bad; I would fain be with him. Hast thou thought of the marvel of it all? Perchance we have lighted on strange times; perhaps it were best that we give up the fishing for good and all."

" Give up the fishing!" quoth Andrew in surprise. " How can we do that?"

" Why," replied the other, " we have ‘enough and to spare; the vineyard beareth well now, and the women are frugal. We do not need the money. If we give up the fishing, we could be with him all the while."

" But, brother," said Andrew, " doth he want us?"

" Nay, I know not. But I think that he needeth some one. Knowest thou not that

beginning behind the great blue hills on the eastern horizon. Before them, seen dimly through the morning mists, rose the towers and walls of fair Capernaum.

As the boats drew near the shore, it could be seen that many people were congregated there, some sitting on the rocks, others walking about—not an unusual sight, for it was the wont of all to rise early so that business might be well over before the heat of the day began. Still there seemed to be something more than the incoming fishing boats to attract so many.

" Seest thou yonder crowd? What dost thou make of it?" asked Andrew.

Simon was silent for a moment, then he answered eagerly, " 'Tis he, the Master; and the people throng him to hear him speak. Let us make haste!" And being now quite close to the shore, he sprang into the water, and pulling the boat after him, quickly made it fast, Andrew following him more slowly.

Meanwhile the other boat, not far behind, and also light because of its emptiness, had been drawn up; and the men in it, dragging their nets behind them, came also to the shore.

When Jesus saw Simon, and Andrew, and the others, and their boats empty, after all the night's toil, he entered into one of the ships, which was Simon's, and prayed him that he would thrust out a little from the land. Then he sat down and taught the people out of the ship.

We may not know what he said that summer morning, so long ago; but we know that he spoke of the things of God. And as he sat there in the shadow of the great sail, his voice sounding clear and sweet across the little space of water which separated him from his hearers, healing fell on many a bleeding heart; children stretched out their tiny hands towards him; and love, stronger than death itself, sprang up beautiful and mighty in many a soul.

Among those who stood on the very water's edge, were two women, one bearing in her arms a rosy babe; with them was a lad of about fourteen, with light golden hair, and great dark eyes. When Jesus had ended his speaking, this lad clasped his hands, and looking at him with a face like that of an angel, murmured:

"Thou that healest, I love thee! I love thee!"

It was Stephen.

Now when the Master had done speaking to the people, he turned to Simon, who, with Andrew, was with him in the boat, and said: "Launch out now into the deep, and let down your nets for a draught."

And Simon answering said unto him, "Master, we have toiled all the night, and have taken nothing; nevertheless at thy word I will let down the net. And when they had this done, they enclosed a great multitude of fishes, so that their net brake. And they beckoned to their partners which were in the other ship, that they should come and help them. And they came, and filled both the ships, so that they began to sink. When Simon Peter saw it, he fell down at Jesus' knees, saying, Depart from me! for I am a sinful man, O Lord! For he was astonished, and all they that were with him, at the draught of the fishes which they had taken. And Jesus said unto Simon, Fear not; from henceforth thou shalt catch men. And when they had brought their ships to land, they forsook all and followed him."

Night again; and with it peace. Far below the solitary watcher on the heights, lay the city, twinkling with Sabbath lights. At sunset, the mellow notes of the trumpet, from the roof of the synagogue, had announced the day of rest. Toil was over for a brief space; the peasants had ceased their labor in the fields; the shops and booths were closed; the fishing-boats lay idle at the wharves.

Hours passed on. The city slept. Still the solitary figure paced back and forth tirelessly, lifting his face to the heavens. Below him the world, full of sin, full of misery, full of ignorance. Above him, God. He—the link between.

CHAPTER VI.

THE reader had finished droning out the eighteen prayers. The men on their side of the synagogue had listened with reverent attention, and responded with devout amens. On the other side of the lattice, however, where the women and children sat, there was a subdued rustling. The place was very full; some were standing, and others crouched along the wall. To many who were present the prayers and psalms had a strange sound; they had never been in the synagogue before, though they had often seen it, and admired the beautiful rose-colored and white marble of which it was built. But all who could crowd into the place had come to-day; for it had been noised abroad that the great worker of miracles would be there, and curiosity to see him, and the hope that he might perform some new wonder, had brought many unaccustomed worshipers.

The Jewish women glanced askance at the foreign women, who, with their little ones clinging to their skirts, had crowded into the best places for seeing.

"The ungodly ones!" whispered one to her neighbor. "Why are they here? If this man be indeed the Messiah, he is not for them."

And now all the prayers had been recited, the lessons from both the Law and the Prophets read, and in the breathless hush of expectancy which followed, the great Healer came forward—the reader, following the custom, having asked him to speak to the people. Every eye was fastened upon him, and as he spoke words of authority, of divine and burning truth, the light of heaven which shone upon his face penetrated the dark hearts in his presence. All were intent, silent, drinking in his words, so different from the vague and stupid utterances of the rabbis. Even the children, though they understood not the words, felt the wonderful fascination of that heart of love, and gazed quietly into his wonderful eyes. Suddenly the sacred hush was broken; a man leaped up from the ground and shrieked:

"Let us alone! What have we to do with thee, thou Jesus of Nazareth? Art thou come to destroy us? I know thee who thou art, the Holy One of God!"

Instantly all was confusion; women shrieked, children cried, and men sprang up, exclaiming:

"He hath an evil spirit, and polluteth the sanctuary. Put him out! Put him out!"

But Jesus silenced the tumult with a word. Then, turning to the demoniac, who was already in the grasp of two or three indignant worshipers, he said:

"Hold thy peace, and come out of him!"

With a great cry and convulsion, the man fell down wallowing upon the floor; but presently, to the great amazement of all, he rose up, calm and in his right mind. Then all the people, being dismissed, went forth talking of the wonderful thing which they had seen; for the man was known to many of them.

"Mother," said Stephen, that same evening, "the trumpet hath sounded and 'tis past sunset; shall we not go forth? I would fain see more of this Jesus."

"I will go with thee gladly, my Stephen," replied his mother. "For truly never man spake as this man. Yet I feel the wonder of it all so keenly, that I think perhaps I am only dreaming. Can it be that thou art really well and strong?"

"It is really true, mother," said Stephen, with a happy laugh. "See how I can leap! And my back hath never an ache in it now; and see my flesh, how firm it is! Oh, mother, what can we do for him to show how glad, how thankful we are? When he said to me, as I lay in the dust that dreadful day, 'Go in peace,' and I sprang up for the first time since I can remember, oh mother, I only clung to him and sobbed—I could not speak for joy and wonder. Then he went away before I could rightly tell what had happened; and all the men were staring at me, and questioning, and others running to see. And then—oh, then, mother—I ran back down the street, and in a moment, it seemed, I found myself with you and Adah."

"Yes," went on his mother, "we thought the little fellow dying, he lay so still, when suddenly the door of the courtyard flew open, and thou didst fly, rather than run, to the spot where the baby lay. My Stephen, I did not know thee! I thought it was some spirit, till thou didst cry out, 'Gogo is saved! and I am well!'"

"And he was well!" put in Stephen.

"Yes, perfectly well," said Prisca. "Not a bruise on him. Ah! how wonderful!"

"Mother!" exclaimed the boy after a little pause, "let us go forth and find some sick ones among our neighbors, and tell them. Thou knowest that he said, 'I am sent to heal the broken-hearted; to preach deliverance to the captives, and recovering of sight to the blind; to set at liberty them that are bruised.' Those were his very words. I cannot forget them. And, mother, if he came for that, would it not please him best if we should help him to do it?"

"Thou art right, my son; I feel that thou art. We will go." And hastily wrapping herself in her mantle, and securing the door of their home, she set forth with the lad.

"We must stop here," said Stephen, pausing before a door.

"Yes," said Prisca, "a blind man dwelleth here."

They knocked, and a voice from within answered: "Enter." Pushing open the door, they found themselves in a courtyard more wretched than their own, for it was untidily littered with straw and filth; several goats and sheep wandered freely about; while a dozen or so of fowls perched aloft.

Sitting against the wall, with his head bowed forward on his knees, and his wretched garments wrapped tightly about him, was a man.

"Greetings to thee!" said the clear voice of the child.

At the sound, the man raised his shaggy head, and turned his face toward the doorway.

"Who art thou?" he said in a husky voice.

"I am Stephen, son of Dumachus. I am come with my mother that we may lead thee forth to find the great Healer. He will cure thee of thy blindness."

"Nay, thou mockest me," groaned the man. "For knowest thou not that my eyes were burned out with a red-hot iron: they be shriveled up in my head. No man could heal me."

"But thou knowest not the power which this man hath," said Stephen. Then he poured forth eagerly the wonderful story of his own healing, and that of the baby.

But the man only groaned and drew his rags more closely about him.

"Come—come quickly!" said the lad.

"Thou wert an innocent child, the babe also," said the man hoarsely, "but I—who am I, that one should heal me! I am accursed of gods and men. 'Twere best for me to die."

"Nay, good neighbor," cried Stephen impatiently, understanding nothing of all this. "Thou must come." And running quickly up to the man, he seized his hand and gave him a gentle pull.

Something in the touch of those soft childish fingers, perhaps the first friendly touch he had felt in years, broke down the barriers in the man's soul—barriers raised by the disgrace, shame and suffering of years—and burying his face in his hands, he sobbed aloud, Stephen still standing by, his childish soul perplexed at the sight of so much misery.

"Come," he said presently, again touching the man. And this time the poor wretch rose from the ground, stretching forth his hands gropingly.

"I will lead thee," said Stephen joyfully, possessing himself of one of the outstretched hands. And so the two set forth, Prisca following.

"Dost thou know where to find him?" asked the man in a trembling voice, a strange hope beginning to stir in his heart.

"Nay," said Stephen, "but we shall find him." Then with a sudden illumination of eternal truth, he added simply: "If we want him truly and seek for him, we cannot fail to find him."

Said Prisca, "I heard one of the women in the synagogue say that he lodgeth at the house of Simon the fisherman. He dwelleth near the lake; I know the place."

As they proceeded on their way thither, they saw many others thronging the narrow streets. Some carried beds on which lay poor sufferers wasted with every woeful disease known to man; others led the blind, or helped half-crippled ones slowly and painfully along. And as the multitude, ever growing, hurried on, the moans of the sufferers on their beds, the shrieks of demoniacs, and the wailing of sick children, made a mighty chorus of misery.

The house of Simon, as Prisca had said, was by the lake-side. It was a modest but thoroughly comfortable dwelling of two stories. Instead of the customary courtyard, a small garden extended in gentle terraces to the water's edge; two or three fine fig trees cast a pleasant shade, while roses, oleanders, and lilies made the spot a sweet and pleasant one. Here dwelt Simon, who was also called Peter, his wife, and the mother of his wife, together with Andrew his brother. And here dwelt Jesus when he sojourned in Capernaum.

On this Sabbath evening the family, with their beloved guest, were sitting in the garden enjoying the cool air, and talking in low tones. That day the Master had done great things for them also. The mother had been taken violently ill with fever, and when Jesus was told of it after his return from the synagogue, he had taken her by the hand and lifted her up, and immediately the fever had left her, so that she was able to rise and minister to them.

As they sat, therefore, James and John being with them, enjoying the Sabbath peace, and listening to Jesus as he talked, they became aware of a confusion of sounds—sounds of hurrying feet, of loud crying and wailing, mixed with shrieks and groans, and ever drawing nearer.

"Hark!" said the wife of Peter, rising in her alarm. "What mean those doleful sounds?"

"The multitude is seeking the Master," said John. "They are bringing their sick with them." And rising, he went to the door of the garden and looked out.

There was near Peter's house a square or market-place, and to this spot the people were hastening. And now they began to lay their burdens down upon the ground, the first-comers crowding as near as possible to the gateway of the garden, calling out as

they did so: "Where is he that healeth?
Let him come forth to us!" With many
other confused cries, such as, "Jesus, thou
son of David, have mercy!" "Master, come
forth, we pray thee!" And through it all
sounded the woeful noise of the wailing of
the sick ones, whose sufferings had been
greatly increased by the hurried journey
through the streets and by the confusion
and excitement.

But now into the midst of all this misery
came the benign figure of the great Physician, divine love, sympathy, tenderness
and healing flowing from his eyes and his
outstretched hands, even as the fragrance
pours forth from the cup of a lily. And as
he moved among the wretched beings, and
touched one here and there, laying his
hands on others with words of forgiveness
and peace, the moans and shrieks changed
to cries of rejoicing and relief. Already
many were going happily away, to make
room for others who were still coming from
every quarter, when Prisca and Stephen
with their charge reached the place.

"He is here," said Stephen joyfully, clasping the hand of the blind man closer. "And
many, oh, many others are here to be
healed; and some are going away well," he
continued.

And indeed the quick ear of the blind
man had already caught the exclamations
of thanksgiving, amid the babel of sound,
and, breaking away from the hands that
still held him, he ran with a quick instinct
to a little open space where Jesus had
paused for an instant, and throwing himself on his knees, caught him by the garment, and cried out loudly:
"Jesus, Master! I beseech thee to have
mercy on me!"

And he answered: "Believest thou I am
able to do this?"

"I believe," murmured the man, turning
his sightless eyes up to the face above him.

Jesus, looking at him, beheld behind the
blind eyes the soul stained with guilt, weary
with suffering, and hungry for love; and,
touching his eyes, he said. "Go in peace."

And the blind man was blind no longer.
He saw; and his first vision was of that
face full of compassion and tenderness.
Then was his soul stirred with a mighty
love for the Healer. And he rose up and
went away, as he was bidden, carrying
with him a memory destined to become a
perpetual fountain of blessing to himself
and others through time and eternity.

CHAPTER VII.

THE morning sun, as it
flickered cheerfully
through the high lat-
ticed window of a room
in the house of Caia-
phas, revealed an apart-
ment of noble propor-
tions. After the fashion
of the times, a divan
extended along the wall
on three sides; the
fourth side, being open, showed between its
light twisted pillars of colored marble,
glimpses of the terrace outside. The floor
was covered with thick rugs of Eastern
manufacture, tapestries of rich hues draped
the walls, while curious low tables, and
chairs of Roman workmanship, rare vases,
and a multitude of costly trifles, completed
an interior speaking of both wealth and re-
finement.

The sole occupant of the room on this
pleasant morning was Anna, the wife of
Caiaphas. Sorrow-laden years had left their
traces, for her hair was streaked with
white, and lines here and there on her fair
face spoke of suffering patiently borne; but
beneath the dark brows her eyes shone
sweet and bright, while the curves of her
noble figure were still perfect and graceful
as in youth.

From where she sat at ease on the divan
with her embroidery, the noble Anna could
look out upon the terrace, where climbing
roses and other fragrant flowers wreathed
the balustrades, and cast pleasant silhou-
ettes of dancing leaves on the marble pavement beneath. The tinkling of a fountain
was borne pleasantly to the ear, mingled
with the twittering of birds. It was very
quiet and peaceful, and the peace seemed
reflected in the face of the lady, as she
worked quietly and steadily, drawing the
gold threads through the rich fabric in her
hands.

Presently there was a sound of footsteps
on the terrace, and Anna, raising her eyes
from her work, saw the tall figure of a man
standing at the entrance.

"Greetings to thee, my wife," he said.

At the sound of his voice the lady rose,
and casting aside her work, came forward
to meet him with a little cry of joy.

"'Tis thou, my husband! And I expected
thee not until evening."

"We traveled by the light of the full

moon, and found it more pleasant than sun-light," said the man. "Is all well with the household?" he continued, "and with thee, my Anna?"

"All is well," she answered. "And how didst thou find our kinsfolk in Capernaum?"

"They are in good health," replied Caia-phas; then frowing darkly, he added, "But Jairus is as strangely infatuated with the man Jesus as are others in Galilee; he de-clares that he believeth him to be the Mes-siah. 'Tis rank blasphemy, and goeth against the Scriptures."

"But is it true about the miracles of heal-ing of which we have heard?" asked Anna with true feminine curiosity.

"There is no end to the marvels which fill the mouth of every Galilean rustic," said Caiaphas contemptuously. "I would that the marvels were all of it, but the pestilen-tial teachings of the man—" Here he checked himself, saying, "But these be not things to trouble thee with. I shall take steps to put a stop to it. Now I must rid myself of the stains of travel; and wilt thou, my Anna, bid the servants prepare me some refreshment, for I have not eaten since before sunrise. But stay!" he added, fumbling in the ample folds of his garment. "I have a letter for thee from the wife of Jairus." And handing Anna a small sealed packet, he hurriedly left the apartment.

Anna regarded the letter in her hand with a smile of pleased expectancy, but forbore to open it until she had made due arrange-ments with her maids for the comfort of her husband; for she was a notable house-wife. Then traversing the terrace, she de-scended the marble stairway which led into the garden, and seating herself upon a bench near the fountain, proceeded to break the seal of the letter which she still held in her hand. It was written upon a fine parch-ment, then tightly rolled, bound about with a silken thread, and sealed with wax in several places; so that the opening of it was a matter which occupied several moments. The last seal being broken, the lady spread open the parchment and began to read.

Sara, the wife of Jarius, unto the noble lady Anna, my sister, beloved of Jehovah, Greetings:

We have had much pleasure in the presence with us of Caiaphas, thy most noble husband, and the High Priest of the Holy Temple. And especially did we rejoice in the knowledge that all is well with thee, and with thy household, and with the household of Annas, our father.

In truth, though this be a fair city, and though our home be very dear to me, I oftentimes long for the things of my youth, and for the faces of my kinsfolk and acquaintance which be at Jerusalem. Of late, there hath been that which hath caused much talk among us: To-wit, the presence in Capernaum of the Naz-arene, Jesus, who hath wrought great wonders of healing, and teacheth new and strange things. My husband, Jairus, who is, as thou knowest, a just man, and one holy and accept-able in the sight of our God, believeth him to be the Messiah foretold by the Scriptures; and I grieve that the matter was one which caused a hot dispute between my husband and the worshipful Caiaphas. As for myself, I have seen with mine own eyes that which hath caused me to be filled with wonder and amaze-ment; for, behold, the lame walk, the deaf hear, and all manner of diseases have been healed by this man. Moreover, he hath cast out many devils from those possessed by them, and the devils themselves have testified of him that he is the Holy One of God.

He is beautiful to look upon, my Anna, but of a mysterious and wonderful presence, so that, while one looks, there seemeth to go out from him an influence which draweth all unto him. Even our little Ruth, who hath seen him, and heard him preach in our synagogue, ceas-eth not to talk of him; and she doth frequently beg me to go forth with her to seek him. This have I not done, for the crowds which attend him at all times are so great that it were not seemly for me, a daughter of Annas, to mingle with them. Notwithstanding, I have taken every opportunity to hear him whenever it hath been possible, and also to inform my-self of his teachings. He teacheth often by stories and parables, and, in brief, that all may return unto God the Father of all. He speaks of himself, sometimes as the Son of God, and sometimes as the Son of man, and declareth that he hath come from God to call sinners to repentance. It is rumored that in Samaria, even, he hesitated not to talk to a woman of their nation concerning this salvation; which thing would not be done by the Rabbis, as thou knowest, for indeed the Samaritans be not of the true faith.

Another strange thing about this man is that he hath selected for his followers certain men of the lower classes, some of whom are fisher-men by trade, and dwell in Capernaum. In truth, my sister, I fear that I cannot make thee clearly to understand why we are in-clined in our hearts to believe that this man is, indeed, the Messiah. But if he cometh up to Jerusalem, be sure that thou makest an occa-sion of seeking him for thyself; then assuredly thou wilt understand.

The little Ruth sendeth greetings, so also doth Jairus, my husband. We hope to see thee at no distant day, for the next Feast day is now not far away, and we shall come up to Jerusalem at that time if all be well with us.

And now, my beloved sister, thou seest how long a letter I have written to thee with mine own hand. Wilt thou, for me, greet Annas, our father; also our brothers, together with their households? May the God of Abraham keep thee and thine. And now, farewell.

As Anna finished reading this epistle, she became aware that someone was waiting her pleasure to speak with her, and raising her eyes, she saw Malchus, the favorite servant of her husband. The man made a gesture expressive of profound respect, and then spoke:

"My lord hath desired me to say unto thee, most noble lady, that matters of importance will detain him until the hour for the evening repast. He will see thee at that time, if it be thy pleasure."

The man after delivering his message was about to withdraw, when Anna detained him with a word.

"Stay!" she said. "Thou mayst tell thy master that it is well, and that the repast will be served in the garden of the inner house, at sunset. I will await him there."

Then as the man still lingered, she added pleasantly—for he was an old and trusted servant—"Didst thou enjoy thy journey to Capernaum, Malchus?"

"I did, most noble lady," was the reply; then rather hesitatingly he added, "I saw there a man whom I knew formerly in Jerusalem. He had been sick with the palsy for many years, and when last I saw him, had lain on his bed unable to move for more than ten years. He was walking about in the streets of Capernaum as nimbly as I myself. I spoke with him, for I thought at first that my eyes had played me false, but it was the same man. His name is Eliphaz, and formerly, before he was stricken with his ailment, he was a servant of the revered Annas."

"And what caused this most notable cure, good Malchus?" said Anna encouragingly.

"I asked him, most noble lady, and he said that one Jesus of Nazareth, which is in Galilee, saw him lying upon his mat at the city gate, and bade him rise up and carry his bed to his home; and that he was able to carry out the command. It was a most amazing thing! Afterward, I myself saw the man who worked the miracle."

"Didst thou see him perform any cure?" questioned Anna.

"Nay; he was telling a story to a crowd of people. 'Twas a pretty tale and easy to be understood. The children who were there—and there were very many of them—listened as quietly as any of the grown folk. I should like to have heard more, but I could not stop, for I was taking a message from my master to one of the rabbis."

Anna longed to question the man further, but restrained herself, and dismissed him with a pleasant word of praise for his faithfulness.

Meanwhile Caiaphas, the high priest, was seriously occupied in his own part of the mansion. Soon after his arrival in Jerusalem, he had sent messengers to men of authority in the Jewish church, with imperative summons to wait upon him at a certain hour in the palace. For some time past, a servant had been ushering these expected guests into an apartment which was especially set apart for such purposes. It was, like the other rooms in the palace, lofty and well lighted, but furnished with the utmost simplicity and severity.

When all were assembled, Malchus acquainted his master with the fact, and he entered the apartment with a mien at once dignified and austere. All but one of the company rose in greeting, and before that one, Caiaphas himself paused, and, bowing his head, said:

"Most revered and noble Annas, I greet thee; and I am especially glad that thou art present with us to-day, for by thy wisdom thou canst guide us in our deliberations."

The man who had sat to receive the salutation of the high priest, was of reverend aspect; his beard flowing upon his breast was of silvery whiteness, while beneath the snowy folds of his turban shone singularly keen and brilliant eyes. Yet despite its dignity, there was in the face of this man that which to the close observer would indicate cunning, obstinacy, and cruelty.

He responded courteously to the greeting of Caiaphas, and as the latter seated himself said: "My son, thou hast called us together to-day to learn the result of thy mission to Galilee. What is now thine opinion of the man who is called Jesus?"

"I found," said Caiaphas, "that the reports of the excitement in Galilee had not been exaggerated, but rather that we had not heard to the full how this man hath stirred up the populace. He hath been teaching not only in the streets of the city, and in the byways of the country round about, but, after the manner of the rabbis, he enters into the synagogues and teaches there. According to the popular reports he hath performed great works of healing. Of these I did not satisfy myself; for I saw nothing, and of that which I heard, I make no account. The credulity of the common people is well known; and more especially in Galilee, they are ignorant and little qualified to judge of such matters."

" But," said a man called Nicodemus, " is it not true that even in Jerusalem this Jesus wrought some notable cures?"

" 'Tis said that he did, most noble friend," replied Caiaphas. " But which of us can prove it? If the cures had been performed upon reputable citizens, they might perhaps be worthy of our note; but, as thou knowest, the ones professing to be healed were beggars. And the word of a beggar—what is it! But after all, it is not of this Jesus as a physician that we would speak. He might heal all the beggars in the country without harm; but his more serious pretensions demand our consideration. I tell thee frankly that the man pretends to be the Messiah, and as such is likely to have a great following among the people."

" His pretensions are blasphemous!" broke in the sonorous voice of Annas. " I have studied the Prophets from my youth up, and nowhere do I find such an one as this foretold. The Messiah is to be a mighty king, who will save the chosen people of Jehovah from the hand of their enemies; and he shall establish his throne in Jerusalem and reign in power. It is moreover prophesied that the prince shall be of the lineage of David, and shall be born in Bethlehem of Judea. This man is a Nazarene."

" If this man were the Messiah," said another, " he would assuredly seek to ally himself with the priesthood of the Most High."

" He not only doth not so seek to ally himself," broke in Caiaphas with an angry frown, " but he hath been heard to speak lightly of the laws and customs of the church, and even of the Pharisees and Scribes. Moreover he observeth not our laws, and doth eat with unwashen hands, and mingleth with publicans and sinners, even going into their houses to eat and to drink. My counsel is, that we require certain wise and prudent ones of the rabbis to watch this man, and report to us of his doings; for there is great danger to the

priesthood, and to the institutions of the God of our fathers, if he be allowed to teach unchecked."

" Thou speakest with wisdom, servant of the Most High," said Annas. " It is our duty to guard the faith of our fathers, and to preserve it from contamination. If this man be a blasphemer, he ought to die. It is our law. Yet must we move with due caution and secrecy in the matter, lest we incur the displeasure of the people."

A murmur of applause followed this sentiment; and then arose a discussion of ways and means, in which all present took part, with the result that certain wise and crafty men, approved by the council, were appointed to go into Galilee and watch the man Jesus, that they might find sufficient accusation against him to warrant putting him to death.

CHAPTER VIII.

IS a wonderful tale, my Stephen, but I must needs believe it, since I have thee before mine eyes, and I make sure that I am not dreaming it all."

The speaker was Titus, and as he said the last words, he gave himself a vigorous shake, as if to prove to himself beyond a doubt that he was in full possession of his waking senses.

The two lads were walking slowly along the lake shore, stopping now and then to throw a pebble into the translucent water which rippled on the beach at their feet. Stephen had been pouring forth the wonderful tale of his meeting with Jesus, and of the healing of Gogo and himself.

" And to think," he went on, " that thou hast not seen him! Nay, but thou must see him when he returns to Capernaum. Oh, Titus, I love him so—better than anyone in the whole world!"

" Better than thy mother, boy?" questioned Titus, somewhat surprised.

" Yes, better than mother; and yet I love mother more than ever before, and thee also, my Titus. He loves everyone. If thou couldst have seen his face, the night when so many sick folk were carried to him to be healed! I was half afraid to look, and yet I longed to, for there was a light upon it like to the light of the sun—and yet not like it; and when he spoke to the blind man, and said to him, ' Go in peace,' I felt in my soul that the man must needs see. No one could remain blind before the glory of that face! Thou knowest," continued Stephen, after a little pause, " that we have had no religion; father speaks of the gods, when he curses. Mother told me once that she was of Jewish blood, yet hath she never gone to the synagogue, save once when she knew that the Healer would be there. I would I knew something of the Father of whom he speaks. One thing I know," he added with energy, " I shall continue to follow him and listen to all that he saith, and perhaps I shall find out soon."

" Hast thou had speech with the man since he healed thee?" asked Titus.

" Nay," answered Stephen, " he is always surrounded with crowds, and so many would speak with him that I know not how he findeth time to take food; but I have followed him day by day here in Capernaum, and when, a few days since, he set forth to visit the villages round about, I went as far as I could with him. I knew the mother would fear for me, if I failed to return by nightfall. Titus, I am sure that something is wrong with mother. She weeps often and so bitterly that I am afraid—yet father hath been away, and I am well."

" Hast thou asked her what aileth her?" queried Titus.

" Often and often," said Stephen, " but she only answers: ' Thou canst not help me, my son, and why should I tell thee?' Wilt thou ask her, my Titus?"

" Perhaps," said Titus briefly.

" And now tell me what thou hast been doing, and where thou hast been; and let us sit here in the shade of this tree, for the sun waxeth too warm for comfort." And Stephen threw himself down beneath a thrifty fig tree.

Titus followed his example, and pulling a stalk of lilies, which grew near, he began plucking it to pieces, throwing the brilliant leaves in showers upon the ground.

" Thou wouldst not do that, hadst thou heard the Master speak of the lilies," said Stephen quietly, stretching out his hand as if to save the flowers.

" And what said he of the lilies?" asked Titus, continuing his work of destruction.

" He said that the Father made them, and that if he cared for the lilies enough to make them so fair, he would surely care for the creatures which he also made. He said, too, that he himself came to teach us of the Father, who is great and mighty, and who loves all of us."

" Humph!" said Titus gruffly, throwing away the dismantled stalk with an impatient gesture.

" What aileth thee, my Titus?" said Stephen tenderly, taking one of the strong brown hands in both his own. " Thou seemest not like thyself. But come, tell me of all that thou didst while thou wert gone."

" 'Twere not a fit tale for thee to hear," said Titus, fixing a gloomy look on the white sails which glittered on the blue surface of the lake. " But what couldst thou expect of such ruffians? Thou didst hear them talk the night we set forth. I was compelled by brute force to do things which I will not tell thee. Nay, may my tongue wither up in my mouth, if I do!" he added fiercely. " I tell thee I hate Dumachus and all of his crew! They

" I have heard them droning out their long prayers."

be devils, and will make me one too. When thou talkest in thy innocent fashion of this great Healer, as thou callest him, I cannot tell thee how I feel. He healeth the lame, the sick and the helpless, while we have been robbing, maiming—yes, even killing!"— the last in a husky whisper, and the lad buried his face in his hands, and wept convulsively.

Stephen sat in perfect silence, all the happy light gone out of his face; but at length he stretched out his hand, and laid it gently on Titus' bowed head.

"Thou wouldst never do such things of thyself, my Titus. Thou hast ever been tender with the mother and with me; in the dark days before I was healed, I could never have borne it but for thee; thou didst carry me in thy strong arms; thou didst sing to me, and tell me tales which eased me of my weariness and pain. Thou art a good lad, and a true, Titus," he went on stoutly, " and thou shalt not go with those bad men again. Stay with the mother and me, and all shall be well with thee."

Titus had ceased his sobbing; straightening himself and half turning away his face to hide the redness of his eyes, he said brokenly:

"I am not good, my Stephen, but thou art good enough for us both. Let us walk further."

"Yes," said Stephen, springing up with alacrity. "It may be that we shall meet him of whom I have told thee. A week since, he set forth to make a circuit of the lake, for I asked one of the fishermen who follow him at all times."

"What fishermen dost thou mean?" asked Titus, interested in the mention of his own favorite craft.

"They be Simon, with his brother Andrew, also James and John, sons of Zebedee. Dost know them?"

"I know who they are; I have oftentimes seen them on the lake fishing, and once, one of them spoke kindly to me at the wharf."

"They do not fish now," said Stephen. "They have given it up, that they may not leave the Healer. I heard the people talk of it. A rabbi in the crowd said, ' Good people, this man selecteth strange disciples; dost see it?' But the people paid no manner of attention to him—they were too busy talking of all that they had seen and heard."

"Then the rabbis love him not?" said Titus with a laugh. "They be jealous for their own teaching—the canting hypocrites! I have heard them standing in the market-places, droning out their long prayers. They must needs draw their robes about them, for fear such an one as I should pollute them with a touch. But what is that crowd of people yonder about? See them running from every direction! Let us make haste and see!"

Saying which, Titus broke into a run, followed by Stephen.

"What is it all about? I see nothing," said Titus, to one who was craning his neck to look up the road.

"Knowest thou not," answered the man, " that Jesus of Nazareth passeth this way?

"Unclean! Unclean!" wailed the voice.

Even now he is coming. Dost thou not see?" And he pointed to a cloud of dust on the highway, where dimly appeared a confused multitude of people. "Thou seest that great numbers are with him," continued their informant. "The people flock after him from every village. There hath never been the like of this man in these parts before; for he doeth wonders of healing, and besides that, he speaketh not as the rabbis, but with such power that even the devils obey him."

"I am one that he healed," said Stephen simply, for he could not help telling his own story to every one who would listen.

The man stared at him. "And of what did he heal thee?" he asked.

"I was a cripple—" began Stephen. But at that moment they were interrupted by a loud and mournful cry, but withal in so strange a voice that all started to hear it.

"Unclean! Unclean!" wailed the voice.

"Room for the leper!" shouted half a dozen voices; and there was an instant scattering among those who were crowding the road in their anxiety to see.

Stephen and Titus shrank back among the rest, and saw the tall figure of the leper, as he limped painfully toward the advancing multitude, still crying at intervals in his hoarse, metallic voice:

"Unclean! Unclean!"

His face was partly concealed by the coarse linen of his head-covering, which he had drawn forward so as to hide as much as possible the ghastly ravages of his malady. But it was evident that he was suffering from an advanced stage of that disease the most horrible and hopeless which has ever afflicted mankind.

By this time the confused crowd of men, women and children, with Jesus walking in their midst, had nearly reached the place where the leper stood. As they approached, again sounded forth the dismal cry:

"Unclean! Unclean!"

The advancing multitude shrank back, leaving Jesus standing alone in the midst of the highway. When the leper saw him, and that he did not turn from him, as did the others, he ran forward, and falling upon his face in the dust, cried out:

"Lord, if thou wilt, thou canst make me clean."

And Jesus put forth his hand and touched him, saying, "I will: be thou clean."

And immediately he rose up and it was seen of all of them that his leprosy was departed, and that his flesh was like that of other men.

In the awed hush that followed, Jesus talked with him that had been a leper; but in so low a tone that no other could hear. Afterward it appeared from the man's account, that the Healer was directing him to go quietly and show himself to the priest, as Moses had commanded, thus fulfilling the law of cleansing; and also, that he charged him strictly to tell no one else of the wonderful thing which had been done unto him.

But as the man departed, a great cry arose from all the people, and they crowded about the Healer more closely than before, so that Stephen and Titus, who still stood at the outskirts of the throng, were pushed to one side.

"Was not that a marvelous thing?" said Stephen, when he could find his voice.

But Titus did not answer, and, looking up at him, Stephen saw that his great dark eyes were brimming over with tears.

CHAPTER IX.

SAY, young man! thou lookest to have a sturdy back—wilt thou not help us with our burden?"

The speaker was one of four men, who were bearing some apparently heavy load between them, and the person to whom he addressed himself was Titus, who, with Stephen, was returning from a fishing expedition on the lake.

The two were well laden with the spoils of their evening's work, and with the fishing nets, yet at the sound of the voice they stopped, and moving toward the spot where the four men stood, they perceived that the burden which they had been carrying was one of the light beds, or sleeping-mats, and that upon it lay the figure of a man apparently helpless.

"Thou seest," went on the first speaker, "that we have undertaken to carry this young man to the house of Simon the fisherman, for it is there that Jesus of Nazareth bideth, and we hope that he may be able to heal him." At this the man on the pallet groaned audibly. "But one of our bearers is an old man and infirm, and he hath not the strength to proceed further; so that we are in a bad case, in that we can go neither forward nor back, unless, young man, thou wilt help us."

"I will gladly help thee," said Titus. "Here, Stephen, canst take my net and these fish?"

"I will carry them for thee," broke in the quavering voice of the old man, who had by this time somewhat recovered himself. "And a father's blessing be upon thee, if thou dost help my poor boy to find the Healer."

" O father," groaned the sufferer upon the bed, "what is the need of it all? Hath not the priest told me over and over again, that I suffer on account of my sins; and that I must needs bear it, for it be laid upon me by the Almighty? Surely it is unrighteous to attempt to escape the judgments of the Most High, for thou knowest that I am a sinner above all men."

"Ah, the rabbis, the rabbis!" grumbled the old man. "I know that they have told thee that; but I know thee that thou art a good lad, as lads go. None of us be righteous altogether, and I am thinking that, were the Almighty so minded, he could put us all on to our beds, and justly; for we have all gone astray. There is not one righteous—no, not one. Is it not true, lads?" The men murmured assent, while Titus felt the blood rise guiltily to his face.

" Come, come, now!" said one of the bearers briskly, "'tis time that we were getting along. Now then, take hold! Steady!" And the four with their burden set off at a rapid pace down the street, the old man and Stephen following with the nets.

" My poor boy! My poor boy!" murmured the old man, as if to himself, shaking his head sadly.

" Hath he been long in this way?" asked Stephen, sympathetically.

" Since he was eight years of age," said the father. " He was run over by a Roman chariot—poor lad! There was some heathen festival or other in Tiberias—where we lived then—and the boy was minded to see it. His mother bade him stay at home, but he 'scaped from her notice, and the first we knew of it, the neighbors brought him to us half dead. Ah, 'twere a pity, a pity! He was a lusty lad ere he was hurt, and never had broken our commands before that day. Since then he hath lain constantly on his bed; for someway, the hurt took all the life and feeling from his limbs, so that he cannot move them. After a while we came to Capernaum, and his mother hath not ceased to pray for his recovery. May the Almighty grant it, as he did the prayer of Hannah! But the rabbis will have it that he is suffering for sin; and in a way he is, poor lad, for it is true that he disobeyed. But we have all gone astray—all gone astray. And he hath been so patient! Thou knowest, boy, that David hath it in one of the Psalms that 'like as a father pitieth his children, so the

Lord pitieth them that fear him.' And I know he must pity my poor patient lad."

" What was it that thou didst say about a father pitying his children?" said Stephen eagerly. " Wilt thou say it to me again?"

The old man repeated the verse; then said somewhat severely, " Dost thou not know the Scriptures, boy? At thy age I could repeat the Psalms and much of the Law."

" Nay, but my father is a Greek, and I have not been taught."

" Then thou art a heathen!" said the old man, slightly drawing away from the boy as they walked. " But thou art a good lad— I know it by thy face—and I am not stiff-necked like the rabbis. It hath been reported that he whom we seek doth teach and heal all who come to him, even publicans and sinners."

" 'Tis a true saying," said Stephen eagerly. " I was a cripple and he healed me. He did not ask me if I knew the Psalms, or the Law, nor whether I went to the synagogue. I did not even ask him to heal me—I was asking for another. And dost think that the Father who pitieth the children, is the Father he speaks of so often?"

" Assuredly," was the answer. " He is also the God of Abraham, of Isaac, and of Jacob."

" And who are they?" asked Stephen innocently.

" Oh, boy, thou art indeed a heathen!" groaned the old man. " Thou must go to the synagogue and hear the reading of the Scriptures."

" I will do that," said Stephen earnestly. " Thou knowest that I could not till lately, for I was helpless."

At this point in the conversation, they saw that the bearers had again placed their burden upon the ground and were straightening themselves to ease their aching backs. The old man came forward and stood beside the bed, looking fondly down upon the wasted features of its occupant.

" Doth the shaking of thy bed as they walk hurt thee, my poor boy?"

" Nay, father; the jolting hurteth me not as doth my sinful soul. He cannot heal me, I am so sinful, so wicked! 'Twere better to take me back and let me die in peace."

" Dost thou see me?" said Stephen in his clear, boyish treble, kneeling beside the bed. " I am a heathen—thy father hath said so— yet he healed me. He healed Philip, the blind man whose eyes had been burned out —for what, I know not—but he was a sinner.

He hath healed multitudes, and none of them priests or rabbis or Pharisees. He will heal thee. Thou dost not know him. He pitieth his children like the Father in heaven, and he loveth them as never a mother loved. Thou wilt see it, when thou lookest into his face."

The young man fixed his great, mournful eyes upon Stephen, and when he had finished speaking, he said:

"Who art thou? Art thou an angel?"

And indeed, in the moonlight the lad seemed not unlike one, as he kneeled by the bed, his hands clasped in his earnestness.

"Nay, nay, lad! He is not an angel," spoke the cracked voice of the old man. "He is only a little heathen lad, as he saith truly, for he knoweth not Abraham, Isaac and Jacob. But for all that, he is a good lad. Thou must cheer up, for it is true that the Nazarene hath healed greater sinners than even thou, my poor child. Here, take a swallow of this wine; it will strengthen thy heart." So saying, he produced a small gurglet of wine from his girdle, and proceeded to administer some of it to the invalid.

Then all set forth as before. They were not far from Simon's house now, and as they approached, it became evident that a great crowd was assembled there, for they met numerous groups coming away, many of them complaining loudly that they could neither hear nor see.

The old man looked anxious. "I fear that we cannot see him, now that we have come so far. My poor boy! My poor boy!"

"Do not let him hear thee," besought Stephen, laying a warning hand on the old man's arm. "Let us go on; we shall surely find him."

Their progress was now necessarily slow, as the crowd grew denser. Finally the four set their burden down for a moment to rest, and that they might consider the situation.

"What hast thou there?" said a passer-by; "a sick man?" And he looked over their shoulders at the bed. "I will tell thee something; 'twere better to take him home again, and as quickly as possible, for he will not be healed to-night. The Master hath healed no one. He is in an upper chamber in Simon's house, and is talking with the rabbis, priests and Pharisees, who have come from all parts, even from Jerusalem, to hear him. Then, even if this were not so, the house and every inch of the garden are packed solid with people: not one of you could step inside the gate, to say nothing of that bed!" And without waiting to see whether or not his advice was taken, the speaker went his way.

"Humph! 'Tis a sorry case!" muttered one of the men who had been helping to bear the bed. "I had not bargained to carry this burden both ways."

"O Benjamin, my son! my son!" wailed the old man, wringing his hands helplessly, "I fear that we must take thee home unhealed!"

"Stay!" said Stephen, again coming forward. "I know that we can find him if we try. Titus, wilt thou go and see if there be not some way to get in?"

Titus was gone in a moment, and in a moment more was back again, flushed and panting with exertion. "There is a stairway leading to the roof, not far from the garden gate," said he. "I had thought if we could take him up there, we might perhaps tear up a piece of the tiling, and lower him into the chamber where the Master is talking. I can repair the breach in an hour, if one of you will help me."

"Oh, Titus!" exclaimed Stephen. "'Tis a good thought; let us go at once."

"Hold!" said the old man. "What right have we to injure our neighbor's roof? Then, too, would it not be a bold and unseemly thing thus to disturb the Master, more especially if he be discoursing to so many learned men? God knoweth that I heartily desire the healing of my son, but I like not thy plan, young man; it savoreth of unlawfulness."

"Oh, father!" said the sick man, with a sob, "if thou takest me back now, I feel that I can never come again. This hath so wrought on me, that I feel the springs of life failing within me. I pray thee try any way that will take me to him!"

The old man hesitated.

Stephen whispered in his ear, "Let us try it, I beg of thee!"

"Well, well! Do thy best; I care not. I will recompense Simon for the roof. It will do no harm to make the attempt."

Lifting their burden, the four once again slowly advanced through the crowd, Stephen and the old man going in front this time, and making a way for them. At length the gateway was reached, then came a struggle through the dense throng that filled every available nook inside the garden. Finally the stairway was gained, and in a moment more they were safely on the roof,—where, strangely enough, no one from below had hitherto come. Now, however, divining the purpose of the party with the sick man, the crowd began to surge up the narrow stairway.

"What art thou purposing, good friends?" called out one.

"To tear up the roof, and lower this sick man into the presence of the Master," answered Titus.

"Then this is the spot to remove the tiling. He is in the chamber beneath. I will help thee," said the man who had spoken first.

In another moment a dozen willing hands were at work. A very short time sufficed to make a considerable aperture; and through it they quickly made preparations to lower the bed containing the sick man. As they lifted him, he murmured in a low tone: "Where is he—the lad that was healed?"

"I am here," said Stephen, coming forward. "Have courage!" he whispered. "I saw him through the hole in the roof. He will heal thee."

"Now then—take a firm hold!" said Titus; and grasping the ropes which someone had brought, and which were firmly knotted to the bed, the sick man was lowered carefully and steadily through the opening till his bed rested on the floor at the feet of Jesus. There was profound silence for a moment; those in the chamber below startled by the strange interruption, and those who crowded about the opening in the roof breathless with anxiety for the success of their bold plan.

The Master had been sitting as he talked, but now he arose, and, stooping over, gazed intently into the face of the sick man. In those pale, pinched features and appealing eyes, he read his whole pathetic story. Laying his hand upon the sufferer tenderly, he said:

"My child, thy sins are forgiven thee."

Instantly there arose a murmur in the room. The words, "He blasphemeth!" "God alone can forgive sins!" "God will smite him!" came from one and another of the bearded and turbaned rabbis who sat about. Then the Master raised himself up, and looking upon them with the eye of omniscience, said slowly:

"What reason ye in your hearts? Whether is easier, to say, Thy sins be forgiven thee; or to say, Rise up and walk? But that ye may know that the Son of man

hath power upon earth to forgive sins,"—turning to the sick man—"I say unto thee, Arise, and take up thy couch, and go into thine house."

"And immediately he rose up before them all, and took up that whereon he lay, and departed to his own house, glorifying God. And they were all amazed, and they glorified God, and were filled with fear, saying, We have seen strange things to-day."

CHAPTER X.

HE worshipful Jairus, ruler of the synagogue in Capernaum, had just completed a careful inspection of the various gardens connected with his house. He was a rich man, as well as ruler of the synagogue; it was therefore meet that all things connected with his domain should be done decently and in order. He had been making remarks to this effect to the servant who filled the office of chief steward in his house, and the man still stood in his presence.

"I am not pleased with the condition of the gardens connected with the inner house, Benoni," he said, somewhat severely. "I saw many withered leaves on the turf, and the shrubbery hath not received the attention which it should have. It is evident that there is fault somewhere."

"If I might venture the suggestion, most noble master, I would say that it would be well to employ another servant. I can buy, if it please thee, a slave, or for a small sum hire some lad from the city. For truly the new vineyard doth require much time and attention, and I have therefore been unable to look to the home gardens as I ought. It is not that the servants are idle, or that I"

—and here the man made a low obeisance—
"am neglectful of my duty."

"Thou hast answered well, Benoni; the
matter of the new vineyard had entirely escaped my memory. Seek out now a lad,
and let it be his duty to attend the gardens,
that I be not further vexed with the matter. And stay!—be cautious in the matter
of selecting the lad, for the little Ruth doth
often play in the gardens, albeit attended by
her maidens, and I would not that the boy
be rough or discourteous."

"Thy commands, most worshipful master,
shall be obeyed; and I thank thee for thy
goodness and forbearance to me in the matter."

So saying, the steward withdrew and at
once made his way to the nearest market-
place. Here he proceeded to make known
the fact that he, Benoni, would engage the
services of a likely lad in behalf of his master, the worshipful Jairus. A number of
lads who were idling about the place
eagerly gathered around him, but the keen
eye of the chief steward quickly pronounced
them, one and all, unfit for the position.

Now it happened that Stephen and Titus
were at one of the numerous stalls, barter-
ing some fish which they had taken that
morning before dawn, Titus as usual man-
aging the business, while Stephen stood by,
looking dreamily at the lively scene about
him; the world, to which he had been so
long a stranger, presenting to his happy
eyes a constantly shifting kaleidoscope of
wonderful pictures. This morning he saw
at once the imposing figure of Benoni as he
entered the market-place, and followed his
subsequent proceedings with an interested
eye. Just as Titus had finished the bargain-
ing to his satisfaction, he caught an excited
whisper from Stephen.

"That man yonder looketh for a lad to
hire! Why dost thou not speak with him?
Then mightest thou be safe from father and
the men."

Titus looked in the direction to which
Stephen pointed, then said: "The man is a
Jew. I care not to hire with him."

"Nay, Titus, now thou speakest foolishly.
Come! Wilt thou not seek him?"

In another moment the two lads were in
the presence of Benoni.

"I heard thee, that thou didst inquire for
a lad," said Stephen hesitatingly, seeing that
Titus did not intend to speak.

"Thou didst hear aright," answered
Benoni with condescension. "But thou art

too young. I require a sturdy lad, more like
to this one,"—glancing, as he spoke, at Titus
—"to work in the gardens of the house of
the worshipful Jairus."

"What work wouldst thou require?"
asked Titus, who had always had a curiosity to see the interior of one of the great
houses, so jealously guarded by their high
walls from the public eye, and which had
often been described to the two lads by
Prisca.

"The work will be, as I said, in and about
the gardens—keeping the graveled paths in
order, and the turf free from weeds and un-
sightly rubbish."

"I think I could do that," said Titus in a
low voice—for he inwardly revolted at the
idea of service of any kind.

Benoni, however, convinced that his hesi-
tation was due solely to modesty, and withal
satisfied with the young man's general appearance, after a few more perfunctory
questions, quickly concluded the bargain,
stipulating that Titus should accompany
him at once, and be introduced to his new
work.

When Stephen was left alone, he stood
gazing after the two, and a desolate feeling
of loneliness almost overcame him for a moment. He suddenly realized that all the delightful hours on the lake with Titus, all the
long rambles, and the pleasant evening
talks on the housetop, were over.

"Why did I ever see that man!" he murmured disconsolately, feeling a strong desire
to run after Titus and beg of him to stay.

But in a moment he straightened himself.
"I am glad he hath gone," he thought. "It
will be best. As for me, I must learn to
manage the boat alone: I am nearly fifteen
now and strong enough. Mother hath need
of me; I must work for her." And he started
out for home at a brisk pace.

Meanwhile Titus and Benoni had reached
the house of Jairus. It was an imposing
structure occupying a whole square, presenting to the street on all sides façades of
massive rough-hewn stone, windowless on
the ground floor, and broken only by a
single entrance on each of its sides. From
the second story projected certain high and
wide windows filled with curious lattice-
work.

Being admitted to one of the strongly-
guarded portals, Titus and his guide found
themselves in an arched passage-way of
stone; quickly traversing this, they proceeded into a courtyard, which Titus—hav-

ing in mind the description of Prisca—perceived to be the court of the household; for here was the great central fountain, there were the stalls for the horses and mules, and on the opposite side the appurtenances for various kinds of work connected with the establishment—the bake ovens, and the grindstones in noisy operation, being most in evidence. It was an animated scene, and everyone seemed to be in the highest spirits, for the men were laughing and talking as they groomed the horses, while the maidens about the fountain chattered as gayly and incessantly as the sparrows which were nesting in the cornice.

As the two entered, all eyes were turned at once upon them, and one damsel, bolder than the rest, came forward, and dropping a courtesy, said saucily:

"And here is our good Benoni, looking none the worse for the interview

Jerusalem as it appears to-day.

which he had with the master this morning! My mistress bade me tell thee that she wished to speak with thee immediately upon thy return. Didst thou know that we are going up to Jerusalem, the next week but one? 'Tis the feast. I am glad, for my part; Jerusalem at feast times hath a gayety which refresheth my spirit after our dull Capernaum."

"Peace, maiden!" said Benoni severely. "Thy tongue hath the sound of waters which run and never cease. But now wilt thou see that this lad hath some refreshment, while I wait upon our worshipful lady? I will return for thee shortly "—turning to Titus—" that thou mayst get to thy work without delay."

The damsel, who was called Marissa,

laughed mockingly, "It would be well, good Benoni, ere our worshipful master return from the synagogue. At least fourscore more of dried leaves have fallen from the shrubbery since thou didst go forth this morning."

But Benoni was already gone, apparently not hearing the last remark.

As soon as he had disappeared, the girl turned to Titus, and with an approving glance at his stalwart figure and handsome face, said:

"Whenever the master hath occasion to chide our good Benoni yonder, he doth mend the matter by hiring a new servant. I heard everything that passed between them this morning from the terrace where I was sewing. Thou art to pick off the yellow leaves from the shrubs; it will require all thy strength!" And again the girl laughed teasingly.

"Nay, I am to attend to the graveled walks, and care for the turf," said Titus with an angry flush.

"Do not be angry," said the girl. "Thou shouldst be glad in these times to have fallen into such a comfortable place; plenty would give their eyes for it. And Benoni is a good master, as thou wilt see, albeit a little stupid. But come, let me give thee to eat, as I was bidden."

Before many days had passed Titus found that Marissa had spoken truly. His work was light and pleasant, and his beauty-loving eyes were never tired of looking at the wonders about him. On several occasions he had seen the mistress of the house in her sweeping robes traversing the terraces; and every day the little Ruth, a pretty child of twelve, played about the shady garden paths. But best of all, Benoni, finding that he was skillful with boat and net, allowed him to supply the household with fish. Stephen invariably joined him in these expeditions, and the two spent many delightful hours together.

"I shall not see thee again for many days," said Titus on one of these occasions, as he pushed off the boat from the shore. "Benoni told me this morning that the family start to-morrow for Jerusalem. Many of the household will attend them. As for me, I have been chosen to lead the mule on which the little Ruth is to ride. Marissa saith that in Jerusalem we shall bide at the palace of the high priest, for the lady Sara, our mistress, is sister to the wife of Caiaphas."

"Thou wilt see wondrous things," said Stephen, somewhat wistfully, but without a trace of envy in his face. "I am glad that I have learned to manage the boat now; I shall go out every day whilst thou art away."

"Thou dost very well with the boat, lad," said Titus, somewhat patronizingly. "But thou must beware of squalls; they come so suddenly, that cooler heads and stronger arms than thine have gone down ere this. Do not go out unless the wind sets in the right quarter, as I showed thee; and never alone at night. The hour of the dawning will be best for thee."

"The Master and his disciples, with many others, have already set forth for Jerusalem," said Stephen presently. Then after a pause he continued: "Thou knowest the man Benjamin, who was palsied, and whom the Master healed so marvelously. He hath not forgotten us. I met him not many days since, as I was coming from the synagogue, and he took me with him to his home. He is going to teach me how to read in the Hebrew Scriptures, so that I shall no longer be a heathen, as his father did call me. He hath given me a roll that he himself did

study when he was my age—albeit he studied lying helpless on his bed. And he taught me a Psalm. Shall I say it to thee?"

Titus assented, and the lad repeated to the musical accompaniment of the water rippling along the side of the boat:

"'The Lord is my Shepherd; I shall not want. He maketh me to lie down in green pastures; he leadeth me beside the still waters. He restoreth my soul; he leadeth me in the paths of righteousness, for his name's sake. Yea, though I walk through the valley of the shadow of death, I will fear no evil: for thou art with me; thy rod and thy staff they comfort me. Thou preparest a table before me in the presence of mine enemies; thou anointest my head with oil; my cup runneth over. Surely goodness and mercy shall follow me all the days of my life; and I will dwell in the house of the Lord forever.'

"Is it not beautiful!" said Stephen softly.

"And there are many more. I shall learn them all. Benjamin saith that I must learn the Law also. But that I like not so well; there are so many 'thou shalt not's,' that it quite bewildereth me to hear them read; and I know not how I could observe them all."

"Thou wilt be a Pharisee yet," said Titus, half bitterly. "I fancy I see thee now with a long robe, and a broad phylactery bound to thy brow."

"Nay," answered Stephen simply. "I would rather follow the Master. He wears no phylactery; and I am sure that he is not a Pharisee."

"Dost thou know, Stephen," said Titus presently, after the two had lowered their net, "that that psalm, as thou callest it, soundeth strangely familiar in mine ears, like something I have heard many times, and forgotten. And the house of Jairus—it is certain that I have seen something like it —in a dream."

"Thou hast heard the mother tell of the great house in which she lived as a maiden; 'tis of that thou hast dreamed, my Titus."

"But the psalm!" persisted Titus. "Did the mother sing it in this way?" And he began a low metrical chanting of the words which Stephen had recited. But he broke off abruptly after a few lines, saying, "It hath gone from me now," then relapsed into silence, which he seemed not disposed to break; though Stephen talked gayly on, apparently unmindful of the fact that he had a very indifferent listener.

CHAPTER XI.

THOUGH the dawn was yet so young that a few stars lingered in the heavens, the great courtyard in the house of Jairus was a scene of the liveliest confusion. Servants were flying hither and thither, and men shouting to each other as they led forth the mules and prepared to load them with the baggage of various sorts which was already lying in great piles on the pavement. In the midst of the court stood Benoni, directing one here, cautioning another there, and keeping a calm and dignified mien, as was his wont on all occasions, however trying. As the beasts of burden were loaded, one after another was led out into the street and stood waiting in a long line.

"And now bring forth the master's horse, together with the mules, and quickly! For time doth fly, and we must accomplish the first stage of our journey before the heat of the day begins."

At this command there issued from his stall an Arabian horse, showing in his full, dark eyes, small head, and slender, clean-cut limbs, all his pride of birth. After the Arabian came a number of large, sleek mules, with luxurious accoutrements, each led by a groom. Benoni had already left the courtyard for the purpose of informing his master that all was ready for a start, and he now hurried forth again, followed in more leisurely fashion by Jairus, his wife—the noble Sara—and their little daughter, Ruth, with several maids laden with wraps of various kinds.

"I am so glad that we are going at last!" cried Ruth joyously, bounding ahead of the rest of the party. "And there is my dear old Bekah! Ah, I believe you know me, you darling!"—caressing, as she spoke, the nose of a snow-white mule, which stood a little apart from the others.

"Wait, darling," said the soft voice of her mother. "Let Benoni lift thee to the saddle."

But the strong arm of Titus had already snugly ensconced the little damsel in her place.

"Titus can do it quite as well as Benoni, as thou seest, my mother," said Ruth gayly.

"I am so glad that thou art to lead my Bekah!" she continued, patting the glossy neck of the animal, "because I can talk to thee as we journey. Last time I had old Asa, and he was too deaf to hear me, even had I cared to talk with him."

Titus showed his white teeth in an appreciative smile, but said nothing. Truth to tell he stood somewhat in awe of the imperious little maiden, who, with her hazel eyes and golden hair, seemed a being set apart from the rest of the world.

At last all were settled to their satisfaction, and one after another moved slowly out from the great gateway, now thrown wide open. Benoni, wiping his heated face, paused for a few last words of warning and advice to the under-steward, who was to be left in charge of the house during his absence; then he too jumped into his saddle and clattered down the street after the procession, which was already well under way.

Ruth rode behind her mother, and was followed by Marissa; while Jairus, with a number of heavily-armed men-servants, traveled in front. The beasts of burden, laden with rich offerings for the feast, and with the tents, cooking utensils, and other things needful for the journey, each under the charge of a man, brought up the rear.

The city was already stirring, early as it was, and the procession, as it wound through the streets and squares, attracted much attention. The wife of Jairus drew her veil more closely about her face, and bade her daughter do the same. The little maiden obeyed, but her bright eyes peeping out from the gauzy folds were intent on losing nothing of the lively scenes about.

Presently, to his surprise, Titus spied Stephen, his fishing nets on his shoulder, waiting, like the others, to see the cavalcade pass. On beholding Titus, his face flushed with pleasure, and holding up a string of fish, that their size and number might be appreciated, he shouted:

"Farewell; and may the gods protect thee!"

"Who is that lad?" asked Ruth curiously. "And why doth he say, 'May the gods protect thee,' as if there were several?"

"'Tis my brother Stephen," answered Titus. "And he saith 'gods' because he hath been accustomed to hear it from his youth. We are of Greek parentage."

"Nay, thou lookest not like a Greek; I have seen many of them," said the little girl. "Thou art a Jew, by thy features;

thou art like someone I know, but who it is I cannot remember. But tell me of this brother—Stephen, thou didst call him." "I can tell thee something wonderful about him," said Titus. " He was a cripple, and could not walk; and the Healer—Jesus —cured him, so that he is, as thou didst see. a strong lad, albeit of a delicate and beautiful countenance—at least," added Titus modestly, " he doth so seem to me."

" Yes, of course," said Ruth, somewhat impatient at the digression. " But was he really healed, so that he can walk? Tell me all about it—everything."

Thus commanded, Titus told, with as much of detail as he was able, the story of the baby and Stephen, Ruth interrupting him at intervals with questions.

" Ah!" said she, drawing a long breath of. pleasure, when he had finished, " I like that story! And the best of it is, that it is all true. I too have seen the Nazarene," she continued thoughtfully after a pause. " I think him the most wonderful, the most beautiful, the best man in the whole world! I have longed to talk with him, but my mother says that we cannot, for he is always surrounded with a great crowd of poor people."

They had now passed out of the city and had begun the ascent of one of the high steep hills which shut in on every side the beautiful little lake of Gennesaret, as it was sometimes called. The way became difficult and stony, so that Titus was kept busy picking the best places for the mule. The wife of Jairus glanced back several times to see that her darling was safe, and that the lad was sufficiently careful, and every time caught a bright smile from the little girl. " The precious one!" the mother murmured happily to herself. " She hath a smile like to the sunlight."

After a hard climb of about an hour, the top of the ascent was reached, and all paused for a few moments to rest. The sun was up now, and the scene spread out before the travelers was one of marvelous beauty. Hundreds of feet beneath them lay the silver expanse of the lake, studded with sails; while on every side the hills, covered with luxuriant foliage and dotted with villages, rose higher and higher, till in the far distance gleamed the snowy head of Mount Hermon.

The days that followed were full of delight to Titus. To his sturdy frame the easy stages of the journey caused no fatigue, while the ever-changing scenery, the picturesque evening encampments, and the growing friendliness of the little Ruth, brought a happiness such as he had never known before. All that had embittered his young life lay far behind now, and his soul responded strongly to the new, sweet influences which surrounded him.

On the fourth day of the journey, it became evident that they were approaching the Holy City, for the bands of pilgrims, together with flocks of sheep and oxen for sacrifice and feasting—which they had met occasionally during the whole course of their journey—became more and more frequent. Many of these pilgrim bands were singing while they marched along, and fragments of their song floated back on the wind, as they defiled through the narrow valleys:

" Our feet shall stand within thy gates, O Jerusalem; whither the tribes go up, the tribes of the Lord, to give thanksgiving unto the name of the Lord. Pray for the peace of Jerusalem; they shall prosper that love thee; peace be within thy walls, and prosperity within thy palaces."

<hr />

CHAPTER XII.

TELL thee that the time for looking lightly on the thing hath passed, for this man doth continually blaspheme the name of the Almighty."

The speaker was Caiaphas. As he spoke, he was striding impatiently up and down one of the roof terraces of his house, while Jairus, his guest, half reclined upon a marble bench near at hand. The two sisters sat at a little distance, placidly happy in each other's society, and Ruth, leaning with elbows upon the parapet, gazed with wide, childish eyes upon the wonderful panorama of the Holy City spread out beneath her.

" Thou didst hear this Jesus to-day, when he was questioned concerning the so-called healing of the impotent man at Bethesda. ' God judgeth no man,' he said, ' but hath committed all judgment unto the Son,'— meaning himself. And further, ' That all men should honor the Son even as they honor the Father.' 'Even as'!—didst note the words? Then he went on to speak of John—who is justly imprisoned, for I believe that he was beside himself. 'There is another,' he said, 'that beareth witness of me, and I know that the witness which he witnesseth of me is true.'"

"He said those words," replied Jairus, who had listened in silence up to this point, "but there was another thing also which he said, and which I have not forgotten; 'twas this: 'But I have greater witness than that of John; for the works which the Father hath given me to finish, the same works that I do, bear witness of me, that the Father hath sent me.' Thou dost in thine accusation of the man singularly overlook the works of healing, assuredly great and marvelous, which he continueth daily to perform. What canst thou say to such a cure as that of the man who, as thou knowest, on reputable testimony, had lain on his bed helpless for thirty and eight years? With a word the Nazarene restored him perfectly."

"Aye, but mark the word!" said Caiaphas with heat. "It was the Sabbath day, and he said unto him, 'Rise, take up thy bed and walk.' In that he both healed the man, and bade him take up and carry his bed, on the Sabbath day, he hath done that which is unlawful. He is therefore guilty of blasphemy and also of profaning the law of the Most High; and thou knowest the penalty of such misdeeds," he added darkly.

Neither of the men noticed that the little Ruth had turned about and was listening with an anxious face to the discussion, until she suddenly startled them with the question: "Dost thou speak of Jesus of Nazareth, Uncle Joseph?"

"Why dost thou ask, my child?" said Caiaphas gently, pausing in his walk to lay his hand caressingly upon her golden hair.

"I know him too, and have seen him. If he is the Son of God, as he doth declare, would he not have the right to heal on the Sabbath day, which is God's day?"

"The child speaketh well," said Jairus proudly. "I would have asked thee that question myself."

"And I should have answered thee that his pretensions are, as I have said before, blasphemous. We know that this man is the son of a common carpenter—nay, more; he is himself a common carpenter, and hath

"Dost thou speak of Jesus of Nazareth, Uncle Joseph?"

followed the trade, working with his hands until lately; his home is in Nazareth; and can any good thing come out of Nazareth?"

"But, Uncle Joseph," persisted the little damsel, her face flushing, "how could he do the wonderful things that he doeth, unless God be with him? I love him!" she continued passionately, without waiting his answer, "and I believe that he is, as he hath said, the Son of God."

"My darling," said her mother softly, "it is not seemly for a babe like thee to discuss this matter with thine uncle, more espe-

32   *TITUS, A COMRADE OF THE CROSS.*

cially as he doth hold the sacred office of
high priest in God's holy temple. Thou must
come with me now, that thou mayst grow
calm before the time to sleep."

So saying, the two women went away
with the child, who was now weeping
softly. As the sound of their trailing garments ceased upon the stairway, Jairus
turned to Caiaphas, who was gazing silently
towards the temple, whose walls and towers
glowed with rosy and golden reflections in
the last rays of the setting sun, and said
solemnly:

"To my mind, my brother, this is a time
of great responsibility to the heads of the
nation. If the child spake truly—as I myself believe—'twere assuredly an awful
thing to reject God's Anointed."

Caiaphas remained silent for a moment,
then he turned slowly and looked at Jairus.

"Thou art a good man, and my brother; it
were well for us not to talk of this matter
further, lest it make between us a breach
which cannot be healed. I will tell thee
plainly, once and for all, that my mind is
made up about this man. He must die; for
'twere better for one to die than for many to
perish." But even as he spoke the prophetic
words, he shuddered slightly and glanced
up towards the heavens.

In the meantime, in one of the great
shadowy chambers of the palace, the two
women, having dismissed the maid, were
putting the little Ruth to bed. The child,
kneeling at her mother's knee, had repeated
her psalms and prayers; and now she was
resting snugly in the stately bed, with its
carven posts and drapery and coverlid of
purple, broidered with gold.

"And now, my mother, wilt thou tell me a
story?" she pleaded. "Tell me of David
and Goliath."

And the mother told the story, so familiar
from her youth that she repeated it in the
language of the Scripture itself.

"I have always liked that story!" said
Ruth enthusiastically when she had finished. "How I should like to have seen
David when he stood up on the body of the
giant Philistine, and grasped his great
sword to cut off his wicked old head." She
paused a moment, as if picturing the scene
to herself, then she added eagerly: "I
think, my mother, that David must have
looked exactly like my Titus."

"How canst thou say that, my child?
Thou knowest that thy Titus, as thou callest him, is a Greek."

"Nay," said the little girl positively, "I
told him that could not be, for he hath the
face of a Jew. Hath he not, now—with his
dark skin, his eagle nose, and those great,
flashing eyes of his? He hath a countenance
like—yes, I know it now—like my Uncle
Joseph's!"—half rising, as she spoke, in her
excitement.

"My child, my child!" said the mother,
gently but firmly, "thou must lie down and
sleep now! Thy brain teemeth with wild
fancies. I will sit outside on the terrace near
thee, but thou must indeed be calm."

"Who is the lad that the child speaketh
of?" questioned the lady Anna carelessly,
as the two settled themselves upon the terrace outside the chamber.

"He is a lad from Capernaum, whom our
good Benoni hath recently employed to
assist about the gardens. My impetuous
little daughter hath taken a great liking to
him, and asked that he might lead her mule
upon the journey. Indeed, he seemeth to be
a kind and careful lad, albeit of a very common Greek family. My Ruth hath had so
much excitement of late, that her tongue
doth doth run overmuch; I must see to it
that she hath more quiet, and some wholesome employment."

"I have seen the lad," said Anna mus-
ingly. "He hath a noble countenance, and
strangely enough of the purest Jewish type.
Thou art assured that he is of Greek parentage?"

"It is certain," replied her sister, "for I
made careful inquiry through Benoni himself. His father is called Dumachus."

Then half guessing her sister's thoughts,
and wishing to divert them from so painful
a channel, she said: "But now that we are
alone, and not likely to be interrupted, I will
tell thee how I heard the Nazarene teach
the people. I had long been anxious to
know more fully what those teachings were;
for as thou knowest, reports oftentimes un-
true reach us from careless listeners. So,
hearing that he had gone forth from the city
towards Tiberias, my husband and myself,
attended only by Benoni, set forth, all three
riding upon mules in true peasant fashion,
for we desired not to attract attention.
After riding for some distance we fell in
with numerous people, all journeying in the
same direction. Every one was talking of
the wonderful works of healing which he
had seen, and many who had been healed
were journeying also, and were pointed out
to me by Benoni, who hath taken a won-

drous interest in this man. We heard finally, that he was to be found at Hattin. Thou wilt remember the place—'tis about seven miles from Capernaum; there is there a small village at the foot of the double peaked hill, called sometimes the Horns of Hattin. The hill can be distinctly seen from our house in Capernaum.

" Upon arriving at this place, we found assembled there a great multitude of people, of all nationalities, and of all grades of society. We quickly learned that the Nazarene was even then upon the top of the mountain, and with him those men who are already known as his disciples. Presently we saw that he was descending the slope, surrounded by his followers; instantly there pressed forward those who had brought their sick to be healed. We were not near enough to see what manner of sickness there was among them, nor exactly what transpired; but from the excitement of the crowd, and the thanksgivings and hallelujahs which burst forth, it was evident that all were healed.

" Meanwhile we edged our way among the throngs, and finally succeeded in getting within hearing distance of the Nazarene. He had seated himself now upon a great rock; and as he gazed around on the assembled multitudes, the look upon his face was such that I could not but think of the great angels of our Holy Scriptures. Presently he began to speak. I would that I could tell thee each word of that discourse, for it was wondrous by reason of its wisdom. If he had been the law-giver Moses, himself, fresh from Sinai, he could not have spoken with greater authority.

" He began with blessings. I do not remember them all, but one stands out in my memory above the others: ' Blessed are they that mourn; for they shall be comforted.' He said, also, that the meek, the merciful, and the pure in heart, were blessed; and all those who should be abused and persecuted for the sake of the Christ. ' Rejoice and exult,' he said, looking at his disciples, ' when men shall falsely reproach you, and say every wicked word against you, on account of me. Your reward shall be great in the heavens, for so did they persecute the prophets of old. Ye are the light of the world. A city builded upon a mountain cannot be hid; and when one lighteth a lamp, they do not put it under a corn measure, but upon a lamp stand, and it giveth light to all who are in the house. Thus let your light shine; that men may see it and praise your Father which dwelleth in the heavens.'

" Then, my sister, I noticed that he said he was not come to abolish the Law or the Prophets, but to fulfill them both; and that not the least thing should pass away, till all had come to pass. And further, that unless our righteousness should be greater than that of the Scribes and Pharisees, we could never enter into the kingdom of the heavens. Then he spoke of the Law in detail, and showed that in his opinion the person who was angry without reason, was as liable to judgment as a murderer; that if a person was engaged in a quarrel with another, he could not acceptably offer sacrifices to God. Moreover, that one should not attempt to resist an evil-doer, but rather shame him with generosity; that we must love, not alone our friends, but even those who hated us and tried to do us harm; and that we must pray for wicked persons, for so might we be children of our Father in the heavens. For his sun riseth on those who are evil, as well as on those who are good; his rain also cometh down on the ground of the bad man, as well as on that of the good. And that if we love and are courteous to our equals only, we are no better than the lowest. In short, we must try to be perfect, even as our Father in heaven is perfect.

" Be careful, he said, not to be charitable in order that your friends may see and praise you for it; if ye give to the poor in this way, God will not reward you. Giving done quietly, and without parade, shall be rewarded openly. He also condemned making a show of prayer; and thou knowest, my sister, how our Scribes and Pharisees sometimes pray even on the street—I have wondered how they could realize what they were doing, as they stand on the corners and pray so loudly. The Nazarene declared that they do it simply to be seen and praised of the lookers-on, and that truly they will get nothing else for their prayers. ' If thou wouldst be heard and answered of God,' he said, ' pray secretly in your own chamber with closed door. And do not suppose that the Father demandeth long prayers, or is pleased with empty repetitions; the heathen pray in that way. God is your Father; he knoweth what things ye have need of, before ye ask him.' He doth not wait to have us ask, for see how he careth for every creature, even for those who, like the heathen, never pray aright. Yet must we pray, for so it pleaseth the Father. Then he said: ' After this manner pray ye: Our Father, who art in the heavens, sanctified be thy name. Let thy kingdom come, let thy will be done, as in the heavens so also upon the earth. The needed bread give us to-day. Forgive us our debts, as also we forgive our debtors. And lead us not into temptation, but deliver us from the evil one. For thine is the kingdom, and the power, and the glory, to the ages. Amen.' "

" 'Tis a wondrous prayer!" said Anna, her eyes glowing in the semi-darkness. " But his teachings are strangely different from what hath sounded in our ears since Moses led forth the people of Israel from Egypt."

" But hath it not the sound of truth? It seemeth so to me," answered her sister. " I can tell thee more, if thou wilt hear it. Art thou not weary?"

" Nay, tell me more—all that thou canst," said Anna.

" I feel that, at best, I can only give fragments, but I will try. He counseled that we should not care overmuch for the treasures of this earth; for such things are liable to be eaten with moths, or rusted away, else stolen. Thou knowest how true that is, my sister?"

" It is indeed true," murmured Anna with a sigh, thinking how her chiefest treasure had been stolen from her.

" Lay up for yourselves treasures in heaven, where neither moth nor rust doth corrupt, and where thieves do not break through nor steal," continued Sara softly. " And do not be over-anxious about the future, for your Father in heaven knoweth that ye have need of food, and clothing, and shelter; and if he clothe the wild lilies, which toil not at all, more gorgeously than even the great Solomon in all his glory, shall he forget his children? The first thing and the most important, is to seek after God and his righteousness. If we do this, all else that is needful shall be given us by the hand that never faileth. Do not criticise others, for often we ourselves are full of faults more evil; we must be judged even as we judge our fellow-men. God will give more abundantly to his children, when they ask him, than earthly parents to their children! So that if we desire anything we must ask it of our heavenly Father. We shall surely receive it, if it be for our good. To keep perfectly the Law and the Prophets —note this especially, my sister, for it is what we are always laboring to perform—' it is only necessary to do unto others such

things as we would wish them to do to us.'

" His closing words were astonishing, for in them he plainly declared himself to be the Heaven-sent One. ' Not every one who shall say to me, Lord, Lord, shall enter into the kingdom of the heavens; but he who doeth the will of my Father who is in heaven. Many will say to me in that day, Did we not cast out devils in thy name, and in thy name perform many works of power? Then shall I say to them, I never knew you. Depart from me, ye who work lawlessness. Every one therefore who heareth these words of mine, and liveth them, is like a prudent man, who built his house upon a rock. Down came the rain; the streams rose; and the strong winds blew; but the house was safe, for it was builded upon a rock. But he who heareth these words, and heedeth them not, is like a man who foolishly built his house upon the sand. Down came the rain; the streams rose; and the tempest raged and beat upon that house; and it fell, and great was the fall of it.'

" When he had finished these sayings a great murmur of amazement arose from that vast multitude. Truly, my sister, it was a marvelous discourse, though I can but dimly and imperfectly repeat it to thee. I would that thou couldst hear the man for thyself."

" I would that I might," said the lady Anna; then she added hesitatingly, " But thou knowest how my husband thinketh, and our father also."

" Yes, I know," assented her sister simply.

After that the two were silent, absorbed each in her own thoughts, while within the child slept peacefully.

CHAPTER XIII.

 HISTLING softly to himself as he worked, Titus was fastening up some long tendrils of a climbing vine; it was a difficult job, and when he had finished, his face was quite hot and flushed. He therefore walked slowly across the turf to the fountain, and, seating himself on the marble ledge which surrounded it, began plunging his hand and arm into its cool depths, withdrawing it at intervals to wet his curly head.

"Ah, that cold water, how good it is!" he murmured to himself; then shaking his head vigorously to rid it of the superfluous drops, he stood up, and looked about the garden with great satisfaction. He had been hard at work since early dawn; and as his eyes wandered from the trim shrubbery to the velvet turf, and then on to the masses of brilliant flowers and graceful festoons of vines, he saw nothing to criticise.

"I see nothing amiss," he said aloud. "But I know not what Benoni will think; he hath the eye of an eagle for a trace of disorder." Then catching sight of some bright-colored object on the ground under one of the marble benches, he stooped and picked it up. It was a ball, gayly striped with blue, scarlet and yellow. As he turned it over and over in his hands, he smiled and said, "I wonder where the little lady is this morning. Ah, there is Marissa!"

The maid was passing rapidly through the garden, bearing a pitcher in her hands. She stopped and turned, as Titus called to her, and as he came near, he noticed that she was unusually grave.

"Here is a ball belonging to our little lady," he said. "Wilt thou take care of it? She hath not been in the garden to play this morning."

"She is ill," said Marissa soberly; "we have sent out for a physician. I am going now for some hot water; do not keep me."

Titus opened the door leading into the passage-way which connected the two court-yards, and followed Marissa as she hastened on with her pitcher.

"What aileth the little one?" he asked, as she paused to dip some water from a steaming cauldron.

"We know not. She hath fever and complaineth of pain in her head. It hath not been well with her since our return from Jerusalem."

"Where is the master?" asked Titus.

"He is with the child," answered Marissa, "also her mother, and old Tabitha, who nursed the mistress in her infancy. She knoweth more about sickness than all the doctors put together. Ugh! I dread to have them come near the child with their loathly nostrums!" And she hurried away with the steaming pitcher, leaving Titus to tell the sad news of the little Ruth's illness to the other servants, who had crowded around.

He left them as soon as possible, for their society was at best distasteful to him, and now their dismal forebodings and ominous waggings of the head filled him with a kind of dull rage.

As he paced uneasily up and down, he saw that the door of the passage-way leading to the street was standing open; and presently, without exactly knowing why, he found himself outside. Once there, he bent his steps toward the quarter of the town where was the poor place he still called home.

"I must see Stephen," he said to himself, as he hurried along.

Meanwhile, in her chamber, which opened upon one of the small inner courts of the house, the little Ruth was tossing wearily upon her bed.

"Oh, mother, my head! my head!" she moaned.

And the mother watching by her side, saw with a sinking heart, the scarlet flush on the child's cheek, and her eyes hourly growing more sunken and brilliant.

The good old Tabitha was wringing out linen cloths from cold water, which she placed upon the sufferer's brow, while at intervals she caused them to put the little feet into a basin of hot water.

"We must keep the heat from the darling's head," she was saying, with the wisdom born of good common sense and long experience. "I have saved many a fever patient, as thou knowest, with water alone."

"Why doth not the physician come?" said Jairus impatiently. "I would be doing something for her, in the way of medicament; the water is well enough, but for such a sickness as this, medicine is assuredly needful."

Even as he spoke Marissa announced the physician, standing aside that he might enter before her.

A tall, heavily-bearded man, magnificently attired, swept into the apartment, attended by a small, black slave bearing the various appurtenances of his craft. He greeted Jairus ceremoniously; then, approaching the bedside of the child, he looked at her, narrowing his eyes, pursing up his mouth, and frowning deeply as he did so. Presently he put out his hand and laid it upon the child's head, then hemmed loudly. The little thing started, and hid her face in her mother's gown.

"She hath a burning heat!" said the great man finally, in a deep, sonorous voice; then he rolled his eyes majestically at Tabitha, as she was about to place a fresh cool bit of linen on the child's burning forehead, and stretched forth his hand forbiddingly.

"Woman!" he said sternly, "cease thy foolishness! Water is indeed good in health, but thou hast imperiled the child's life by thy folly."

Tabitha turned her broad back upon him, and was heard to mutter something unintelligible.

The physician now beckoned to his slave, and, taking from him a small brazen vessel, he proceeded to mingle in it a number of dark liquids, together with a grayish white powder. When he had finished, he again turned to his familiar, who immediately produced from another receptacle a dead snake. This the great man proceeded to skin. When he had finished the operation, which he performed with marvelous deftness, he again hemmed loudly, and said:

"Thou shalt make of this snake-skin three portions; one portion shall be bound upon the forehead of the child, and one upon the side of each foot. Also of the draught which I have mingled, give her, at intervals of an hour, one great spoonful. If it be the will of Jehovah, she will recover within seven days. I shall return again at the evening hour. And stay!"—here again his eye sought Tabitha—"'Twere better to remove yon contentious woman from the apartment." Then bowing deeply, he was about to leave the room, when Jairus stopped him with an imperious gesture.

"Good sir!" he demanded, "I would know what hath entered into the potion which she is to swallow."

The physician frowned and shook his head, but finally said majestically:

"'Tis not our custom to reveal the secrets of our craft; but for thee I will even make exception. Know, then, that the draught—which thou wilt find most wholesome—containeth first, the gall of a wild sow dissolved in vinegar; second, the ashes of a wolf's skull mingled with the fat of a viper; and lastly, and most important of all, a stone taken from the head of a sea eel, caught at the time of the full moon. This stone hath been powdered together with a portion of scorpion's legs, and hath been known to be efficacious when taken alone; but compounded as I have described, maketh a nostrum of such rare virtue, that without doubt the patient will speedily recover. Should she not recover, it will be because of the folly of yonder woman." So saying, and

again bowing profoundly, he swept from the chamber, followed by his slave.

When he had finally gone, Tabitha came forward, and, throwing herself upon her knees before her mistress, sobbed out:

"Oh, send me not away! I will do anything, if only I may remain. Surely I have not hurt the child—thou knowest that the wet linen soothed her. And how can the skin of a snake be better than cool, fresh water?"

"Hush, Tabitha!" said her mistress, the tears running down her cheeks. "Thou shalt stay; indeed I could not do without thee. But oh, my husband! what dost thou think of the draught? I cannot bear to give it to her. And that dreadful slimy skin!"

"I think this of it!" said Jairus fiercely, rising and seizing the skin and the brazen vessel, and tossing them both out of the window. "If she must die, she shall die unpolluted with such vileness! Go on with thy nursing, Tabitha, and in thine own way. And do thou, Marissa, give orders to the porter not to admit that man when he cometh at evening. Stay!—tell him to give the fellow this gold."

But now the little patient, either because of the fright and agitation, or because of the progress of the disease, began to talk wildly. Now she fancied that she was in Jerusalem, and wandered on incoherently of the processions, the temple, the singing. Now she thought she was riding her mule, and that Titus was gathering great bunches of wild-flowers for her. Presently she half raised herself in the bed, and shading her eyes with her hand, cried out joyously:

"Oh, Titus! I see the Master! He is coming through the meadow. See how the lilies bend, as his garments pass over them! I shall speak with him at last!"

Then she fell back upon her pillow, her voice sinking into a low, incoherent murmur.

But like a flash of light came the thought of the great Healer to the despairing mother. Rising, she crossed the room to the window, before which stood her husband, his head bowed upon his breast, and laying her hand upon his arm, she half whispered: "My husband, in our terror we had forgotten the Nazarene; could he not heal our child?"

Jairus started and turned toward his wife, a gleam of something like hope in his eyes.

"True!" he said. "We had most strangely forgotten. I believe that he, and he alone, can help us now. I will go at once and make inquiries concerning him. Benoni is even now waiting outside for orders."

Titus was sitting motionless at the side of the fountain, his eyes fixed upon the door of the inner court. He had been there for hours, waiting for some one to come out. When, therefore, Benoni issued forth, prepared to do his master's bidding, Titus sprang forward to meet him.

"How doth our little lady fare?" he asked.

"Alas! I fear that she doth not mend. She will die, unless she hath help, and that quickly. I am going forth to seek the Nazarene. We hope—"

"He is not here," said Titus in a tone of dull despair. "This morning, when first I heard of her sickness, I sought Stephen, my brother—for he always knoweth the best thing to do—and he said at once, 'Let us seek the Master.' We sought far and wide, and found at last that he had taken shipping yesterday to go to the other side of the lake. It may be that he hath gone away into Samaria, or even back to Jerusalem. I know not how we could find him."

Benoni looked grave. But at length he said: "I must go forth, even as I was bidden; it may be that he hath returned since the morning."

"Go if thou wilt," said Titus wearily. "But Stephen was to keep watch, and bring me word should the Master return; he will not fail to do so."

"I also must go," said Benoni.

But he returned within an hour, and his grave countenance showed that he had failed in his mission.

CHAPTER XIV.

LOWLY the hours dragged by. Night came on, and, as slowly, wore away. Still Titus watched and waited for some word from Stephen, while within the sick-room the watchers, with despairing hearts, saw the steady and relentless approach of the dread destroyer.

The child lay motionless now, her eyes half opened and glassy; but for the sound of her difficult breathing which filled the chamber, they would have thought her dead. The mother had thrown herself on her knees at the foot of the bed, her face hidden in the draperies. She had been praying at intervals all night, the words of the Master in her thoughts: "God is more willing to give good gifts to his children, than are ye to give good things to your children." And now her heart was full of bitterness. "I have prayed, and God hath not heard me. My child is dying. The Master hath healed scores of worthless beggars, but now that my pure, innocent child is suffering, he will not come. If he were the Christ, would he not know of this?" And over and over again the cruel thoughts repeated themselves; till her brain was half crazed with pain.

At length she arose, and swiftly approaching her husband, who was sitting motionless watching the child's face, she said:

"Wilt thou not go forth and search for the Nazarene? Do not wait! It may be that he hath come even now."

Jairus rose, and without a word left the room. It was morning now, and the bright sunlight struck painfully on his throbbing eyeballs.

Outside the faithful Benoni was pacing up and down on the terrace. At the sound of a step he sprang forward, but the question died on his lips as he saw his master's face.

"Has anything been heard of the Nazarene?" asked Jairus.

"Nothing, my lord," answered the man mournfully. "I have been out to inquire many times, and the lad Titus also."

"I am going now. It may be that I shall find him," said Jairus. "Do thou remain within call. I will take the lad with me."

Titus had just made one of his fruitless excursions into the street, and was about to return sorrowfully for the twentieth time, when he heard a noise as of light, rapid footfalls on the stone pavement. Some one was coming! He stood still and listened. In another moment Stephen approached the gate, running at full speed. When he beheld Titus, he cried out joyfully: "He has come!"

Titus did not stop to hear more, but, calling to Stephen to wait, ran back through the court into the garden, and was about to knock boldly on the door which led to the inner court, when it suddenly opened and Jairus himself came out.

"The Healer hath come!" cried Titus excitedly, without waiting for his master to speak. "My brother hath but just brought word. He is waiting outside and can tell us where the Nazarene is to be found. Shall I go for thee?"

"No, lad," said Jairus; "I will go for myself; but thou mayst attend me."

The two passed quickly into the street, where they found Stephen waiting.

"Come this way!" he said. "He hath but just landed outside the city, and was approaching the eastern gate when I heard of it."

All three hurried on in silence, Jairus slightly in advance of the two lads, as though he would outstrip them. Never had the way seemed so long. Streets, squares, alleys; mansions and hovels, amphitheatre and synagogue—they were all alike to him now. He had neither eaten nor slept for more than twenty-four hours; and things loomed up huge and horrible through a mist of pain. At last they reached the eastern gate.

"Hath the Nazarene passed this way yet?" he asked the gate-keeper hoarsely.

"No," said the man. "He hath stopped yonder to talk to the people, who already throng him, though he hath but just landed." He pointed eastward as he spoke, and the three hurried on toward a little rise in the ground, which was crowded with people.

They presently reached the outskirts of this throng and could see the face of the Master himself, as he stood upon an elevation in the midst.

"In God's name, let me pass, good people!" cried Jairus. "I must speak with the Master!"

The crowd gave way respectfully, for many of them recognized the speaker, and all saw that he was in deep trouble. And now he has fallen at the feet of the Master, and is crying out:

"Jesus, thou son of God, I beseech thee to hear me! My little daughter lieth at the point of death; I pray thee come and lay thy hands upon her, that she may be healed; and she shall live."

Immediately Jesus put forth his hand and raised him up, and they began to move toward the city gate; and with them, all the multitude, which was constantly increasing, as one and another, scenting some new excitement, joined it.

Their progress was necessarily slow now, for the crowd was surging on all sides of them. Presently they stopped altogether, for Jesus was standing still in the midst. Turning, he said:

"Who touched me?"

At first no one answered, for all were astonished at the question. Then one of his disciples, Peter by name, said:

"Master, the multitude throng thee and press thee; and sayest thou, Who touched me?"

But Jesus answered: "Somebody hath touched me; for I perceive that power hath gone out of me."

As he spoke, he fixed his eyes upon a poorly-dressed woman who stood near. When she saw that he was looking at her, she trembled, and coming forward, fell down before him, and sobbed out:

"Oh, Master! I beseech thee to forgive me! I have been in misery for twelve years by reason of an incurable disease, and have suffered many things of many physicians. I have spent all that I had, and was nothing bettered, but always made worse. And I thought in my heart, that if I could but touch the hem of thy garment, I should be healed. And it was so, for no sooner had I touched, than I was made whole."

When Jesus heard this, he put forth his hand and raised her up, saying:

"Daughter, be of good courage; thy faith hath made thee whole. Go in peace, and be healed of thy scourge."

While he was yet speaking to the woman, Jairus, who had been waiting in an agony of impatience, saw Benoni approaching. And Benoni, when he spied his master, rent his clothes with a loud cry of grief.

"Alas! my lord," he said, "thy daughter is dead. Trouble not the Master further."

The face of Jairus blanched to a ghastly pallor when he heard these words, and he would have fallen to the earth, had it not been for the quick hand of the Master.

"Be not afraid!" he said to him gently. "Only believe!" Then turning, he spoke authoritatively to the crowd, forbidding them to come any further.

Again they went on; Jesus with three of his disciples and Jairus; the two lads, with Benoni, following them at a little distance.

"What can the Healer do now to help?" muttered Titus bitterly. "But for the woman, we might have been in time."

"The little one breathed her last just after the master left the house," said Benoni sadly.

"But didst thou hear what the Master said to the father of the child?" said Stephen. "'Fear not. Only believe'! He will do something to help—thou wilt see."

"But what can he do, now?" repeated Titus.

"He can help them to bear the will of our Father which is in heaven," said Stephen softly.

By this time they had come to the house of Jairus; and entering in after the others, they found the court of the household almost deserted. Passing through into the garden court, they could hear the piercing wails of the women from the death-chamber, for the door leading to the inner court stood wide open. The garden itself was filled with excited women, wailing and gesticulating, while the men with rent garments were weeping aloud, and strewing ashes upon their heads and beards in token of their grief.

Within sat the mother by the bedside of her dead child—for she had resisted the well-meant efforts of her women to take her away—her wide, tearless eyes fixed upon the waxen beauty of the face upon the pillow. Amid all the wailing and tumult she was stonily silent.

"Soon she will be forever hidden from me," she was thinking. "I must not weep now, while she is sleeping so quietly."

Presently she became dimly aware of another presence in the room, and of a deep, authoritative voice. What was it that he was saying?—"Why make ye this ado, and weep? The damsel is not dead, but sleepeth."

And the strident wailing ceased; and there was a blessed stillness in her tortured ears.

Not dead! Sleeping! She started to her feet, and leaning over the little form, listened breathlessly. Alas! she slept indeed, but it was the chill and pulseless sleep which would know no waking. She raised her eyes, dim with anguish, to his face.

"Thou knowest that she is dead, Master," were the words which shaped themselves on her lips; but they were never uttered. Something in those fathomless eyes forbade them.

And standing by the bedside, Jesus took the little icy hand in his, and said:

"My child, I say unto thee, arise!"

And at the words, lo! a rosy flush swept over the marble beauty of the face, the long lashes trembled, and the eyes—but lately closed for their long, long sleep—flashed wide open, bright with joy and health. They fixed themselves upon the Master's face, and a smile slow and sweet dawned in their starry depths.

"'Tis thou at last!" she said. "I have been dreaming of thee."

Who could describe the scene which followed!—the happiness, the gratitude, the well-nigh delirious revulsion from the depths of a grief so profound, to the heights of a joy so transcendent.

The child gazed at her parents in solemn wonder, as they fell at the Master's feet, covering them with tears and kisses. She had slept; she had dreamed; she had awakened. But what meant this strange weeping, this tumult in the garden outside? Was she dreaming still?

The Master seeing her look, and divining her thoughts, spoke to the mother, his words recalling her instantly to herself:

"The child is an hungered; wilt thou not give her to eat?"

Then charging them straitly that they should not noise the thing abroad, he left them alone with their joy.

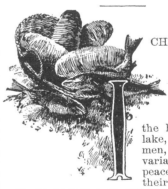

CHAPTER XV.

IN one of the green and pleasant solitudes near the head of the lake, a group of men, strangely at variance with the peaceful beauty of their surroundings, sat, or sprawled at full length, around a small fire. There were ten or a dozen of them, great hulking fellows, low-browed, swarthy with wind and weather, and disfigured with the scars of many a sinister combat. They were engaged for the moment in the peaceful occupation of broiling some fish, while on the grass near at hand lay several half emptied wine-skins.

"And so the lad hath given thee the slip, Dumachus? 'Twere a pity; he hath the making of a bold fellow in him," said one of the men, leaning forward to heap fresh fuel on the fire. "Where didst thou get him? He is of no kin to thee."

"He is my son," said Dumachus sullenly.

"Come, come, now; comrade! Why take the trouble to lie to us about a trifle like that? If thou hast stolen him from some rich Jew, why not demand a ransom for his return? Men are plentier than gold nowadays."

Dumachus made no answer for a moment, then replied sneeringly:

"And thou, my good friend, wouldst share the gold, perhaps?"

"I am he, and these be my disciples!"

"That would I!" said the other, with a great laugh. "Come, tell us the man's name."

"Fool!" hissed Dumachus. "If I had chosen to restore the boy, as thou sayest, would I not have done it years ago? I love my revenge better than the yellowest gold ever coined. He shall not escape me, and when the time is ripe I shall—" Here he stopped abruptly, while so hideous an expression overspread his countenance that even his guilt-hardened companions stared at him in momentary wonder.

"I envy not the lad his future with such a guardian as thou art," said the first speaker, shrugging his shoulders. "I believe there is not another such brute in

Galilee! Thou wilt be crucified yet, my worshipful chief!"

But he had his hand on the haft of the short two-edged knife in his belt, as he spoke, and Dumachus, who had started up at the words, sank back again, muttering threats and curses under his breath.

"Come!" said another. "Hast thou not had blood enough, that thou must knife each other, now we are at rest? Let us eat!" And the speaker helped himself to one of the fish which were sizzling on the coals.

The others followed his example, and soon all were eating and drinking, the rude feast being enlivened with snatches of coarse song, and bursts of coarser laughter. Presently, one of the men stopped, with a morsel half way to his mouth.

"Hist! I hear some one coming!" he said.

Instantly all were on their feet; and one, creeping lightly to the verge of a little declivity fringed with bushes, peered out cautiously. In a moment he returned.

"'Tis the Nazarene rabbi with his band; they have just landed on the beach below."

"What can they be doing here, think you?" whispered another. "Shall we—?" And he drew his glittering knife with a significant gesture.

"No, fool!" snarled Dumachus. "They have no booty. Besides," he added, "the man may be useful to us. Thou knowest that he hath a great following already, and greater every day. With him for king, we could make ourselves masters of the country. He hath magic powers; and could, from the grass of the field, make swords enough to arm every man who should join us. The Romans themselves fear him!"

"They say," said another, "that he hath made a compact with Beelzebub himself, and that is why he hath such marvelous powers. I heard a rabbi from Jerusalem explaining the matter to a multitude who were marveling because the Nazarene had healed one of their number from a blind and deaf spirit."

"Well, for my part, I care not to whom he hath allied himself. I am ready for anything wherein is a prospect of plunder," exclaimed a third. "But what causeth the tumult which I hear? Stay! I will see." And scrambling up a tall tree which grew near, he presently called down to his companions below: "'Tis a wondrous sight! There be thousands upon thousands of men, with women and children, both riding upon beasts, and walking,—and all coming this way!"

"They are seeking the man yonder," said Dumachus, jerking his thumb over his shoulder. "Now thou seest that I spoke truly! Let us wait here, and see what shall follow. To-day the time may be ripe for action."

Even as he spoke, a man broke through the bushes near at hand. He started back in dismay, when his eye fell upon the savage group; but regaining his confidence in the knowledge that the rest of his company was close at hand, he advanced and called out in a loud voice:

"Have any of you knowledge of the whereabouts of the man who is called Jesus of Nazareth?"

"I am he," said Dumachus mockingly, "and these be my disciples. What dost thou require of us?"

The man stared; while the others burst into a great roar of laughter at his discomfiture.

"The Nazarene is yonder on the hill!" said Dumachus finally, seeing that he was about to run.

The man glanced upward, and then cried out joyfully to those below:

"He is here! Come this way!"

In a moment two—three—a dozen men had pushed through the bushes, and with glad cries pressed up the hill. These were quickly followed by an indiscriminate throng of men, women, and children—all hurrying — pushing — struggling upward. Dumachus and his men joined the multitude, shouting lustily for the great Healer as they maliciously trampled down some of the weaker ones in the throng.

Meanwhile Jesus, with his chosen followers, was resting quietly in a little nook of the mountain slope. Faint, and exhausted with uninterrupted toil and excitement, they had sought this peaceful solitude for a little time of rest. As the first sound of the approaching multitude reached their ears, Peter was on his feet in an instant, and springing to the top of a high rock, he shaded his eyes with his hand, and looked off in the direction from which the noise came.

"What is it? What seest thou?" cried half a dozen voices anxiously.

Peter scrambled down from his lofty perch without replying, and approaching the Master, who sat a little apart from the others, his eyes fixed peacefully on the wide landscape, he said:

"Master, I see a great multitude approaching. They seek thee. Shall we not escape them while yet there is time? We can withdraw further up the mountain, or take to our boats again."

Jesus made no answer, but rising, moved toward the edge of the slope, and looked down. The noise was louder now, and floated up to him in a confused roaring like to the sound of the sea. Already the bright colors of the moving masses could be seen through the green foliage; in another moment the throng would be upon them. He sighed deeply, and murmured with a look of divine compassion:

"They are as sheep having no shepherd!"

"Master, thou art sorely in need of rest; wilt thou not come?" again urged Peter.

But even as he spoke, the crest of the first wave of that ocean of wretched humanity broke sobbing at their feet.

The hours that followed were crowded, as were always his hours upon earth. Verily, "He had a work to perform, and how was he straitened till he should perform it." He healed those that had need of healing; after that he taught them many things concerning the kingdom of God.

And now the day was far spent, and the shadows were lengthening upon the mountains. Still the people lingered, listening to his words, while only the fitful cry of a tired or hungry child broke the hush.

The disciples, who had been holding a whispered consultation, now came to him; and one of them, who was called Philip, said:

"Master, this is a desert place, and it is already late; wilt thou not send the people

away, that they may go into the country round about and buy themselves bread? for they have nothing to eat."
And he said: "Give ye them to eat."
"Two hundred pennyworth of bread would not be sufficient, that everyone of them might take a little. How then can we give them to eat?" answered Philip.
"How many loaves have ye? Go and see," replied the Master.
"I will go," said Andrew. Presently he returned. "There is a lad here, which hath five barley loaves and two small fishes; but what are they among so many!"
"Make the people to sit down on the grass by companies," was the answer.

But what of Dumachus and his fellows, on this memorable afternoon? Having crowded themselves, by means of brute force, into a place where they could both see and hear to the best advantage, they had stared with open mouths and many a muttered oath, as the Master healed the sick and injured which were brought unto him. But when he began to talk to the people, one by one they had slipped away—save Gestas. He, the day being warm, and himself very comfortable as he lounged back against a tree, had sunken into a doze, and from a doze had passed into a heavy slumber; and as the Master spake the words of eternal life, he sat with head sunken upon his breast. His ears were heavy and he did not hear.
"What is the Master going to do now?" was the question which flew from mouth to mouth, when the multitude were bidden by the disciples to sit down by hundreds, and by fifties. Every eye was fastened upon him, as he took the five loaves and the two fishes; and as he looked up to heaven and blessed them, and began to break them into fragments to give to the disciples for distribution, the wonder grew. Awe-stricken they watched. Behold! under those gracious hands the loaves multiplied themselves! Again, and yet again, and many times over, the twelve returned to him for fresh supplies, till at last all of the five thousand men, together with the women and children, had been fully satisfied.
After all had eaten, the Master gave command that the remnants of the feast should be gathered up, that nothing might be lost. And they took up of the fragments that remained, twelve baskets full.
Dumachus and his followers had eaten also.

"Thou art right," said one of them, who was called Gaius. "This is the man for our king; if he can make for us barley loaves and broiled fish, could he not give us honey and wine in abundance, and other good things also? Let us even now crown him!"
And the Jews, moreover, which saw it, said, "This is, of a truth, that prophet which should come into the world; for, behold, he hath fed us in the wilderness, even as Moses fed our fathers."
But he knew their thoughts; and directing his disciples to get into the boat and go unto Bethsaida, which was on the other side of the lake, he commanded the people that they should depart quietly, and go each man to his own house. Then he, himself, went alone up into the mountain to pray.
Now while some of the people obeyed him, and departed, even as he had bidden them, many lingered, hoping that he would presently come again into their midst, for they had seen the disciples go away in the boat, and knew that he was not with them. And as they waited, the wonder and excitement grew apace, till at length Dumachus, seeing the temper of their minds, sprang upon a lofty rock, and thus addressed the throng:
"Galileans!" he shouted, "hear me! Thou hast seen how this man hath been able to create before our very eyes, and from nothing visible, an abundance of food for this great multitude. If he is able to do this, think ye not that from the grass of this place he could presently make swords enough to arm every man of us? Let us make him our king! Then will we sweep down from the mountains, gathering in the people from every town, and city, and village. Nothing can stand before us! The Romans shall flee! Their rich palaces shall be a prey unto us! Hail to the Nazarene! Hail! Hail to the Nazarene! Hail to the King!"
When the people heard this, there arose a mighty cry, which rang out over the waters of the lake, and rolled back to the mountains, reverberating in thunderous echoes to the very stars.
To a solitary figure, far above on the mountain heights, that cry brought the old, subtle temptation of the wilderness. The kingdoms of the world and the glory of them! A throne—and not a cross! But the victory had been won, once and forever. He saw, in the sure light of eternity, his earthly road, and it led to Calvary.

" Now it was dark, and the ship was in the midst of the sea, and he alone on the land. And the sea arose by reason of a great wind that blew. And he saw them toiling in rowing; for the wind was contrary; and about the fourth watch of the night he cometh unto them walking upon the sea, and would have passed them by. But when they saw him walking upon the sea, they supposed it had been a spirit, and cried out; for they all saw him and were troubled. And immediately he spoke and said unto them, Be of good cheer; it is I; be not afraid. And Peter answered him and said, Lord, if it be thou, bid me come unto thee on the water. And he said, Come. And when Peter was come down out of the ship, he walked upon the water to go to Jesus. But when he saw the wind boisterous, he was afraid; and beginning to sink, he cried, saying, Lord, save me! And immediately Jesus stretched forth his hand and caught him, and said unto him, O thou of little faith! wherefore didst thou doubt? And when they were come into the ship, the wind ceased. Then they that were in the ship came and worshiped him, saying, Of a truth thou art the Son of God!''

CHAPTER XVI.

TELL you that he is not to be found upon the mountain.'' The speaker was Dumachus, and he was addressing a motley crowd of Galileans. " My men know every inch of the region hereabouts, a n d they have made thorough search.''

"There was no boat, so that he could have gotten away by the lake,'' said another. " He must have gone over the mountain, and descended upon the other side; in that case we cannot find him, for the present. It may be that he will stop in the villages; 'tis his wont.''

" Let us go back to Capernaum, for it is there his disciples dwell; he will be there sooner or later,'' suggested a third.

And seeing drawn up on the beach below, some great barges from Tiberias, which had been driven out of their course by the storm of the night before, as many as were able crowded into them, and a few hours later landed in the village of Capernaum.

As they made their way up into the city, they perceived that there was a great noise and confusion, people hurrying in crowds through the narrow streets, or gathered in dense throngs in the market-places.

" What is the ado, neighbors?'' shouted Dumachus, as they paused near one of these knots of people. " We have just landed, and are seeking the miracle-worker; dost know his whereabouts?''

Two or three had turned at the sound of his voice, and now one answered eagerly: " The Nazarene is here. He came this morning, and hath wrought many signs and wonders in our midst. For as he passed through the villages of the plain, people brought out their sick and laid them in the streets that they might touch the border of his garments; and as many as touched were made whole. Afterward he came to Capernaum, and the whole country-side hath followed him thither. Is not this man he that should save Israel?''

" He can assuredly work wonders; and why not to-day wonders greater than any we have yet seen?'' answered Dumachus, cunningly. " Let us seek him and see if he will not presently give us some sign that shall be greater than the healing of these sick folk. Let him give us an abundance of gold and treasure; and let him take these fine houses and lands from the rich, and give them to us, who are his servants. Then shall we delight ourselves in rivers of wine; and eat, and drink, and satisfy ourselves with pleasures.''

" If he be the Messiah, he will do all this, and much more,'' said the man. " It hath been promised us by the prophets. Surely the time hath come for Israel to claim her King; and confusion of face shall be to all heathen who would rule over our nation!''

" Amen! and Amen!'' cried they that heard him; and with a common impulse, all began to run in the direction of the synagogue, for it was one of the holy days of the week. " We shall doubtless find him there!'' they said, as they hurried along. " Let us hasten, that we may speak with him!''

As they approached the place of worship, the excitement grew more and more intense; it was almost impossible to move in the dense throng. The synagogue was already filled to its utmost capacity, though the hour for service had not yet come—Scribes and Pharisees, Sadducees and Doctors of the Law, publicans, fishermen and laborers, with women and children—and every tongue employed with the one theme, Jesus of Nazareth.

"He is coming! I see him! Make room!" arose from one and another of the multitude outside, together with a vast uneasy murmur of sound.

Dumachus had succeeded in elbowing himself to a place just outside the door of the synagogue through which the Master must pass to enter; and now, when he saw him ascending the steps with his disciples, he thrust himself forward rudely, saying, "Rabbi, when camest thou hither, and how? There was no boat for thee to cross by."

Jesus looked at him; then turning, he glanced at the multitude. Greed, vulgar curiosity, mean self-interest, ambition, cruelty, hatred, unbelief—all this might have been seen by any keen-eyed observer; but how, think you, looked the multitude to the reader of hearts?

Then he spoke slowly, decisively: "Verily, verily, I say unto you, Ye seek me, not because ye perceived the signs; but because ye did eat of the loaves and were filled. Strive not for the bread which perisheth, but for that bread which shall abide unto life eternal, which the Son of man shall give to you; for him hath God the Father sealed."

Then from out of the throng came another voice—a clear young voice—and the question was one which the speaker had been pondering in his heart for months: "What shall we do, that we might work the works of God?"

And the Master saw the face of the questioner among the sinister faces which surrounded it, like a star in the darkness of night; he saw and knew it for his own. And looking steadfastly into the clear eyes lifted to his, he answered: "This is the work of God, that ye believe on him whom he hath sent."

"What sign showest thou, then," broke in the brutal voice of Dumachus, "that we may see, and believe thee? What dost thou work?"

And a turbaned rabbi, who stood near, added cunningly: Our fathers did eat manna in the desert; as it is written, He gave them bread from heaven to eat."

The Master made answer: "Of a truth I tell you that Moses gave you not bread from heaven. But my Father giveth you now the true bread from heaven; for the bread of God is he which cometh down from heaven, and giveth life unto the world."

"Like the benediction after prayer," came again the clear tones of the boy's voice: "Lord, evermore give us this bread!"

Then the Master passed into the sanctuary, and the solemn hush within proclaimed that the service had begun.

In obedience to the imperative commands and gestures of those in authority, the crowd now drew back, somewhat, from the entrance and approaches to the synagogue; and as they did so, a clamor of voices broke out.

"How doth he say that he came down from heaven?" demanded one. "We know who he is; he is Jesus the son of Joseph, from Nazareth yonder."

"He came down from heaven no more than I did," cried another. "I am a silversmith; and he is a carpenter, as I happen to know."

"Now are ye wise, good people!" said a smooth-tongued emissary of the Sanhedrim. "This man hath not ceased to blaspheme God, in that he maketh himself equal with God; and as for coming down from heaven, he hath a devil and is mad."

"If he be not mad," one answered, "he at least is not the Messiah, as we hoped; for he hath not the ways of a king."

"'Twere an evil heresy to so suppose him," said the rabbi again. "Thou shouldst have studied the Law and the Prophets, and have listened to the words of those wiser than thou art. This fellow is dangerous to the people, in that he is in league with the prince of darkness, and doth continually work iniquity."

"I can bear it no longer!" rang out a clear voice. "Thou liest, and that foully, when thou sayest such things of the Nazarene!"

Every one started and turned toward the speaker. "Have thy say, lad!" shouted two or three, delighted with the fresh excitement. "Now shalt thou stand here and answer the worthy rabbi." And a dozen hands lifted the boy to the top of a stone wall near at hand, so that he was above them, and in sight of all.

He stood for a moment abashed; then the words of the rabbi coming back to him, he again flushed red in his boyish indignation. "Thou sayest that he hath a devil," he cried. "Can a devil do such works as doth this man? For thou knowest that he hath healed the sick and helpless; he hath opened the eyes of the blind; he hath cleansed the lepers; and even raised the dead to life! He hath done good, and not evil, to all. How canst thou say that he worketh iniquity?"

"He doth blaspheme God; for he declareth that he is the Son of God, and hath come down from heaven," answered the rabbi angrily. "Cease thy prating, foolish boy, ere I have thee arrested for disturbing the peace!"

"Nay, good master! Let the lad have his say, as thou hast had thine; we will answer for him!" cried half a dozen at once.

"Thou knowest him not," said the boy. "He came down from heaven; and he worketh even as he is bidden by the Father, who dwells on high."

"Then, let him give us a sign, and he shall be our king!" shouted a man in the outskirts of the crowd.

"Hath he not given you signs in abundance? I am one of them! Behold, I was a cripple, and he healed me with a word, so that I am as straight and strong as any of you."

"Who art thou?" cried a rough voice. "By all the gods! I believe it is my own boy, Stephen! Here, let me come near, that I may make sure." And the man began elbowing his way toward the lad.

The boy had grown deathly pale; he stood irresolute for a moment, then jumped down from the wall, and advanced through the crowd, which opened to let him pass.

"Thou art my boy, Stephen! And straight and strong! Nay, but I can scarce believe it!" said Dumachus, grasping the lad by the arm. "Now, by all the powers of Olympus! I will make a man of thee; for I like thy spirit! Come along with me."

They walked along for a moment in silence; then Dumachus broke out with a savage oath: "Why dost thou not speak? Art thou not glad to see thy father? Thy mother hath taught thee to hate me; and I cared not as long as thou wert a helpless cripple. But now thou shalt know that thou hast a father, and must obey him."

"My mother did not teach me to hate thee," said Stephen in a low voice.

"Nay, thou dost whine like a woman! Speak up, as thou didst but just now to that purse-proud rabbi; thou didst answer him boldly. And so the Nazarene healed thee, did he? Tell me how it was."

Stephen's face lighted up again at the mention of the Master, and he poured forth his story eagerly, almost forgetting his listener for the moment.

"So that was the way of it!" said Dumachus, running his fingers through his shaggy locks. "Now the Nazarene, if he would do that for thee, will do more; dost thou not think it?"

"Oh, yes," cried Stephen joyfully, remembering the look in the Master's eyes, as he answered him from the synagogue steps.

"Then thou shalt ask him for gold, Stephen lad; and we will buy us a vineyard and a house, and live like the Romans."

"I think that he is very poor," said Stephen, hesitatingly. "I should not like to ask him for gold."

"He can make it, boy. Did I not see him make out of five little loaves, and two small fishes, food enough to glut five thousand? He hath made a compact with the foul fiend, and he helpeth him to do these wonders."

Stephen started back in horror, and fixed his eyes on his father's face. "I cannot talk with thee, father, if thou sayest such things!"

"Cannot talk with me!" said Dumachus mockingly. "And how wilt thou help thyself, my fine fellow? But now shalt thou tell me where I can find Titus." And his face darkened ominously. "Answer! Dost thou know where he is?"

"Yes, I know where he is—but—I shall not tell thee."

"What!" roared Dumachus, grasping the boy by the shoulder so roughly that he almost lost his balance. "Dost thou dare to defy me!—thine own father!"

"Father!" said Stephen, fixing his steady dark eyes on the man's face, "I would gladly render thee my obedience, but when Titus came back after being with thee and the men, he told me that thou didst compel him to take part in horrible crimes; in that thou didst him a great wrong. He is safe now, and hath an honest employment."

"An honest employment, hath he!" broke in Dumachus, with a sneering laugh; then suddenly, with a savage look, he turned. "Thou wert a cripple; and now thou art recovered, by the diabolical arts of yonder fellow from Nazareth. But listen!—if thou dost not presently tell me where Titus is to be found, I will do that to thee which will put thee beyond cure! Aye! look about thee as thou wilt, thou canst not escape me!"

Stephen had cast a furtive look around; and realized, with terror, that his father had been so directing their steps during the conversation, that they were now in a lonely spot outside the city walls.

"Wilt thou tell me?" continued the man, suddenly dropping his threatening tone. "Then will we be friends and comrades. I

"Oh, father! have mercy!"

swear it. Thou art no better than a baby; but thou shalt go with me, and I will make of thee a man. Now what thinkest thou of this?" and he drew from under his tunic a gold chain of fine Etruscan workmanship. "This shall be thine, and many other things as well; for am I not chief, and art not thou mine only son?"

"Thine only son!" echoed Stephen in surprise. "Is not Titus—"

"'Tis none of thy business, boy, what Titus is to me. He is nothing to thee. But

there is no time for this folly. Where—is—Titus?"

Stephen hesitated. "What dost thou purpose concerning him?" he asked.

"My purpose concerns thee not," answered Dumachus. Then fixing his eyes on the boy, he continued slowly, and with savage emphasis, "Thou hast need of a scourging; I will, therefore, scourge thee. Then if thou art not purged of thine obstinate folly, I will break each bone of thy body, and leave thee here for the wild dogs to take care of."

Stephen was as colorless as death, but he said not a word. The man proceeded to bind him securely to a small tree which grew near, then cutting a heavy stick, he began to strip it of its foliage with great deliberation.

Titus was returning from the hill farm, whither he had been sent with a message by Benoni. He was striding briskly along, stopping now and then to add a choice blossom to a great sheaf of wild-flowers, which he had gathered for the little Ruth.

"There are some wild roses—the first I have seen," he said to himself, scrambling down a little bank covered with short grass. "I must have them." But as he reached out his hand to gather the flowers, he heard a sound which caused him to start back and listen. It was a low, wailing cry, and seemed to come from a thicket of trees close by. As he came nearer, the cry was repeated, accompanied by the sound of a heavy blow, and the words—"Oh, father! have mercy!" were sobbed out in a voice which Titus knew. He clenched his fist savagely, and peering through the branches, saw a sight that fairly froze the blood in his veins.

For an instant he was tempted to dash forward; but sturdy as he was, he could not hope to match his boyish strength with the savage giant yonder. Another blow, and yet another, while the innocent victim wailed aloud in his agony. Titus stooped, and picking up a large, round stone which lay at his feet, hurled it with all the strength and precision of which he was master. It struck Dumachus just behind the ear, and he fell forward with a crash to the earth. To dash through the bushes and cut the thongs which bound Stephen, was the work of a moment only; then he turned to look at the fallen Dumachus.

"Oh, Titus! have you killed him?" cried Stephen tremulously, the tears running down his white cheeks.

"Killed him? No. I only wish I had—the vile brute! He is merely stunned, but I will keep him here till we can escape."

So saying, he quickly and skillfully bound the prostrate man with the leathern thongs which he had just taken from Stephen. "Come along now!" he said roughly, for his blood was still boiling with passion. "How camest thou into the hands of that devil?"

Stephen quickly told him all that had occurred.

"So he would have killed thee!" said Titus fiercely, when he had finished.

"No! No!" answered Stephen. "He could never have killed me; he only meant to frighten me."

"Thou dost not know him, boy, as I do," answered Titus. "Hark! Dost thou hear that?"

They paused for a moment, and heard the distant sound of frantic yells and curses.

"Now we must run for it!" said Titus. "For he hath the strength of ten men, when he is in a rage like that."

And the two broke into a pace which soon brought them to the city gate. Once safely inside, Titus turned to Stephen. "Thou must take mother and get thee away for awhile. He must not find thee at home to-night. And stay! Thou wilt need money. I have my wages; take this and go—go quickly." And he thrust a small purse into Stephen's hand as he hurried away.

CHAPTER XVII.

"WE have very little to-day so far," said the child; "only a few farthings." And he rattled the coins in a small brass cup, and cried out to a passer-by: "Wilt thou not have pity on a blind man?—

No, he hath gone by without even looking."

"Well, child," said the blind man wearily, "thou knowest that there are so many of us beggars in Jerusalem."

"But not born blind," insisted the child in a tone of pride.

The two were sitting in one of the beautiful porches of the temple; assuredly a pleasant spot, for the pillared portico sheltered them from the sun, and the breezes blew softly in this lofty place, when the heat in the city below was well-nigh unbearable.

Day after day they came there, the man and the tiny child with his dark curls blowing about his eyes. Early in the morning they waited for the te ple gates to open. Once admitted, they s. all day under the shadow of the portico; at noon sharing the scanty meal of bread and olives which the man brought in his wallet, and at night trudging home with the earnings of the day.

To the blind man the temple was home, and he loved it. The child had told him, over and over, of the wonderful great stones of pure, white marble of which it was built; of its courts shining with gold, and of the priests in their gorgeous robes. They could hear the chanting of the almost never-ending service from their place on the porch, and catch spicy whiffs of the incense, as it floated out on the warm air. Morning and evening, the child led him into the court of the temple, where he took part with the congregation in the service of the hour; and now, as he sat leaning back against one of the great pillars, fragments of the prayer of adoration came back to him:

"Blessed be thou by whose word the world was created; blessed be thou for ever! Blessed be thou who hast made all out of nothing! Blessed be he who has pity on the earth; blessed be he who has pity on his creatures; blessed be he who richly rewards his saints; blessed be he who lives forever, and is forever the same; blessed be he the Savior and Redeemer. Blessed be thy name; blessed be thou, O Eternal! Our God, King of the universe! All-merciful God and Father."

"Ah, if he would but have pity on me—a blind, useless clod! Yet am I strong, and shall live—yes, live long, and beg." And the man silently clenched his strong hands.

"Here are more passers-by," said the child. "Have mercy, kind masters! Have mercy on one born blind!"

The quick ear of the blind man heard the steps of a number of men coming along the marble pavement. Now as the cry of the child shrilled forth, they paused.

"Master, who did sin, this man or his parents, that he was born blind?"

The head of the blind beggar sank upon his breast, as he heard these words. The old question!—had he not heard it from his youth? "I am accursed," he thought. "He

Pool of Siloam as it appears to-day.

who hath pity on his creatures, yet punishes the innocent for the guilty."

But what was it that the rabbi was saying? Assuredly something new and strange: "Neither hath this man sinned, nor his parents; but that the works of God should be made manifest in him. I must work the works of him that sent me, while it is day: the night cometh, when no man can work. As long as I am in the world, I am the light of the world."

"The light of the world"! The man had raised his head now, and was straining his sightless eyes in the direction of the voice. Presently he felt the touch of something cool and soft on his sunken lids.

"Go," said the mysterious voice again, "wash in the pool of Siloam." And the sound of the steps died away.

"Come!" said the beggar, rising and stretching forth his hand to the child. "Come!"

"They gave us no money," said the child complainingly, "and he put wet clay on thine eyelids. Why did he do it?"

"Hold thy peace, child!" said the man. "Take me to the pool. I will wash even as he bade me."

Down—down—the marble steps, went the twain.

"I heard them call the man Jesus," said the child softly. Then after a moment, he cried, "Stay, master! Here is the pool. Kneel down; I will hold thy robe. Now if thou wilt reach out thy hand, thou canst touch the water."

The man plunged his hand and arm deep into the gurgling water, and dashed it over his eyes. Then he drew back silently, with so strange a look on his face, that the child cried out:

"What is it? What hath happened to thee?"

The man did not seem to hear him; for without answering, he raised his hands to heaven, and cried in a loud voice:

"We would praise thee, eternal Lord God! We would laud and magnify thee with songs of thanksgiving and praise! We do homage to thy name, our King! our God! The only One! He who liveth forever! O Lord, whose name is glorious forever and ever! blessed be thou, O Eternal! For thou hast, by the hand of thy servant, saved me out of darkness, and out of the blackness of night. My sin is hidden; and the sin of my parents is covered. Verily, thou hast in thy mercy remembered one who was cut off and accursed. Praised be the Lord, who is ever and eternally worthy to be praised!"

The child regarded him with awe, for he saw that the closed and sunken eyes were open, and that they were full and bright even as his own. "His name was Jesus!" he repeated, not knowing what he said; for his childish brain was dazed with wonder.

The man now turned and regarded him steadfastly. "Thou art the child," he said at length. "I am he who hath led thee forth at morn-

"I heard them call the man Jesus," said the child.

ing and at evening," answered the child, trembling.

"Thou shalt lead me forth no more. Thanks be to the Eternal One! From henceforth I shall care for thee."

"Wilt thou come with us before the Pharisees, and confess this thing, even as thou hast told it to us?"

"Assuredly," answered the beggar. "I will gladly make known my deliverance. Would that I knew my deliverer, that I might kiss the hem of his garment!"

"I believe him not!" said one of the group of neighbors who were gathered around him. "'Tis one who resembleth the blind man, and that marvelously."

"But why should he lie to us in the matter?" questioned another. "What would it profit him?"

"Nay," said the man earnestly, "I lie not; I am he that was born blind, and my eyes were opened, even as I declared unto you."

"Most worthy and revered members of the council," said a Pharisee, whose pious mien, broad phylactery, and flowing robes, marked him a zealous religionist, "I have brought before thee, for examination, a man who reports a miracle wrought in his behalf. In that this miracle was unlawfully wrought upon the Sabbath day, it merits thy consideration."

"Thou hast done wisely, good sir," said Caiaphas, with a stately inclination of the head. Then turning to the beggar, he continued: "Speak, fellow, and make known thy case for our judgment."

"I have little to tell," said the man simply. "One who is called Jesus made clay and anointed mine eyes, and said unto me, 'Go to the pool of Siloam and wash.' I went and washed, and I received sight."

This statement was received with ominous frowns and solemn shakings of the head by the august assembly. Finally one spoke:

"This man, Jesus, is not of God, because he keepeth not the Sabbath day. He hath repeated this offense many times already, as is known to all of us."

"But how," said Nicodemus, "can a man that is a sinner do such a miracle? What sayest thou who wert healed of this Jesus?"

"I think that he is a prophet," replied the man.

"Let me advise," said another member of the council, "that an officer be sent to fetch the parents of this man, that we may question them of the matter."

This being approved and acted upon, the members of the council engaged in whispered consultation one with another, while the beggar stood apart and watched the scene with his quick, bright eyes.

Presently the officer returned, accompanied by an old man, and a woman heavily veiled. As they entered the room, they cast a furtive glance at their son, then made humble obeisance to the assembled dignitaries.

Caiaphas regarded them in silence for a moment, then demanded with a frown: "Is this man in our presence thy son, who ye say was born blind? How is it that he doth now see?"

The old man again made obeisance; and spreading abroad his hands, and lifting his shoulders apologetically, answered: "Most noble lord, we know that this is our son; and that he was born blind. But by what means he now seeth, we know not; or who hath opened his eyes, we know not. He is of age, therefore ask him; he shall speak for himself."

"Stand forth!" said Caiaphas imperiously to the beggar.

The man came forward and stood beside his parents. The high priest looked at him threateningly, but the bright eyes did not flinch.

"Thou shalt be dealt with after thy deserts, if thou hast not a care," at length said the high priest. "Confess the truth concerning this matter, and give God the glory for thy cure—if such it be; for we know that the man Jesus is a sinner."

The beggar straightened himself. A clear light blazed from his eyes; and in a tone which rang through the council chamber like a trumpet, he made answer:

"Whether this man be a sinner or no, I know not; but one thing I know, that whereas I was blind, now I see!"

For a moment there was silence in the place; then an old man who had hitherto not spoken, craned his neck forward and said patronizingly: "What was it that he did to thee? How opened he thine eyes?"

And again the beggar made answer: "I have told you already, and ye did not hear; wherefore would ye hear it again? Will ye also be his disciples?"

"We are disciples of Moses," said Caiaphas, his eyes flashing with anger. "'Tis such low-born beggars as thou, who are disciples of this man. We know that God spake unto Moses; as for this fellow, we know not from whence he is."

"Why, herein is a marvelous thing!" said the beggar sneeringly, "that ye know not from whence he is, and yet he hath opened mine eyes! Now we know that God heareth not sinners; but if any man be a worshiper of God, and doeth his will, him he heareth. Since the world began, was it not heard that any man opened the eyes of one born blind. If this man were not of God, he could do nothing."

"Vile wretch of a beggar!" said Caiaphas, rising in his wrath, "thou wast altogether born in sins, and dost thou teach us? Get thee hence from this sacred place, and dare not to again enter it on pain of thy life!"

And the man went forth, sad at heart; for he longed with a great longing to see the glories of the temple.

Now as he walked, continually lifting his eyes to the shining walls from which he was henceforth to be shut out, he heard a voice speaking to him; and turning, he saw one who looked at him with a grave and yet sweet look, so that his heart was mightily stirred within him, though he knew not why. And the man spake to him, and he knew the voice—it was that of him who had bidden him wash in the pool of Siloam!

"Dost thou believe on the Son of God?"

And the beggar, trembling, made answer: "Who is he, Lord, that I might believe on him?"

And Jesus said unto him, "Thou hast both seen him, and it is he that talketh with thee."

Then the beggar fell down at his feet and kissed the hem of his garment, crying out, "Lord, I believe!"

Now it happened that some of the Pharisees who had cast him out of the temple were standing near, and heard it. And Jesus, seeing their angry looks, and reading the thoughts of their hearts, turned and said unto them: "For judgment I am come into this world, that they which see not might see; and that they which see might be made blind."

Then the Pharisees answered him scornfully: "Are we blind also?"

Jesus said unto them: "If ye were blind, ye should have no sin; but now ye say, We see; therefore your sin remaineth."

———

CHAPTER XVIII.

OWARD the close of an early spring day, two travelers were toiling up the steep, rocky path which led to the little mountain village of Nazareth. The way was rough and difficult, and the woman sighed painfully, as she moved slowly onward; the boy turned and looked anxiously at her face, which gleamed white in the waning light.

"Thou art weary, mother; we should have stopped for the night in the village below. Sit here, and rest awhile."

With a sigh of relief, the woman sank down on the rough stone which the boy had covered with his sheep-skin coat. "Yes," she said at length, with another long-drawn breath, which was almost a groan, "I am very tired; my strength faileth me for toiling up these hills."

"Thou wilt feel better presently, when thou hast had time to rest," said the boy tenderly. "We have wandered too widely of late; it may be that we can bide in yonder village till thou art stronger. Is it not beautiful here! See the hills, how green they are; and the flowers—let me gather some for thee while thou art resting."

The woman smiled patiently. "Dost thou not need to rest, my Stephen? We have yet a hard climb, to reach the town."

"I am never tired now, mother," said the boy, gayly, springing up as he spoke.

The mother's eyes followed him fondly, as he climbed a steep bank for some bright-hued blossoms. "The dear one!" she murmured to herself. "He is almost a man now, but he hath the heart of a loving child still."

"Look, mother!" said the lad as he laid a great sheaf of blossoms in her lap. "Here are roses—pink, white and yellow; are they not sweet? And cyclamen and mignonette too, and these tiny yellow flowers, like little stars. From the high rock where I gathered these pink roses, I could see the scarlet blossoms of the pomegranate, and orange trees as white as snow. Wouldst thou not like it to live in such a spot? I can work hard now, and surely I could earn enough to buy bread for the two of us." After a pause, he added dreamily: "Nazareth is where he lived; we shall see his home."

"I think, my Stephen," said his mother presently, "that we must hasten on our way; for the sun hath gone down an hour since, and the night will soon be upon us."

"Thou art right, mother," answered the boy, springing up. "Let me help thee."

Half an hour more of hard climbing brought the travelers to the edge of the village. There, where the water from a spring in the hillside gushed forth with a musical tinkle into a stone trough below, the woman stopped short.

"I can go no further," she said faintly, sinking down on the grass. "I am ill."

"Oh, mother," cried Stephen, "we are almost there now! Let me give thee some of this water; it will revive thee."

View of the city of Nazareth.

But the woman made no reply. Her head had fallen back against the grassy bank behind her; and the boy, as he bent over her, saw with terror that she was unconscious.

"What shall I do!" he cried aloud, wringing his hands helplessly. "Mother, oh mother!"

"She hath fainted," said a voice near him. "Let me give her water."

He looked up, and saw standing at his side a woman, bearing on her shoulder a water-pot. This she hastily dipped into the fountain, then stooping over the prostrate form, sprinkled the white face with the fresh, cool water.

"See! She is reviving. She will soon be herself again!" said the new-comer. "Fill thy cup and give her to drink."

Stephen obeyed, and to his great joy his mother sat up and looked about her; but almost immediately she sank back again, moaning faintly.

"Hast thou friends in the village?" asked the woman.

"Nay," said Stephen. "We were going to

the inn. Is it far from here?" he added anxiously.

" 'Tis in the upper street; too far for her to walk to-night," was the answer. " But my house is near,"—pointing, as she spoke, to where a faint light twinkled through the dark foliage. " If thou wilt help me to get her on to her feet, a few steps will bring us to the door. Thou shalt bide with me for the night."

" Thou art good," said Stephen, " and I thank thee."

Between them they helped the exhausted Prisca to her feet, and supported her faltering steps till they reached the cottage, which was, as the woman had said, close at hand.

" She sleeps, and will be better by morning," said their hostess as she came from the little bedchamber, where she had been ministering to the wants of her guest, into the room where Stephen was waiting.

He had had time to look about him, and saw that, while the appointments of this home were very humble, it was as daintily pure and neat as a flower. And now he looked more closely at the woman herself. She was tall and of noble proportions; and though past middle age, her face was beautiful, with its clear, hazel eyes, firm yet tender mouth, and waving reddish-brown hair, slightly tinged with gray.

" Thou too art weary," she continued, with a smile which irradiated her face like sunshine. " Thou must eat, then thou shalt sleep also." So saying, she set before the boy a wooden bowl containing milk, and some cakes of barley bread. " Tell me," she said, when the boy had finished, " how is it that ye are traveling alone, and so far from home? For thy mother tells me that ye dwell in Capernaum."

Thus encouraged, the boy poured forth the whole story, telling the wondrous tale of his healing by the Nazarene.

" We had to go away from Capernaum, as thou seest," he said. " And we came to Nazareth, because I wanted to see his home. I thought perhaps we should find him here. Dost thou know this Jesus?"

The woman's eyes filled with tears, yet again a smile transfigured her face, kindling it to a beauty almost divine.

" He is my son," she said simply. " And this is his home."

CHAPTER XIX.

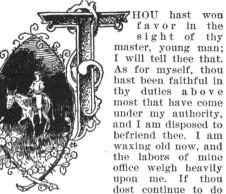

HOU hast won favor in the sight of thy master, young man; I will tell thee that. As for myself, thou hast been faithful in thy duties above most that have come under my authority, and I am disposed to befriend thee. I am waxing old now, and the labors of mine office weigh heavily upon me. If thou dost continue to do well, and art discreet and wise, I see no reason why in time thou shouldst not become steward in my place. For I have been prudent with my wages; and have bought a vineyard of mine own, whither I can retire when old age shall overtake me."

The speaker was Benoni; he was sitting at ease on a bench in the garden, while Titus stood before him respectfully.

The lad flushed with pleasure at these words, but he made no reply, for he saw that the old man had more to say.

" I have an important commission for thee," continued Benoni, " and I entrust it to thee by special request from the most noble Jairus himself—for I do not deny that I should have selected another to perform it. Not that I do not trust thee, but that thou lackest wisdom, by reason of thy youth. The commission is this: that thou shouldst visit the vineyard which lieth a little beyond Tiberias, carrying with thee moneys which shall be paid to the man Caleb, whom thou wilt find in charge of the vineyard. He will dispose of them according to the directions which I have written herein, and which thou shalt deliver to him together with this bag. In the bag are the moneys of which I spoke; thou must secure it to thy person, and go heavily armed. I shall place at thy disposal a fleet-footed mule, and the journey can be made between now and moonrise, if thou gettest speedily on thy way."

" I shall be ready within half an hour," said Titus briefly. " Thou wilt give me plain directions how to find the place?" he added.

" I will do more," said the old man, looking thoughtful. " I will give thee Asa for company; he knoweth the way, for he hath been there many times on the like errand." "And when he went on errands of the like, went he alone, or did another go with him?" asked Titus. "He went alone," replied the old man unguardedly. Then, seeing the angry flush on the cheek of Titus, he added soothingly: "Thou knowest that the country is infested with robbers; surely it would be safer for two than for one." "If thou canst not trust me to go alone, I will not go at all; let old Asa take the bag, and go as heretofore." "Nay, nay, lad! Now art thou in an unseemly temper; thou must bridle thy tongue and thy temper if thou wouldst do well. Did I not tell thee that I trusted thee? Nay, more—I love thee, lad, as if thou wert mine own son; but something tells me that thou shouldst not go forth alone to-day." "But am I not strong?—fit to meet robbers if there be any?" demanded Titus, drawing himself up to his full height, and throwing back his broad shoulders. "I know the ways of robbers and their haunts better than thou thinkest, my good Benoni," he added to himself; then aloud, "The excellent Asa would actually be in the way, should we be unfortunate enough to fall among thieves. I can imagine him in the grasp of such an one as Dumachus." "What sayest thou?" asked Benoni abstractedly. Titus bit his lip. "'Tis time for me to be off, good Benoni," he said. "And if it please thee, I would not be burdened with the company of the worthy Asa." "Well, thou shalt have thy way in the matter; and may Jehovah protect thee." "'Tis a pious wish, assuredly; and I will back it up with my stout staff and a brace of knives," said Titus, laughing. But old Benoni shook his head. "'Tis a pity that thou art a Gentile, lad; thy words savor of heathendom." Half an hour later, the young man, mounted on a strong and speedy mule, was clattering out of the great courtyard; the money-bag securely bound about his waist under his tunic, his wallet well stocked with lunch, and a couple of formidable-looking knives thrust into his belt. "I shall be back long before moonrise. Fare thee well!" And he waved his hand at Benoni, with a gay laugh at sight of his anxious face. The old man shook his head as he went back into the house, and muttered to himself: "My heart misgiveth me in the matter; someone should have gone with the lad."

In the meantime Titus had reached the gate of the city, and was climbing the stony bridle path which led to the hill road. It was a blithe spring morning; the sunshine lay warm and bright on field and vineyard, green with that vivid emerald tint seen only in spring. The roadsides were gay with blossoms, pink, yellow and blue, over which floated great butterflies—living blossoms. Birds, busy with nest-building, flitted hither and thither in hedge and thicket, while overhead the lark "flooded a thousand acres of sky with melody." Titus drew in long breaths of the fragrant air, then throwing back his curly head, he too began to sing lustily. Assuredly 'twere a good thing to be alive and young, on such a morning. Towards noon, he began to leave behind the region of vineyards and cultivated fields alive with busy peasants, and entered upon a comparatively uninhabited and desolate tract of country. Here the narrow road, or bridle track—for it was little more—wound among rugged hills, amid dense thickets of oleander, tamarisk and wild olive trees. Titus knew the place well. He was silent now and alert. Presently he stopped, and fastening the mule, crept cautiously through the underbrush to a little open space, which was perfectly concealed from the roadway. Here a tiny spring, clear as crystal and ice-cold, gushed out of the side of the hill, trickled into a rocky basin beneath, then overflowing, lost itself among the flowers and grasses, which grew lush and rank in this favored spot. Titus laid his ear to the ground and listened; then he climbed a tall oak and looked out over the forest. From his lofty perch he could see the road by which he had come, winding like a narrow ribbon along the hillside; the fresh green leaves dancing in the sunshine; glimpses of blue water hundreds of feet below him; while out and away, beyond the hills flecked with shadows, lay Hermon like a snowy cloud on the far horizon. He slid down the tree well satisfied; and pushing through the branches, seized the bridle of the mule. "Thou shalt have water, and that the best thou hast ever tasted!" he cried cheerily, slapping the sleek neck of the animal; then having attended to the wants of the beast, he dropped down on the soft turf and began to refresh himself with the contents of his wallet.

The spot was deliciously cool and sweet, the silence broken only by the distant twitter of birds, the trickling of the water, and the steady munching of the mule, intent upon his noonday meal. Titus felt a soft drowsiness stealing over him; he glanced sleepily at his beast, and seeing that he had disposed of only about half of his provender, he stretched himself out comfortably, and,

His awakening was the signal for a burst of loud laughter and mocking jeers.

"Art thou refreshed, my pretty youth?" said one.

And another: "In truth we did not think to find thee here; but 'tis an old tryst, and well known to thee. Thou wert awaiting us, no doubt."

Titus made an ineffectual struggle to free himself from his bonds, glaring fiercely at his captors as he did so.

"Art thou refreshed, my pretty lad?" said one.

pillowing his head on his arm, fell fast asleep.

How long he slept he did not know, but he awaked with a dim sense that something was wrong. Moving uneasily, he opened his eyes; then the full extent of his folly burst upon him. He was bound securely hand and foot. Against a tree trunk near by, lounged Dumachus, regarding him with a hideous leer of triumph, while the rest of the band stood, or sprawled at full length on the ground, around him.

"With thy mule and thy money-bag, thou art quite a pretty prize," quoth Dumachus, shaking the bag which he held in his hand, till the coins within clinked musically.

"And all the more welcome, since we have had nothing but bad luck of late," growled another.

"We must push on to Jerusalem without further delay; if all goes well there, we shall soon see an end to it," said Dumachus. "This,"—giving the bag another shake— "will serve us for the present."

" Shall I loose the lad?" asked Gaius, with whom Titus had always been a prime favorite.

" Loose him? No!" roared Dumachus. " I have a score to settle with him first. Some time ago," he added, planting himself in front of Titus, and gazing at him ferociously, " I had occasion to scourge my son Stephen for disobedience; whilst I was so scourging him, someone stunned me with a blow, then bound me hand and foot while I was helpless."

" Aye, 'twas handsomely done too," broke in Gaius with a huge laugh. " He lay there shrieking like a demoniac, till I myself happened along and loosed him. By my faith! he was so securely bound, that he might have lain there yet, had the dogs spared him."

" 'Twas the fate that thou didst intend for Stephen," said Titus, boiling with indignation at the remembrance.

" So thou wert the one who did it! I knew it, thou dog of a Jew!" hissed Dumachus.

Then, quite beside himself with rage, he hurled his long, two-edged knife at the helpless boy. It barely missed his head, striking with a dull thud the bole of the tree just behind him, where it stuck fast, quivering with the force of the blow.

" What dost thou mean, man!" cried Gaius, starting forward. " Wouldst thou murder the lad for a trifle like that? Thine own son, too—as thou hast always declared."

" I tell thee he is not my son. He is an accursed Jew and I hate him!" shrieked Dumachus.

" 'Tis no news to any of us," said Gaius, with a short laugh. " But thou shalt not murder him, for all that. What sayest thou? —Shall I loose him and let him go? Or shall we take him with us to Jerusalem?"

" We will take him to Jerusalem," said Dumachus sullenly, pulling his knife from the trunk of the tree, and cutting the cords which bound the lad's feet. " I shall ride the mule; as for this fellow, let him try to escape me, and I will kill him with my hands!"

The whole party was presently under way; two of the men going ahead as scouts, Titus walking with bound hands between two of the others, while the remainder of the band, with Dumachus riding comfortably on the mule in their midst, brought up the rear.

Titus was too much wrapped up in his own unhappy thoughts to pay any heed to his companions. " Fool that I was," he thought, " to sleep in that place of all others! But I made so sure that they were nowhere about. Why did I not take the other road? What will Benoni think when I fail to come to-night?—when he finds that I never reached the vineyard with the money? If they had only taken me after I had paid it!" And he groaned aloud.

" Do the cords hurt thy wrists?" asked one of the men kindly enough.

" No," said Titus shortly; then, with a gleam of hope, " Thou wert always my friend, Gaius—wilt thou not help me to escape?"

" Thou talkest like a fool, boy! Why dost thou wish to escape from us? We are thy friends; thou hast passed many a merry day in our company ere now. Use thy wits to placate our worthy chief yonder, and all will yet be well with thee."

" Nay; that I cannot do," said Titus sullenly. " He hates me; and for my part, I hate him. I wish I had killed him the day he beat Stephen."

" The world might have spared him," said the man, chuckling. " And I doubt not, 'twould have been better for him in the end."

After a pause, Titus turned to his companion abruptly: " Canst thou tell me who I am? Thou didst hear him twice call me a Jew."

" Now thou askest me something I fain would know myself," replied the man thoughtfully. " For I doubt not that a handsome sum would be paid for thy return. I opine that thou wert stolen from Jerusalem; for when I first fell in with the worthy Dumachus, he had recently come from Judea, and was a stranger in these parts. Thou wert then about three years of age; once in my presence thou didst strike Dumachus, in a fit of puny rage, because he called himself thy father."

Titus made no reply. " I am glad I am not the son of yonder brute," he thought gloomily. " But whose son am I? He hath taught me to hate the Jews. I am a Jew. Stephen is not my brother; and mother—is not mother. She must hate me, too, for she hath known this thing, and kept it from me all these long, unhappy years."

It was night now; and lifting his eyes, he saw the moon rising, large and yellow, behind the dark masses of the hills. The hot tears rose to his eyes. " 'Tis moonrise. Benoni is expecting me now. I shall not come. They will think me—a thief!"

CHAPTER XX.

THE band of robbers, with Titus always closely g u a r d e d, pushed on as rapidly as possible toward Jerusalem, traveling chiefly at night by the light of the moon, which was now at its full. Daytimes they skulked in thickets or ravines, lying in wait for their prey. Several unlucky travelers thus fell into their clutches during the journey; these were promptly stripped of their possessions, their subsequent fate depending upon their behavior during the stripping process. If they submitted quietly, they were allowed to go, albeit half naked. But woe to the man who dared to resist, or make any outcry! A dozen ready knives quickly quieted him, the wicked old saying, " Dead men tell no tales," being a favorite maxim with Dumachus.

At dawn of the fourth day, they reached the hills lying to the west of Jerusalem, and encamped in one of the narrow valleys for a few hours of rest and refreshment.

" I shall go into the city alone," said Dumachus, after he had eaten. " The rest of you will await me here. Let there be no disturbance amongst you, lest we be foiled in our purpose ere it be undertaken."

Then he drew Gaius aside, and talked with him in a low tone for a few moments. Titus felt sure that the conversation referred to him, but he made no sign; he hoped in the excitement which would shortly follow, to be able to make his escape. His brain was already teeming with vague, impossible plans for seeking out his parents—if indeed they were to be found in Jerusalem—and for making himself known to them. How he was to do this he did not know; but he was full of unreasoning hope.

After some hours Dumachus returned. " All is well," he announced shortly, but with an air of triumph. Then after draining a cup of wine, he threw himself down in the shade and slept heavily.

The men conversed in low tones, snatches of their conversation at times reaching the ears of Titus.

" There be already above five hundred men in the plot; 'tis sure to succeed."

" Will the attempt be made to-night?"

" Before the moon rises—when 'tis dark."

" We shall force the temple gates with ease. 'Tis the plan of Barabbas to tear down the golden eagle from the inner gate. Herod hath set it up; 'tis an abomination in the eyes of the Jews."

" What care we for the golden eagle, or for the Jews! 'Tis plunder we want!"

" Hist! Once inside the gates, man, 'twill go hard with us if we cannot secure some of the golden vessels with which the temple is crammed. Then there is the other."

Here they lowered their voices, so that Titus lost what followed. Then one spoke a little louder.

" 'Tis there still?"

" Yes. Pilate hath not yet dared to put his hands upon it; though the aqueduct must be finished, and he hath not the means to do it."

" 'Tis a goodly sum?"

" A goodly sum! 'Tis a great treasure, man! 'Twill make us all rich for life. Our plan is to get away with it in the confusion of the fight and make for the sea; once there, we can escape into Greece. After that —a long life, and a merry one!"

" 'Tis a plan worthy of our chief; hath Jesus Barabbas any knowledge of it?"

" Not he! He is a devout Jew, the son of a rabbi, and thinketh only to rid the temple of the golden eagle, which, in his notion, desecrateth it. He is a turbulent fellow though, and hath an unsavory reputation with the authorities."

" All the more reason why he should have no share in our plunder. We be reasonably unknown in these parts, and can therefore hope to get away. Let them take him and crucify him if they like; 'twill be the better for us."

" May Jove help us!" said Gestas devoutly. " I vow a golden chain at every shrine in Greece, if we be successful."

" I also!" shouted another.

Dumachus roused up at the sound, and rebuking them savagely for their folly, called for wine and food.

As he ate and drank, he now and then cast a fierce look in the direction of Titus. The boy paled, and clenched his hands tightly, for he guessed his thoughts, or fancied that he did.

" What shall we do with the lad here?" asked one of the men presently, observing these glances.

" 'Tis in my mind—" began Dumachus, fixing his red eyes upon Titus with an evil smile.

But Gaius, thoroughly understanding his chief, interrupted him hastily: "Taste this wine, my Dumachus; thou wilt find it good and sound. Hold thy cup, and let me fill for thee—what thinkest thou of that?"

Dumachus drained the cup slowly, then held it out to be replenished. "'Tis a goodly vintage; where got we it?"

"From the Samaritan wine-merchant, yesterday," answered Gaius, filling the cup to the brim. "We shall need every arm in our venture to-night," he continued. "There is none bolder in a fight than the lad Titus here, as thou knowest; dost remember how he fought the giant Ethiopian single-handed last year, when we so narrowly escaped being taken? Aye, and downed him too! We shall have need of him. What sayest thou, lad? Wilt thou fight the Romans with us to-night?"

"That will I!" said Titus, trembling in his anxiety. "Only give me that with which to fight."

Dumachus held out the cup to Gaius for the fourth time. "I have a mind to leave him here," he said slowly, "and to so leave him, that he will not again escape me, nor again foil me in my purposes."

"Nay, my good chief," said Gaius, laying a warning hand on Titus' shoulder. "We can scarce leave him with safety. I will take him under my charge to-night; let the fellow dare try to escape me!" And he glared at Titus with assumed ferocity.

"If we succeed in our venture, I care not what becomes of the boy!" said Dumachus, who was beginning to be merry with the wine, with which Gaius still continued to ply him. Let me find Prisca—the woman hath escaped me. She can tell him of his parents. If we win to-night, I shall be avenged of my wrong! Ha, ha! But come! 'tis time we were away; we must enter the city by twos and threes to avoid suspicion. We will meet in the wine-shop of Clopas, in the upper market. There we shall find Barabbas, and there will the others come as soon as it waxeth dark. Fill all around and let us drink. What is left shall be poured out as a libation to Mars; may he, and all the gods, help us!"

"Let them help us, I say! 'Tis a pious act to seize the treasure from the God of the Hebrews; our own gods shall profit by it!" cried Gestas.

Dumachus now rose to his feet, and with drunken solemnity poured out upon the ground what was left in the wine-skin, call-ing loudly upon all the heathen deities for assistance in their unholy enterprise.

The wine-shop of Clopas, in the upper market-place, sent out a broad glow of cheery yellow light into the darkness, as Titus, together with Gaius, and another of the band called Joca, paused near by to make sure of their bearings.

"Yonder is the place," said Joca. "'Tis well enough known to me. Many is the merry night I have passed there in my youth."

"Then thou art Jerusalem-born?" asked Gaius.

"Jerusalem-born and bred," replied the other. "My father was a silversmith and wrought sacred vessels for the temple use. 'Twas in the shop of Clopas that I first met Dumachus. He was a handsome fellow in those days. Something befell him—I know not what; he fled to Galilee, carrying a woman and child with him. The child was the lad here. Once in my hearing the woman called him David. Afterward he was known to us as Titus, but I doubt not that David is his true name."

Titus was listening with all his ears, but he said nothing, for he hoped that the man would speak further. Gaius had armed him with one of his own knives. He could have slipped away in the dark easily enough, and was half-minded to do so. Then he reflected that he might learn something more of his mysterious birth and parentage, if he stayed; besides, he had a strong curiosity to see the much-talked-of Barabbas; and underneath all, was an unconfessed desire to share in the exciting events which were soon to follow.

"If I go now," he argued further with himself, "I shall have to find my way back to Capernaum alone, and confess to Benoni that he was right and I was wrong. Moreover, the mule and the money are both gone, and how could I replace them? I will, at all events, wait for a few hours; something may happen to my advantage."

By this time they had entered the wine-shop, and the opportunity for escape had, for the moment, passed.

"Yonder is Barabbas! He is even now speaking with Dumachus," whispered Gaius. Titus looked, and saw a man of giant stature, whose bold features and quick, brilliant eyes were in marked contrast to the bloated, brutal face of Dumachus. Titus felt instantly drawn to the man; and edging his way through the crowd, managed to get near enough to hear what was being said. " He will not dare to restore it, once it is torn from its place," Barabbas was saying in a low-toned but powerful voice. " The symbol of Roman supremacy hath long enough insulted the house of our God. It shall be torn down, and broken into pieces so small that no one shall be able to put it together again. I myself will cast the fragments into the courtyard of the palace. I tell ye that Pilate is, at heart, a coward.

"We have been betrayed!"

He feareth us. Did he not yield to us at Cæsarea? Did he not yield to us when lately he would have seized the sacred treasure of the temple for his own purposes?"

" Thou speakest truly!" shouted half a hundred voices. " Let us go forth, and tear the accursed image from its place!"

With a common impulse all rushed into the street. Titus, who had managed to keep near Barabbas, saw to his astonishment that the square was crowded with men, their fierce, determined-looking faces revealed by the light of flaming torches brandished here and there over the heads of the throng.

A low, hoarse murmur ran through the assemblage, as they recognized their leader. Barabbas paused, and with a few short, de-

cisive words, explained the plan and method of attack; then commanding that the torches should be extinguished, all set forward at a rapid pace toward the temple, under cover of the darkness.

They had advanced no great distance, when the clang of shields reached them, and a loud voice was heard demanding the password.

" Death and confusion!" muttered Gaius, who, with Titus, was pressing forward immediately behind Barabbas. " 'Tis the Roman guard!"

" Forward, men! Seize the Romans; there are but a handful of them!" shouted Barabbas.

With a great cry the mob rushed on; and in a moment the noise of a fierce conflict was heard--the clashing of swords, the clangor of shields, savage yells, together with the shrieks of the wounded, who were trampled ruthlessly under foot. Barabbas had pushed forward into the thick of the combat, where he fought like a madman; but before many moments, it was apparent that the mob was giving way.

" We have been betrayed!" said Dumachus in the ear of Gaius. " Let us get away speedily; we can do nothing to-night. The Romans are thicker than bees." And without waiting for an answer, he darted swiftly away through the crowd.

Almost instantly followed a great cry from the front: " The Romans from the citadel are upon us! Barabbas is taken! Run for your lives!"

The mob was now in the wildest confusion, each thinking only of his own safety. Titus was hurried along with the rest, and scarcely knowing what he did, darted down a narrow street in the darkness. Presently finding himself unpursued, he paused for an instant to recover his breath, and listening intently, heard the frantic yells of the mob, and the sound of the pursuing soldiery growing momently more distant.

His heart beat high with hope. "I am safe now!" he thought. "I have only to keep out of sight till morning; then I can easily find my way out of the city. I will go back and confess the whole thing to Benoni; he shall believe me."

The thought of the quiet Capernaum home was very sweet to him, as he stood there alone and unfriended in the thick darkness. But why was his tunic so warm and wet? And now he became conscious of a stinging pain in his head. "I am wounded," he thought; and feeling cautiously in his thick curls, he discovered a deep gash which seemed to be bleeding freely.

"Strange!" he muttered to himself, "I do not remember that I was wounded in yonder fight!"

Presently he began to feel faint and light-headed. "I must have help," he thought, "and that quickly, or I shall perish in the street."

Moving cautiously, he advanced down the street, feeling his way along by the wall. The moon was rising now, and by her dim, uncertain light he saw that he was about to emerge into an open square; on the further side of this place there was a light, as of a fire burning, and dark figures moving near it.

Titus uttered a cry of joy, and staggered forward, forgetting his danger, and thinking only that help was at hand. The next moment he fell half-fainting to the ground, crying out feebly for help.

"What was that sound?" said one of a number of Roman soldiers, who were gathered about the fire.

"I heard nothing," answered another. "What was it like?"

"'Twas a cry, and sounded near."

"'Tis the insurgents," said the centurion. "They are still pursuing them in the lower town. They have taken many prisoners; the ring-leader Barabbas among others. We shall have a pretty show for Passover week."

"What meanest thou?"

"Why, of crosses, to be sure; 'tis the way Pilate taketh to keep down this turbulent people. 'Tis a wholesome sight for the crowds that come to the city at feast times,

and doth more to keep order than an extra legion."

"Hist! I heard the sound again!" said the other; and plunging a torch into the fire, he began a hasty search in the neighborhood. "Here, comrade!" he shouted. "'Tis a wounded man; lend me a hand with him!"

Between them they brought the lad to the fire, and began to examine him roughly by its light.

"What dost thou make of him?" asked one.

"He is a Jew, by his features—one of the insurgents. We must not let him escape us," replied the centurion. "Tear a strip from his tunic, and bind up his head; he hath a nasty cut. And hand me yonder wine; I will give him a sup."

"Verily, Marcus, thou art as handy as a woman," declared one of the others who stood by looking on.

"I am saving him for Passover week," said he who was called Marcus, with a brutal laugh. "To die with a cut in his head, were too good for such an one!"

Titus had revived under the combined influences of the warmth, the wine, and the stanching of the cut.

"Canst thou stand?" asked the centurion, seeing that he had opened his eyes.

Titus replied by standing up, albeit somewhat unsteadily.

"Wert thou in yonder fight?"

"I was," said Titus in a low voice. "But—"

"Take him to the prison, Caius and Brutus!" was the prompt order. And before Titus could protest, he was marched away between the two soldiers, and shortly found himself thrust into a cold, damp dungeon. Here he sank on to a pile of mouldy straw; and despite his fears, and the pain in his head, soon fell into a heavy slumber.

CHAPTER XXI.

ITUS had passed more than a week in his dungeon, when one morning he was roused from an uneasy slumber by the entrance of a guard of Roman soldiers. These commanded him to come forth, then marched him rapidly and silently through the streets till they reached the palace of the governor. Passing through the great entrance, which was heavily guarded, they found themselves in the prætorium, or judgment hall.

Titus glanced hastily around, then his head sank upon his breast. In that brief survey, he had seen that the great hall was thronged with people, and that seated high aloft in imposing state was a man whom he at once divined to be Pontius Pilate, the Roman governor.

For a moment he almost forgot his surroundings in the maze of confused and fearful thoughts which thronged his brain. Again aroused by the suppressed but fierce murmur of excitement about him, he looked up and saw the imposing figure of Barabbas. Heavily manacled, and guarded by four soldiers, he stood forth in the sight of all in a slightly elevated space immediately before the judgment seat.

" Thou art accused of having incited an insurrection against the government, on the evening of Adar the twenty-seventh, and of having committed murder, in that thou didst with thine own hands feloniously slay certain soldiers of the Roman guard, who were in lawful fulfillment of their duty. Hast thou aught to say for thyself?"

" Who are mine accusers? Let them stand forth," said Barabbas boldly, looking at the governor with unflinching eyes.

" Produce the witnesses," said Pilate shortly.

Several men now advanced to the front, among whom Titus was amazed to recognize Gestas. The testimony practically agreed that the prisoner was, on the night mentioned, engaged in feloniously plotting against the government; and that he was personally responsible for the death of an unknown number of the Roman soldiers, who were slain in the conflict.

" What sayest thou to the testimony of these witnesses?" asked Pilate. " Is there any reason why I should not presently inflict upon thee the just penalty of thy misdeeds?"

" What were these, mine accusers, doing on the night of Adar the twenty-seventh?" demanded Barabbas, with a scornful smile.

" That concerns thee not," replied Pilate sternly. " Speak for thyself now, if thou wilt, or hold thy peace while I pronounce sentence upon thee."

" I will say this," said Barabbas, knowing that his case was hopeless; " that I only regret that we accomplished not our purpose, which was to rend the golden eagle from the temple of Jehovah. And furthermore, if the Romans which desecrate the holy city of Jerusalem were possessed of one single neck, I would gladly hew it asunder with my sword, that the land might be rid of an abomination which riseth to heaven."

This incendiary speech was received with a storm of hisses from the Romans, and an irrepressible murmur of applause from the Jews who were present. Pilate's face paled and his voice trembled with rage as he said:

" Out of thine own mouth thou art condemned; it only remaineth for me to pass sentence upon thee. Thou shalt be nailed to the cross on Friday, the fifteenth day of Nisan next, and remain thereon till life be extinct. Thou shalt also be scourged upon being removed from my presence, and again before the execution taketh place." Then turning to the guard, he commanded them to remove the prisoner.

Titus was sick and faint at these fearful words; but Barabbas, apparently unmoved, passed from the presence of the governor with as lofty and undaunted a front as he had worn on the night of the riot.

Then followed the examination of a number of witnesses against forty or fifty of the insurgents. These had been seized by the soldiers as they fled after the capture of Barabbas. Pilate disposed of their case very quickly, sentencing them one and all to a heavy scourging, and a night in the stocks.

After these had been removed, for the infliction of their sentence, Pilate consulted for a few moments with the officials who surrounded him, then said in a loud voice, " Let the other prisoners be brought forward."

Titus was now roughly pushed to the space in front of the judgment seat, and lifting his eyes, he saw standing beside him the familiar figure of Dumachus. The two stared at each other in mutual surprise; then Dumachus smiled, and the smile was an evil thing to see.

" Prisoners," said Pilate, " ye are accused of three crimes—highway robbery, murder and rioting. Let the witnesses against you testify; then shall ye speak for yourselves."

The first witness was the identical Samaritan wine-merchant whose vintage Dumachus had so highly praised. He deposed, that in his journey from Samaria to Jerusalem, he had been set upon by thieves, who had stripped him of his possessions, consisting of certain skins of choice wine which he was conveying to the Jerusalem market; and even of his clothing. That after beating him, and subjecting him to various indignities, they had left him lying half dead by the roadside. He had subsequently been rescued and cared for by one of his own countrymen, who happened to be journeying that way. He recognized the prisoners at the bar as members of the band which had thus feloniously assaulted him.

The next witness swore to having seen the prisoners at the wine-shop of Clopas on the night of the riot, and afterward in the company of Barabbas at the time of the encounter with the Roman guard.

Then the centurion who had captured Titus recounted the circumstances of his arrest, and also stated that the prisoner had confessed that he had taken part in the riot.

The last witness to be brought forward, was Gestas. He carefully avoided the eye of Dumachus, as he stood forth, and stared stolidly at the governor in his ivory chair of state.

"Thou shalt suffer with the others; the world will be well rid of thee."

"What sayest thou concerning the prisoners?" asked Pilate.

Gestas looked down upon the ground, then rolled his eyes uneasily at the guard which stood near the prisoners; he seemed to feel the murderous look with which Dumachus was eying him. At length he began to speak in a low, hoarse voice.

"I was promised that if I told all, I myself should escape. Is it so, Excellency?"

"Thou shalt escape, even as was told thee. Speak on!" said Pilate impatiently.

"Well, then," continued the man, "Dumachus, yonder, was chief of our band. There were twenty of us in all, but about a dozen did most of the business. We had our headquarters in Capernaum; but put in most of our work on the great highways leading to Jerusalem, where there is always plenty of plunder for the taking. We took much booty, and disposed of our prisoners as seemed best at the time. Many we allowed to go free; but if any made outcry or disturbance, our chief commanded them to be put to death as quickly and quietly as possible."

"How many did ye so dispose of?" questioned Pilate.

The man scratched his head reflectively,

then replied, "I do not rightly know, Excellency. We never counted them."

"Was this young man a member of the band?" asked Pilate, indicating Titus, with a motion of his hand.

"He was until lately, Excellency. He is called Titus, and was known as the son of our chief; but 'twas thought by all of us that he was stolen in his infancy, and was therefore of no kin to Dumachus."

"As a member of the band, took he part in the robbery and murder of which thou hast spoken?"

The man hesitated for a moment, then said:

"He was a good-hearted lad, and would have been an honest one, had he been suffered to be so; but he had a bold spirit, and a ready hand in a fight."

"By that thou meanest that he did take part in the business, as thou callest it?"

"'Tis true that he killed an Ethiopian," was the reply, "but 'twas in a fair fight; the fellow had killed him else."

"Ye hear what these witness against you," said Pilate, now addressing the prisoners. "Thou, the chief, mayst speak first."

Dumachus lifted his shaggy head, and began to speak rapidly, and in a whining voice. "The man hath lied, Excellency; 'tis all a foul lie. I am a fisherman by trade, and an honest man. This young man here is my son. He is a wayward lad, and hath caused me great sorrow. He hath undoubtedly done much evil; I came up to Jerusalem to endeavor to wean him from his bad companions. 'Twas my errand in the wine-shop of Clopas. It paineth my father's heart thus to testify against mine only son, but—"

"Thou hast said enough," said Pilate, interrupting him. "Thou art undoubtedly a valuable citizen, and a sorrowing father—'tis written all over thee. But we must even spare thee to entertain our Passover visitors. On Friday, Nisan the fifteenth, thou shalt suffer with Barabbas, and in like manner. Guard, remove the prisoner!"—as Dumachus began to bellow like an animal.

"And thou, wayward son of a righteous father, hast thou aught to say for thyself?"

Titus looked up into the sneering face of the man on the judgment seat, then around on the hostile faces which hemmed him in, his injured head throbbing painfully.

"Oh, Stephen!" he cried aloud, "Oh, mother!"

Pilate was thoroughly tired of the whole affair. Besides, it was nearly time for the noonday repast, and he expected guests; it was therefore the more necessary for him to have time to compose his spirits, after the painful scenes of the morning. With a gesture of disgust, he arose to his feet and said sharply:

"Enough! This is no place for a scene! Thou shalt suffer with the others; the world will be well rid of thee. Guards, remove him! And clear the hall."

Titus lay on the mouldy straw of his dungeon once more. He was quiet now; he was thinking, not of the scenes of the morning, nor of the frightful doom which hung over him, but of the old, sweet days with Stephen on the lake; of Prisca, the only mother he had ever known; of the rosy, laughing face of little Ruth; of the good old Benoni. And as he thought of all these, another face arose before him; 'twas that of the Nazarene, Jesus—beautiful, mysterious, tender, with a love beyond all earthly love—and he fancied he again heard those words which, light-hearted and happy, he had heeded so little: "Come unto me, all ye that labor and are heavy laden, and I will give you rest." Over and over, he repeated the words aloud, and their sound seemed to soothe his tortured brain. His eyes closed, after a time, and with the healing words still on his lips, he slept profoundly.

And as he slept he dreamed. He thought that he was with Stephen, and that they two were walking alone in a great and wide meadow. 'Twas a pleasant spot, for flowers of every form and color bloomed profusely about them, while the air was filled with the heavenly melody of the lark, high above their heads.

Stephen was talking, as was his wont, in his sweet, silvery voice: "Dost thou remember how the Master said, 'Consider the lilies, how they grow; they toil not, neither do they spin; and yet I say unto you that even Solomon in all his glory was not arrayed like one of these'? And our Father in the heavens loveth us better than he loveth the lilies, for we are his children; the Master hath said it, not once, but many times."

"Thou art his child," Titus answered, with an eager longing at his heart. "But I —I know not whose child I am."

Then he lifted his eyes and saw coming toward them the figure of a man clad in raiment of a dazzling whiteness.

"Who is it?" he said to Stephen, yet in his heart he well knew.

"'Tis the Master!" cried Stephen joyfully, and he hastened to meet him.

But Titus stood still where he was, longing, yet afraid; for he knew that he had sinned. As he looked, he saw Stephen fall down at the Master's feet in an ecstasy of joy. Then Jesus put forth his hand, and raised him up, and the two, talking lovingly together, came towards him amid the lilies. Then he thought that he hung his head, not daring to look again, for his sin was heavy upon him.

"My child!"

He raised his eyes slowly at the sound of that voice, and as he looked, lo! the bitterness and guilt of his heart melted away, and his soul expanded with a mighty love. Then the Master, leaning forward, touched him on the brow, and said:

"Thou, too, art mine!"

And he awoke, and it was a dream! But his eyes shone in the darkness of the dungeon, and his lips smiled.

"Behold, mine eyes have seen the King in his beauty," he murmured. "And I am his."

CHAPTER XXII.

IT was more than a month, now, since Stephen and his mother had climbed the rocky road leading to Nazareth; and still they abode in the house of Mary, the mother of Jesus. Prisca had never risen from the bed on to which she had sunken so thankfully the night of her arrival, and it became more and more evident to the experienced eyes of Mary that her days were numbered. Once, as she bent over the invalid to perform some trifling service, she said gently:

"I would that we might send word to my son; he could heal thee."

But the sick woman caught her hand. "No, no!" she cried earnestly, "I am going to die, and I am glad of it. My life has not been so happy that I would fain live longer. Let me die here, where it is so quiet and peaceful."

And in truth, it was a peaceful haven that she had reached, after the troublous voyage of her life. As she lay in the humble bed fragrant with spotless linen, suffering no pain, but growing daily weaker, she was almost happy for the first time in years.

Often after the duties of the little home had been performed, Mary would bring her spinning into the chamber where the sick woman lay, and sitting by her bedside, work silently while she slept. Sometimes they talked together. Once she told Prisca the wondrous story of Bethlehem, of the star, the song of the angels, and the visit of the wise men. Another time, when Stephen was sitting by his mother, she told them of the angelic warning, and the hurried journey into Egypt: of the strange people and customs of that far-away land; and of the return—not to their old home and friends in Judea, but to this little mountain village of Nazareth.

Stephen never tired of listening as she talked of the childhood of Jesus, of his boyhood, and the years of his young manhood.

"This bench under the shade of the fig tree is where he studied when he was a child," she said one day, "and here I used to bring my spinning in the long afternoons. He always loved to be with me; while the other children of the village liked best to play in the fountain, or hunt birds' nests, or play noisily in the streets. Yet was he the happiest child in the world, always singing about his work, and with a smile like sunshine. The others all loved him dearly. No one could tell such beautiful stories as he; and there was no other so ready to soothe a sick baby, or comfort a crying child, or bind up a cut finger, in the whole village. So that while he loved best to be near me, as I have said, and spent much of his time in helping me about the house and garden, the neighbors' children flocked about him as thick as bees about a rose. I remember me how he used to sit on yonder bench with one or two babies in his arms, and a dozen other little ones crowded about him, some sitting at his feet, leaning against his knee, and all listening with eyes and ears wide open, as he talked to them of the birds—how they built their homes so patiently and lovingly, and worked hard to bring up their young ones all through the long bright days; about the flowers that grew so fair and sweet in the lonely valleys, where no one but God could see them; about the snow that fell white and silent from the clouds in the winter time, yet every tiny flake a thing of beauty. Sometimes on the Sabbath days he would repeat Psalms to them, and tell them long stories from the Scriptures—of Moses in his little ark and the beautiful princess; of Goliath and the bold young David; of Samson, the foolish strong man, and many others."

"Ah!" said Stephen, with shining eyes, and a pathetic look of wistfulness, "how I wish I might have lived in Nazareth then!"

Mary smiled her beautiful gentle smile, and laid her delicate hand caressingly on his thick curls. "Dost thou know," she said after a little pause, "thou art like him in some of thy ways. When thou art working so busily in the garden, singing softly to thyself, or sitting as thou art now at my feet, I always think of him as he was at thy age. That is why I talk of him to thee so often."

"I would rather be like him," cried Stephen passionately, "than to be the Cæsar on his throne!"

"In that art thou wise," said Mary, and her deep eyes beamed with a mysterious light. "The Cæsar on his throne is at best a sinful man, while Jesus is—"

"He is the Holy One of God!" said Stephen reverently.

Then a silence fell between them for a time. But always after that, the mother of Jesus noticed how he tried, humbly and unobtrusively, but ever faithfully, to fill that vacant place. And in her heart she loved him for it.

As for Prisca, she felt for her a tender pity, for she divined that the woman had somewhere a dark page in her history. One day as she sat silently by the bedside of the invalid, busied with her spinning, glancing now and then at the white worn face on the pillow, she saw that great tears were stealing slowly from beneath the closed lids. Rising, she leaned over the bed, and taking the thin, chill hand of the sufferer in both of hers, said gently: "Wilt thou not tell me thy trouble?"

Instantly the dark eyes opened and looked long and earnestly into the loving face above her. "Yes!" she said slowly, "I will tell thee all. I did a great wrong years ago, and it hath weighed me to the earth all my life

since. Yet have I never had the courage to make it right."

Then she told the story of Titus, and how she had stolen away by night to meet her lover, taking the child with her.

"Why didst thou take the child?" questioned Mary.

"Dumachus bade me to," answered the woman feebly. "And I loved the little one, and could not bear to part with him; so I obeyed. I always meant to restore him to his mother, but I never dared. Once when I said that I must do it, my husband in a fury struck me down; and worse than that, he hurt my baby Stephen, crippling him hopelessly. He was always helpless and suffering after that, till, as thou knowest, he was healed by the goodness of thy son. Ah, what do we not owe to thee! And now thou wilt hate me! I am not fit to be under this roof."

Mary was silent for a moment, but she kissed the sufferer tenderly on the brow; then she said firmly, "Thou must even yet make this wrong right. Let thy son Stephen go to Capernaum and bring the young man David hither. Thou shalt tell him all, and give into his hand the proofs that the story is true. Hast thou them here?"

"Yes," said Prisca, reaching under her pillow and drawing out a little packet, securely wrapped in linen, and bound with a silken thread. "I have never let it go from me; 'tis the little tunic which he wore when I fled with him. His mother wrought it with her own hands; she will know it. And with it is a chain of wrought silver, which she gave me to wear, when she selected me from all her maidens to care for the little David. And how have I betrayed my trust! What will become of me!"

"Thou hast indeed sinned grievously," said Mary. "But God will forgive thee, even as he forgave King David, who was guilty of murder, if thou wilt but humble thine heart before him."

"God knoweth that my heart is humbled, even unto the dust; but, alas! it bringeth me no peace!"

Mary looked troubled. She raised her dove-like eyes. "Ah, Son of God!" she murmured, as if to herself, "would that thou wert here to minister to this sin-sick soul! As for me, I know not what to say unto her." Then she spoke again to the sick woman. "Dost thou know my son, who is called Jesus?"

"I have seen him," answered Prisca.

"And I always longed to speak with him, that I might thank him for the healing of my Stephen. But I dared not; the sin in my heart was too great. I had almost put it under my feet, till I saw him in Capernaum."

"He is the Sinless One," said Mary gravely. "But didst thou never hear him say that he had come to this world, out of

"Thou wilt find Titus—give him this."

heaven above, to save those that had sinned?"

"Said he that?" cried Prisca eagerly. "And how save them?"

"He hath said, not once but many times, that 'whosoever believeth in him, should not perish, but have everlasting life,'" said Mary simply.

"Thou art sure that he said 'whosoever'?"

"He hath said it—not once, but many times," answered the mother of Jesus.

"And what is it that I must believe?" asked Prisca, trembling in her eagerness.

"That he came down from God, to seek and to save that which was lost; and that he is able to accomplish that for which he came," answered Mary.

"How could I help but believe that?—did he not save my Stephen from worse than death!" Clasping her thin hands, she cried out joyfully: "I believe that he is able!" Then she closed her eyes and lay so quiet, that Mary thought she slept. Presently Stephen stole into the room, and stood beside the bed, looking down at his mother.

"What thinkest thou?" he asked in a low voice. "Doth she mend?"

At the sound of his voice, the sick woman opened her eyes. "I have been a great sinner above most," she said faintly. "But he came to save me, and I am at peace. Thou wilt find Titus— give him this. She will tell thee all."

Then the dark eyes closed again, and for the last time. The two sat beside the bed and watched the quiet sleeper through the long hours of the night. Just at dawn, the pale lips moved, and Stephen, stooping down, caught two words: "Stephen— Jesus." Then the faint breath stopped altogether. She had entered into everlasting life.

After the simple funeral, which took place, in accordance with the Eastern custom, at evening of the same day, Stephen heard from the lips of Mary the story of Titus.

He was greatly moved. "Poor mother!" he said. "No wonder she wept, with such a burden on her heart. She was a timid soul and lived always a life of terror."

Then he told the mother of Jesus all that he knew of his father's evil life. "He is all I have left now," he said bitterly when he had finished.

"Dost thou mean that?" said Mary.

"No! A thousand times no!" cried Stephen impetuously, as he caught her meaning. "Didst thou hear my mother's last words? In that moment when with her dying breath she coupled my name with his, I knew what I must do. I shall give my whole life to him."

"Thou shalt indeed," said Mary, gazing away over the hills with a solemn look in her deep eyes. "But I know not what the future hath in store for him. He hath bitter enemies; sometimes I fear for his life." And she turned to Stephen with a tremulous quiver of her sweet, firm mouth. "Is he not the Beloved of the Father?" said Stephen simply. "And is the Father not able to save him from the hand of his enemies?"

"'He shall make his enemies his footstool,' even as it is written," answered Mary in a firm voice, "and he shall triumph gloriously."

Stephen regarded her with awe.

After a little silence she said: "To-morrow thou must go forth even as thy mother bade thee, that thou mayst find the young man David, and acquaint him with all that hath happened. As for me, I am going up to Jerusalem. Something tells me that he will have need of me."

And so it happened that in the morning early, Stephen set forth alone on his journey, bearing with him the little tunic wrought by the mother of Titus, and the silver chain which had belonged to his own dead mother. And when he departed Mary blessed him and kissed him; and he wept, as he bade her farewell, for he was but a lad after all, and the world was wide and lonely.

<hr />

CHAPTER XXIII.

CAIAPHAS was striding up and down the floor of his own private apartment, his hands clasped behind him, his head bent forward on his breast. His eyes were blazing with an angry light beneath his brows, and now and then he muttered fiercely to himself, "Blasphemer! He shall be crushed! Have I not vowed it—I, Caiaphas, the high priest? He shall not defy me longer!"

Hearing a slight sound outside, he strode rapidly to the door of the chamber, and flung it open.

"Ah, Malchus! 'Tis thou. Enter! Well, what hast thou to say?"

The man bent his head humbly. "Most worshipful master, I went as I was bidden to Bethany. When I reached the place, I had not the slightest difficulty in finding the abode of Lazarus; the streets were thronged with people going and coming to the house, which I found to be one of the humbler cottages of the town, albeit comfortable and tidy."

"I care not what sort of a place it was," interrupted Caiaphas irritably. "The man! —didst thou see the man?"

"I saw the man Lazarus—alive and well," continued Malchus. "He was in the garden of his house talking to the people."

"Talking to the people, was he!" sneered the high priest. "The country is full of orators nowadays. And what said he?"

"He was telling the story of his resurrection. He said that the four days which he passed in the tomb were as a sleep. He hath still a faint memory of wondrous dreams, but cannot tell clearly what they were like. He was also praising and blessing God, and ascribing equal praises to the Nazarene, whom he called the Son of God, and the Consolation of Israel."

Caiaphas ground his teeth. "And the people?"

"The people all cried aloud, 'Hallelujah!' and 'Hosanna to the Son of David!' All Bethany hath gone mad over the thing; such a wonder hath never been heard of."

"'Tis a palpable lie, and hath been invented by this fellow and his followers to make an uproar at feast time! Didst thou question others concerning the thing, as I bade thee?"

The man looked gravely at his master. "'Tis regarded as a veritable miracle in Bethany," he said. "I made the most careful investigation, even as thou didst command me, questioning many discreet and prudent persons concerning the matter. I also examined the tomb in which he lay. The man was unquestionably dead, and had been buried four days; but how the Nazarene was able to restore him to life, except by the power of God, I know not; nor could any one tell me."

"Keep thy senses, man! Let not the evil one prevail over thee!" said the high priest, looking sternly at his favorite servant. "No disciple of the blasphemer shall serve me."

"I am not a disciple," replied Malchus, looking down upon the ground. "But the thing is beyond my understanding."

"Enough!" said Caiaphas, with an impatient gesture. "Leave me; and prepare the council chamber. Let it be in readiness within an hour."

"We have dealt gently with this thing too long already; the man must be put out of the way, and that speedily!" The speaker was the venerable Annas. He was the centre of an excited group in the council chamber of the high priest. "If we let him thus alone, as we have been doing for almost three years now, all men will believe on him, and the Romans will come and take away both our place and nation; and deservedly so. He should have been dealt with long ago—'twas my advice then, and could have been easily followed in the beginning; but the matter hath now assumed such an aspect, that it will be exceedingly difficult to bring about his death."

"I am not in favor of putting the man to death," said Nicodemus, in his mild tones. "For in my opinion he hath done nothing worthy of death."

"Thou knowest nothing at all!" broke out Caiaphas, passionately, "nor dost consider that it is expedient for us that one man should die for the people, and that the whole nation perish not."

Nicodemus looked at him for a moment in silence. "Thou art the high priest," he said solemnly. "Jehovah speaketh through thy words; but God forbid that we put an innocent man to death. For my part I will have nothing further to do with this thing."

"We have long suspected that thou art one of his disciples," said Annas with a sneer. "Thou art therefore out of place in the council of the Sanhedrim. Go hence, and join thy illustrious master, the carpenter, and his followers whom he hath gathered from the refuse of the earth."

"Enough!" said Caiaphas. "Leave me; and prepare the council chamber."

Nicodemus made no reply; but he arose and passed out of the council chamber in dignified silence.

"Let him go!" said Jochanan. "'Tis not meet that we lose time in discussing what is sufficiently obvious to all the rest of our number." As he spoke, he glanced around the circle, and a little murmur of applause followed.

But there was one who did not join in the applause. He was looking steadily upon the floor at his feet, his fingers busying themselves uneasily with his long beard. The name of this man was Joseph, and he was a native of Arimathea.

"Now as to the case of this fellow Lazarus, who is making quite an uproar on his own account," continued Jochanan, "what think ye? It seemeth to me that he were better off in the tomb from which he was taken. If he were indeed dead, then was it the will of God, and he should have remained so. We shall not be doing unlawfully if we carry out upon him the sentence of death which Jehovah had himself already imposed."

"Thou hast spoken wisely," said Annas. "The man had evidently reached the proper limit of his days; it is more than probable that his body is now animated by a devil, which thus speaketh blasphemously through the flesh. He should be put out of the way, and that speedily. See to it; for he leadeth away much people after him."

"Moreover, being a dead body, which hath no longer any right on top of the earth, he defileth every man with whom he cometh in contact," said another, piously.

"Let the man Lazarus alone!" said Joseph of Arimathea, unable to restrain himself any longer. "I know him well; he is an honest man and a just. I have also seen him since his resurrection from the dead—if so it was. He hath not a devil; and believing what he doth, he justly praiseth God for his deliverance, and glorifieth with him his savior from the tomb."

"The matter can be discussed later," said Annas smoothly. "Can any one here inform me of the whereabouts of the Nazarene?"

"He hath come even to-day to Bethany, where he sojourneth with the same Lazarus," said Caiaphas. "I was informed of the fact as I entered the council chamber. He undoubtedly purposeth to be in Jerusalem for the feast. He must be seized in secret, that there be no uproar among the people. And there must also be some evidence secured against him, which shall bring him under Roman jurisdiction. For, as ye know, this tribunal hath not the power to put any man to death."

The eyes of several present flashed dangerously, at this reference to the Roman supremacy and the national degradation. But Annas hastened to say blandly:

"The Romans have not shown themselves unfriendly to the church of the living God—our temple beareth witness to the fact; we must not forget it, nor blindly risk being crushed by the iron hand of Rome. We must rather seek to ally ourselves to them in every way in our power. If this man Jesus can be convicted of plotting against the government, our work will be practically done. We can then deliver him over into the hand of Pilate, assured that he will be dealt with after his deserts. To-morrow, especially, let him be watched closely; in such a case as this, the Sabbath laws must be relaxed, so that we shall be enabled to perform this work—which is assuredly one of necessity."

At this moment a loud knocking was heard at the door of the council chamber. Caiaphas looked astonished. "Who dareth to interrupt us in our deliberations!" he said aloud. "But stay! It must be something of importance!" And he beckoned to one of his brothers-in-law to open the door.

The man returned almost instantly, and said in a low voice: "'Tis one of the followers of the Nazarene. He would speak with the high priest."

Caiaphas hesitated.

"Wilt thou not command that he be brought before us?" suggested Annas. "It may be that he hath repented himself of his folly in joining the man; he might in that case be disposed to give us timely assistance."

"Let him be brought in," said Caiaphas.

There was a silence in the chamber, broken only by the footfalls of the man who now entered. As he stopped and hesitated at sight of the imposing assemblage, it could be seen that he was of low stature, and of a singularly sinister cast of countenance.

Annas smiled genially as his eye fell upon the new-comer.

"Wilt thou not come forward and acquaint us with thy desires?" he said in his most honeyed tones.

The man looked at him. "Art thou the high priest?" he asked hoarsely.

"I am the high priest, fellow! What wouldst thou with me?" demanded Caiaphas impatiently.

But Annas touched him warningly. "Thou hast come, my good man, to speak with us in regard to the Nazarene; is it not so?" he asked.

The man's face brightened, and an evil light shone in his eyes. "Aye!" he said in a loud voice, "I have! I can no longer abide his presence. It hath been made known to me that thou art his enemy, therefore am I come."

"Ah!" said Annas softly, "thou wouldst fain return to the bosom of the church of thy fathers, and cease thy wanderings in by and forbidden paths; am I not right?"

"I care not for the church!" was the bold reply, "any more than the church careth for me. But I want money; what wilt thou give me if I betray him into thy hands?"

Caiaphas started to his feet, while joy sparkled in his eyes. "What will I give thee?" he exclaimed. "Why, man—"

But Annas checked him, saying in a low voice: "Let me manage the fellow, my son; I understand this sort as thou dost not." Then he went on judicially: "It were worth no great sum, assuredly, my good man, since we already know where he is to be found. Still, thou mightest be of assistance to us, and we are disposed to be generous. What sayest thou to twenty pieces of silver?"

The man looked down. "'Tis too little," he said sullenly. "Thou knowest not his haunts as I do."

"True," said Annas smoothly. "I will even increase the amount by half. Deliver him into our hands safely, and at a time when there shall be no uproar of the people, and we will give thee thirty pieces of silver—'tis a goodly sum and not to be despised."

The man shuffled uneasily on his feet, and looked furtively about him at the evidences of wealth on every side. But he made no answer.

Caiaphas, in a fury of impatience, was about to burst out into speech, when Annas again spoke, and this time his cold, even tones had a shade of sternness in them: "Thou must decide quickly, for we are considering other plans. Wilt thou have the thirty pieces or wilt thou not? Thy Master is doomed in any event."

The man was silent for a moment longer, then he said slowly:

"Well, I will do it; 'tis a small sum, but I am a poor man; I must look out for myself. I have wasted many months in following this Jesus. I thought him the Messiah; but he is not—he is not—he is not." And his voice died away into an inarticulate murmur.

"Thou hast done right and wisely, both for thyself and for us," said Annas warmly,

rising and approaching the miserable wretch, who was trembling in every limb. "Thou shalt have food and wine before leaving the palace. But first, what is thy name? and what art thou to the Nazarene?"

"My name is Judas Iscariot. I am one of the twelve who are always with him," replied the man, in so low a voice that Annas could hardly catch the words.

"One of his immediate followers!" said Annas, rubbing his hands, and looking about the circle of attentive listeners with a triumphant smile. "Ah, this is better than I thought; it is indeed well! Now, my good man, it is important that the Nazarene should suspect nothing of all this—thou seest that, of course, for thou art a shrewd fellow —therefore attend strictly to what I shall say. Go back to him and attend him as usual, till such a time as thou canst safely— mind, I say safely, with no disturbance, nor outcry to arouse the people—deliver him into our hands. We will take care of the rest. And the silver shall be paid thee immediately thereafter. This is the earnest of the larger sum which shall be thine." And he pressed a coin into the man's hand.

He clutched at it greedily, muttering something unintelligible.

But Annas was content. "Here, Malchus!" he said cheerfully, opening the door of the chamber, "take this good fellow and see that he hath an abundance both of food and wine."

At this, the man turned fiercely upon him. "Nay, I am not a beggar! I want only what is justly due me." Then looking full into the eyes of Annas, he hissed: "Thou shalt have him! Do not doubt it; for I hate him, even as thou dost!"

After that he turned and went swiftly away, without once looking behind him.

CHAPTER XXIV.

WANT to go home, mother! Why must we stay here so long?" and the child tugged impatiently at his mother's robe.

"Nay, my child, thou must be patient. We have not long to wait now. See, here is a cake for thee; eat it while I tell thee again why we are here, for thou must remember this day to thy latest breath."

"Tell me," said the child, between his mouthfuls, looking up into his mother's face. "When thou wert a babe, my Gogo, thou wast nigh unto death; and this Jesus healed thee."

"Thou hast told me that many times! Give me another cake; I am hungry."

"Yes, my son, I have told thee many times, for had it not been for this Jesus, thou wouldst even now be lying in the grave—and I should be childless! My child! My love!" And the mother embraced the little form with passionate tenderness "Why dost thou hold me so tight, mother?" asked the boy, shaking the curls out of his eyes. " Oh! see that lovely bird!"

"Never mind the bird, child, but listen! This Jesus is a king—the Messiah. To-day he is coming along this road, and thou shalt see him."

"A king! Will he wear a crown?"

"I know not. It may be. We shall see. But look at the people!—thousands upon thousands of them! We have a good place here. We shall be near him."

"Nay, I like it not; I care not to see a king. I would rather play. Let us go home!"

"Hark! Dost thou hear that?" cried another woman who stood near. "They are coming! What is it that they are saying— 'Hosanna! Hosanna to the Son of David! Blessed is he that cometh in the name of the Lord! Hosanna in the highest!' Ah, 'tis a blessed day! To think that we should live to see it! But see the people running! They are stripping down the palm leaves!"

"Why do they do that, mother?" again questioned the little one.

"Thou shalt sit on my shoulder and see. Now art thou as tall as a man, and can see further than I. What seest thou?"

"I see many people coming—and a man riding upon a mule," replied the child.

"Yes! yes!" said the other woman, "I see also. Can it be he? The people are shouting and throwing the palm branches before him! See! they strip off their garments, and lay them also in the road!"

And now the procession was close at hand; and the whole multitude of the disciples began to rejoice and praise God with a loud voice for all the mighty works that they had seen, saying:

"Give thou the triumph, O Jehovah, to the Son of David! Blessed be the kingdom of our father David, now to be restored in the name of Jehovah. Blessed be he that com-

eth, the King of Israel, in the name of Jehovah! Our peace and salvation are from God above! Praised be he in the highest heavens! From the highest heavens send thou now salvation!"

"Look at him, child! 'Tis the King—the Messiah! Shout now with me—Hosanna to the King! Hosanna to the Son of David!"

"Hold thy peace, woman! Art thou mad, that thou teachest thy innocent babe to blaspheme?"

The woman, startled by these harsh words, turned about and fixed her eyes, large with fright, upon the speaker. She saw that he was a Pharisee, and clasping the little one closer to her breast, she said: "I know not what thou sayest. He is the savior of my child; therefore I praise him."

But the man paid no heed to her answer; he was pressing forward into the throng which surrounded the Master. "Hearest thou what these are saying?" he shouted angrily. "Bid them hold their peace!"

The Master turned, and looking upon him, said: "I tell you that if these should hold their peace, the stones would immediately cry out."

"And when he was near, he beheld the city, and wept over it, saying, If thou hadst known, even thou, at least in this thy day, the things which belong unto thy peace! But now they are hid from thine eyes. For the days shall come upon thee, that thine enemies shall cast a trench about thee, and compass thee round, and keep thee in on every side, and shall lay thee even with the ground, and thy children within thee. And they shall not leave in thee one stone upon another; because thou knewest not the time of thy visitation. And when he was come into Jerusalem, all the city was moved, saying, Who is this? And the multitude answered, This is Jesus, the prophet of Nazareth of Galilee."

As the procession passed within the city gates, and the sound of the chanting and acclamations died away, one of a group of men in foreign dress who had been intent witnesses of the scene, turned to his companions. "What say ye to this, friends?" he asked earnestly.

"'Tis a wondrous sight. And the man! —his countenance hath a look upon it that is not of earth. Know ye aught concerning him?"

"I have heard, mine Apelles, that he is

in deed and in truth the Prince long expected of the Jews, and foretold in their Scriptures. Even now they look to see him establish his throne in Jerusalem. I would fain see him, and stand in his presence."

" I also, my Andronicus," said another. " But how may that be? We are Gentiles— albeit converts from the pagan faith of our fathers to the one only and true God. Would this King of the Jews suffer us to approach him?"

" Nay, I know not," answered Apelles. " But he hath not yet hedged himself about with the grandeur of a king. Didst thou see how even the children and the women approached him fearlessly?"

" 'Tis true," said one who had hitherto been silent. " If he be a king, he is a king apart from the kings of this earth. His followers be humble men. One of them is known to me. He hath a Greek name— Philip. Let us seek him and inquire further of this matter." And forthwith they all entered into the city and sought the temple. For there they hoped to find the man Philip.

As they passed into the court of the Gentiles, the quick eye of Rufus caught sight of the man of whom he had spoken, about to pass into the inner court, whither these foreigners could not come. Starting forward hastily, Rufus touched him on the shoulder and said in a low voice: " A word with thee, good friend."

Philip turned himself about, and as his eye fell upon the swarthy face of the Greek, he drew back a little, and said somewhat coldly:

" Ah, Rufus, 'tis thou! What wilt thou?"

" I would have speech with thee for a moment," replied Rufus. " I and certain of my countrymen—like myself converts to the religion of the Jews—have come up to the feast, and to-day we saw the man who is called the prophet of Nazareth as he entered into the city, and certain strange things concerning him have come to our ears. Sir, we would fain see this Jesus for ourselves, that we also may learn of him."

Philip looked troubled. " Friend, thou art a Gentile notwithstanding that thou hast turned from idolatry to the true faith. I know not whether this may be. And yet— stay! I will consult with another of our number. Wait here; I will return speedily." So saying, he turned away and was quickly lost to view in the crowd which filled the place.

The Greek beckoned to his companions.

" Thou wert right, mine Apelles," he said bitterly: " these Jews cannot forget that we are but strangers within the gate."

" He will not receive us, then!" said Apelles in a tone of deep disappointment. " Let us depart out of this place, and I care not whether I ever return."

" Nay, friend—thou art over-hasty," said Rufus, smiling at the impetuous young man. " We have directions to wait here until the follower of the Nazarene hath made sure of the matter. Nevertheless he reminded me that I was a Gentile. 'Tis a name that I hate! But see! he is returning."

" We have spoken with the Master concerning thee," said Philip, " and since it is unlawful for thee to come to him in the inner courts of the temple, he will even come forth unto thee. He is ever merciful and hath compassion on the lowliest," he added.

The proud, sensitive face of Apelles flushed at these words, but Andronicus made answer:

" Thy Master doeth us honor. It may be that even we, Gentiles though we be, shall yet render him some service which shall be acceptable unto him."

Philip bowed his head gravely, but made no answer. Then, lifting up his eyes, he said: " The Master is at hand."

And the Greeks, looking earnestly in the direction to which he pointed, saw approaching them the Jesus whom they had longed for. They bowed in lowliest reverence before him, and Jesus, lifting up his face to heaven, said:

" The hour is come that the Son of man should be glorified."

Then looking searchingly into the earnest faces before him, he continued, " Verily, verily I say unto you, except a grain of wheat fall into the earth and die, it abideth by itself alone; but if it die, it beareth much fruit. He that loveth his life loseth it, and he that hateth his life in this world shall keep it unto life eternal. If any man would serve me, let him follow me; and where I am, there shall also my servant be. If any man serve me, him will the Father honor."

Here he paused for a moment, evidently lost in thought; then again lifting his face toward the cloudless spring heavens, he said in a tone of pathetic patience: " Now is my soul troubled; and what shall I say? Father, save me from this hour. But for this cause came I unto this hour. Father, glorify thy name."

Then sounded forth a great and melodious voice, filling all the infinite space of the sunlit sky above them:

"I have both glorified it, and will glorify it again."

The Greeks were awe-stricken at the prayer and at its wondrous answer. Instinctively they covered their faces with their hands, and sank upon the earth.

"It thunders," said one of a group of Jewish rabbis who stood by, enviously watching the scene.

"An angel hath spoken to him," murmured others beneath their breath.

And the Master answering said: "This voice hath not come for my sake, but for your sakes. Now is the judgment of this world: now shall the prince of this world be cast out. And I, if I be lifted up from the earth, will draw all men unto me."

"We have heard out of the law that the Christ abideth forever," said one of the rabbis; "and how sayest thou, that the Son of man must be crucified? Who is this Son of man?"

And Jesus made answer:

"Yet a little while is the light among you. Walk while ye have the light, that darkness overtake you not; and he that walketh in darkness knoweth not whither he goeth. While ye have the light, believe on the light, that ye may become sons of light."

Then he went away and was seen no more of the multitudes that day.

And the Greeks departed out of the temple, communing earnestly together of all that they had both seen and heard.

"Let us tarry in Jerusalem," they said, "that we may again speak with him."

But the Jews believed not, for their eyes were blinded to the light, and their souls were filled with bitterness and envy.

Yet because of the voice from heaven some even of the rulers believed; but they durst not confess it, because they feared the Pharisees. Verily, they loved the glory of men more than the glory of God.

CHAPTER XXV.

YONDER is a man bearing a pitcher. Dost see him? He is about to turn up the street."

"I see him," said Peter, looking earnestly in the direction in which John was pointing. "Let us follow quickly, lest he escape out of our sight."

So the two followed the man, who presently paused before the gateway of a house, seemingly that of a well-to-do family. The two entered boldly in after the pitcher-bearer, who turned to stare at them with amazement.

"We would see the master of the house," said Peter authoritatively.

The man made obeisance. "Wait here for a moment, good sirs, and I will fetch him," he said, looking curiously at the two.

Presently he returned, followed by an elderly man.

"If thou art the master of the house," said Peter, fixing his eyes upon him, "I have a message for thee."

The man bowed his head. "Speak," he replied, "and I will listen."

"This is my message," continued Peter. "The Master saith unto thee, 'Where is the guest chamber, where I shall eat the Passover with my disciples?'"

"'Tis the word I received in my dream," murmured the man, as if to himself. "Lo, I have prepared the chamber, and it is ready. Follow me."

They followed him, and he showed them a large upper room, furnished with everything needful for the feast. And they made ready the Passover.

And when it was evening Jesus came with his disciples, that they might eat of the supper. As they reclined at the table, Jesus being in the midst, he looked about upon the twelve and said: "With desire I have desired to eat this Passover with you before I suffer. For I say unto you, I will not any more eat thereof, until it be fulfilled in the kingdom of God."

And as they were eating, he said: "Verily I say unto you, that one of you shall betray me."

And they were all astonished and exceeding sorrowful, and began every one of them to say unto him: "Lord, is it I?"

Now John, who was especially beloved by the Master, was next to him at the table. Peter, looking at him attentively, motioned that he should ask Jesus who it was of whom he had spoken.

And John said very softly, so as to be heard by no one save the Master, "Lord, who is it?"

And Jesus, in the same low tone, made answer: "'Tis he to whom I shall give a morsel of bread, when I have dipped it in the dish."

Then breaking from the thin cake of bread before him a fragment, he rolled it up, and dipping it into the dish, gave it to Judas Iscariot.

As Judas accepted this little token of friendship from the hand of him whom he had once loved, all the awful passions of his soul broke their bonds. He started up, his eyes blazing with an evil light. Jesus looked at him, and said, still in a low voice: "What thou doest, do quickly."

And unable to bear the look in those eyes, Judas slunk out of the room and hurried away in the darkness, muttering fiercely to himself.

When he had gone, Jesus said to the eleven: "Now is the Son of man glorified, and God is glorified in him. Little children, yet a little while I am with you. Ye shall seek me; but whither I go, ye cannot come. A new commandment I give unto you, That ye love one another, even as I have loved you."

And he took bread and blessed it, and brake it, and gave to the disciples, and said: "Take, eat; this is my body, which is given for you. This do in remembrance of me."

And he took the cup, and gave thanks, and gave it to them, saying, "Drink ye all of it. For this is my blood of the new testament, which is shed for many for the remission of sins. This do ye, as often as ye shall drink it, in remembrance of me. But I say unto you, I will not drink henceforth of this fruit of the vine, until that day when I drink it new with you in my Father's kingdom."

Then Peter said to him: "Lord, where is it that thou art going?" For he was perplexed and sorrowful, as were they all.

Jesus answered him: "Whither I go, thou canst not follow me now, but thou shalt follow me afterward."

"Lord, why cannot I follow thee now?" insisted Peter anxiously. "I will lay down my life for thy sake."

Jesus looked at him sorrowfully, as he answered: "Every one of you shall be offended because of me this night. For it is written, 'I will smite the shepherd, and the sheep of the flock shall be scattered

Garden of Gethsemane as it appears to-day.

abroad.' But after I am risen I will go before you into Galilee."

"Though all men should be offended because of thee," declared Peter passionately, "yet will I never be offended!"

"Simon! Simon!" said the Lord warningly, "behold, Satan hath desired to have you, that he may sift you as wheat. But I have prayed for thee, that thy faith fail not. And when thou art converted, strengthen thy brethren."

But Peter answered him yet again: "Lord, I am ready to go with thee both into prison and to death."

Then said Jesus sadly: "Verily I say unto thee, that this day—even in this night—

before the cock crow twice, thou shalt deny me thrice."

"If I should die with thee," cried Peter, vehemently, "I will not deny thee in any way."

And all the others said the same.

Then Jesus had compassion on them, as he thought of all that they must suffer in the future; and he said many sweet and comforting things to them, which though they forgot in the terror and confusion that shortly followed, John afterward remembered and wrote of it all. And it hath come down to us, even to this day. Likewise he prayed with them. After that they sang a last hymn together, and went forth into the night.

Now when they were come to the Mount of Olives, they went into a garden there, called Gethsemane, which is, being interpreted, the oil press; for many great olive trees grew therein; and there was also a stone trough, where, in the season, it was the custom to tread the oil from the ripe fruit.

It was a calm and peaceful spot, well beloved by the Master as a place of prayer and rest. Overhead the great Passover moon shed a flood of mellow light, which, sifting through the new leaves, lay in silvery patches on the ground beneath.

As they entered the garden, Jesus said to his disciples, "Sit ye here, while I go and pray yonder."

Then taking Peter and James and John, he passed further on among the gnarled trunks of the olives.

"My soul is exceeding sorrowful, even unto death," he said at length, his eyes dim with anguish. "Tarry ye here and watch."

And the three stopped, as they were bidden, throwing themselves down on the soft spring grass, to wait his pleasure.

And he went from them about a stone's cast, and kneeled down; and they heard him praying:

"Abba, Father, all things are possible unto thee; if thou be willing, remove this cup from me; nevertheless not my will, but thine be done."

And as they sat apart, and watched him there, a confused drowsiness and heaviness of spirit fell upon them, so that they could no longer see nor hear distinctly. They fancied that they discerned dimly the radiant figure of an angel, stooping over that prostrate form—or was it but the silver light of the moonbeams falling interruptedly

through the branches? Their spirits were drowned in that strange slumber which held them fast, so that they could not move, though they dimly knew his agony.

Was it only the sleep of tired men, or was it that Omnipotence deemed the scene too sacred for mortal eyes to look upon? Be that as it may, the man Jesus sorely longed for human sympathy, and when he came—his brow crimsoned with the anguish of his soul—and found them asleep, he cried with bitter disappointment:

"What, Simon! Could ye not watch with me one hour? Watch and pray, that ye enter not into temptation." Then tenderly: "The spirit indeed is willing, but the flesh is weak."

Then he went away the second time and prayed, saying: "Oh, my Father, if this cup may not pass away from me, except I drink it, thy will be done!"

And he came and found them asleep again, for their eyes were heavy; neither could they, when he awoke them—in the dim confusion of their senses—make him any answer.

Verily might he have said, in the words of David: "Thy rebuke hath broken my heart. I am full of heaviness; I looked for some one to have pity on me, but there was no man; neither found I any to comfort me."

And he left them, and went away again, and prayed the third time, saying the same words.

Afterward coming to his disciples, he found them still sleeping. Looking upon them compassionately, he said: "Sleep on now, and take your rest; behold, the hour hath drawn near, and the Son of man is betrayed into the hands of sinners."

Then he raised himself up, and listened intently. The hour was even now come; for he heard the sound of tramping feet, and caught the glimmer of torches through the darkness. Turning to the sleepers he cried aloud, "Rise! Let us be going! Behold, he is at hand that doth betray me."

"How knowest thou that we shall find him yonder?" queried Jochanan impatiently, as he stumbled along at the side of Judas through the half darkness.

The man looked up, and by the irregular flame of the torch which he carried, Jochanan caught the look on his face; and hardened as he was, he recoiled from it.

"He will be there. I know the place well. He goeth there—to pray."

"Thou knowest that we must lose no time," said Jochanan, half apologetically. He had an unaccountable horror of this man.

"'What thou doest, do quickly.' They were his words to me," said Judas.

And again Jochanan felt that icy shiver. "Ugh! The wind is chill!" he said, wrapping his cloak closer about him.

Judas laughed, long and loud, and muttered something to himself.

"How shall we be sure of seizing the right man, if we be fortunate enough to find him?" continued Jochanan.

The man laughed again, a mirthless sound and terrible to hear. "I shall kiss him!" he answered.

Jochanan wrapped his cloak still closer about him. "The man is a devil!" he muttered. "I wish I had compelled Issachar to come. He is too dainty fine, though, for an errand like this."

Then he spoke no more, save to give a few sharp orders to the mob of temple police and Roman soldiers, which followed them.

"This is the place," said Judas at length, pausing before what dimly appeared to be a stone gateway. "Follow where I lead." And he strode away into the uncertain darkness of the garden.

"The fellow is mad!" said Jochanan impatiently to Malchus. "'Twere impossible to capture the man in a place like this. He hath a thousand chances to escape."

But even as he spoke, he caught at the arm of the high priest's servant. "Who is that, yonder?"

Malchus looked, and saw in the half darkness the figure of a man. Did he imagine it?—or was there a mysterious brightness—a dim shining? Hark! There was a voice!

"Whom seek ye?"

All were silent for a moment, save for the hiss of an awed whisper among the superstitious soldiers. Then Jochanan, gathering courage, said boldly:

"We seek Jesus of Nazareth."

And the answer came calm and clear, "I am he."

Something in that voice struck terror to the cowardly hearts of the mob. Starting back with a common impulse, they stumbled confusedly over one another, with muttered imprecations, and cries of fear.

Again the voice and the question: "Whom seek ye?"

And again they made answer: "Jesus of Nazareth."

"I have told you that I am he; if therefore ye seek me, let these go their way." That the saying might be fulfilled which he spake: "Of them which thou gavest me have I lost none."

And Judas, peering sharply into the darkness, saw that the other disciples were there also, albeit shrinking fearfully in the background. Then all the old, long-smothered hate and envy burst forth within him. He started forward with a bound like that of a wild animal, and grasping the arm of Jesus, cried aloud, "Hail, Rabbi!" and kissed him.

The others looked to see him smitten to the earth; but the Master only said sorrowfully: "Judas, betrayest thou the Son of man with a kiss?"

At this Peter started forward impetuously. "Lord! shall we smite with the sword?" he cried. And without awaiting the answer, he drew his weapon, and with a fierce but badly aimed blow, struck off the ear of the high priest's servant, who was advancing to lay hold of Jesus.

"Peter, put up thy sword into the sheath," said the calm, authoritative voice of the Master. "The cup which my Father hath given me, shall I not drink it? Thinkest thou that I cannot now pray to my Father, and he shall presently give me more than twelve legions of angels? But how then shall the Scriptures be fulfilled, that thus it must be?"

Then turning to the soldiers, who had grasped him tightly by the arms, he said: "Suffer ye thus far." And reaching forth his hand, he touched the wounded man, and healed him.

Jochanan and the officers of the temple, forgetting their fears, were now crowding about him with insulting curiosity. To them he said:

"Are ye come out, as against a thief, with swords and with staves for to take me? I sat daily with you, teaching in the temple, and ye laid no hold on me. But this is your hour, and the power of darkness."

When the disciples heard these ill-omened words, they were panic-stricken. Giving one last terrified glance at their Master and Lord, apparently helpless in the brutal grasp of the mob, they all forsook him and fled.

Now it chanced that a friendless lad, weary after a long day of wandering, had sunken down in the shelter of the wall to sleep. He had removed his outer garment, using it as a coverlet from the cold night dews, and had rolled others of his garments into a pillow for his head.

Steeped in the heavy slumber of sorrow and loneliness, he had heard nothing of the disturbance at first; but the triumphant shout as the mob passed out of the gateway aroused him, and a chance word from one of them brought him to his feet in an instant.

"The Nazarene"! Could it be! Without stopping an instant to reflect, he seized his abba and, flinging it over his shoulders, ran after the retreating throng. In a moment he had caught up with them, and the red glare of a torch falling upon him, revealed him plainly to the soldiers who brought up the rear. Starting forward, one of them seized him by the garment, crying out as he did so:

"Here is one of them now! Let us take him also."

But at that, he slipped away, leaving his linen abba in the hands of the soldier, who gaped stupidly after him, as he fled half naked into the darkness.

CHAPTER XXVI.

TOP here!" commanded Jochanan, ringing the bell at the massive p o r t a l loudly and imperatively as he spoke.

After some delay, the porter opened the door cautiously—for it was now late in the night—and peered out.

"Tell thy master to come down quickly!" cried Jochanan impatiently, for he was weary.

"Ah, 'tis thou, worshipful lord!" said the man. "I have orders to admit thee." And he threw the door wide open.

The temple officers, together with Malchus and Jochanan; the two soldiers, who were grasping the prisoner between them; and lastly, the betrayer, Judas, filed into the gateway. The others, obeying the command of Jochanan, waited outside.

They had scarcely entered the great court-yard when Annas came hastily in. "Thou hast the man!" he exclaimed joyfully, as his eye fell upon Jesus. "'Tis well!"

Then turning to Judas: "Thou art indeed a shrewd fellow, and much to be commended for the discreet way in which thou hast managed this affair. The thirty pieces of silver are thine; take them and begone. We have no further need of thy services." And carelessly tossing a small purse toward the man, he drew nearer the prisoner, that he might feast his eyes on the welcome sight.

Judas stooped, and snatching the purse from the ground, skulked out into the darkness. He had not once looked at Jesus, but he felt those eyes upon him. They were following him. The purse in his bosom burnt like a living coal. "God!" he shrieked aloud. And again and again he shrieked, as he rushed madly on in the black night. His punishment had begun.

"Thou hast bound the man most carelessly," said Annas at length, drawing back as he spoke.

He had intended to make a preliminary examination of the prisoner; but now he suddenly determined that it might be better to wait. He felt strangely shaken and faint. "I am an old man," he thought, "and overweary; I must spare myself. Besides, there is to me something most unpleasant about the aspect of this man, though he is quiet enough."

Then he continued aloud: "See thou to his bonds; make them secure, then remove him to the house of Caiaphas. I myself will take some refreshment and be there at once."

"Is it thou, Peter?" said a voice.

"'Tis no other. Hark! Have they gone? Where are the rest?"

"Nay, I know not," said John, sorrowfully. "'Twas even as he said: 'Smite the shepherd, and the sheep are scattered'—I know not why I fled; 'twas a cowardly act. I am going to seek him; it may be that they will let him go in the morning."

"They will not let him go in the morning —nor at all," said Peter bitterly.

"But it may be that he will escape out of their hands. He hath the power," said John hopefully.

"He hath had the power, but what if he hath it no longer?" answered Peter. "He hath said many things of late, hard to be understood. Said he not, even as they bound him, 'It is your hour and the power of darkness'?"

John was silent for a moment. Then he

said in a firm voice: "I shall find him; wilt thou go also?"

"Yes, I will go," answered Peter gloomily. "But what can we do alone? and where wilt thou seek him?"

"At the palace of the high priest. I heard them give the order, as they passed me in the darkness."

The two men were silent, as they strode rapidly on towards the city. It was no time for words and each was absorbed in his own unhappy thoughts.

"This is the place," said John at length. "We will go in,"—knocking upon the portal as he spoke.

The door opened almost immediately. Peter shrank back into the darkness.

"Go thou in," he whispered. "I will wait here; it may be that he is not there."

John passed in without replying; and soon Peter heard the portress greet him by name, as she closed the ponderous door.

He leaned back against the stone wall, and the moments dragged slowly by. He was growing weary and cold. He half wished that he had gone in with John. "I will go away," he thought. Then the words which he himself had spoken in a happier day, flashed back into his mind. "Lord, to whom shall we go? Thou hast the words of eternal life." Where indeed should he now go! All was gone—all lost.

At this moment the door opened and John came out. Peter saw his face by the light which streamed from the open passageway; it was pale and grave.

"He is there," he said. "Even now they are questioning him before the high priest. Wilt thou come in?"

"Yes," answered Peter, "I will go in."

John spoke briefly with the portress, and she admitted them both, looking curiously at Peter as he passed. "Go in yonder," she said, pointing with her finger.

"Ah, there is a fire!" said Peter. "I am cold." And without waiting for John, he walked rapidly toward the cheerful blaze, around which stood a number of persons.

He shivered as he spread his hands over the fire, and glanced furtively about him. He saw nothing of Jesus; and presently feeling more at his ease, he sat down, as did some of the others.

They were all talking among themselves. "Hast thou seen Malchus?" said one.

"Yes, I have seen him."

"Didst thou know that one of the disciples of the Nazarene smote off his ear?"

"No! Is it so?" broke in another.

"He smote it off with a single blow of his sword," continued the speaker. "And the Nazarene touched the wound and it was whole."

"What meanest thou—the ear?"

"In truth, just as it was before the blow was struck."

"A marvel indeed! But not more wonderful than many other tales they tell of him."

"Why do they seize the man and bring him hither? What hath he done amiss?"

"For one thing he hath spoken against the priesthood; in my own hearing, he called them no better than whited sepulchers—fair without, but within full of pollution."

"Little wonder then that they are his enemies; he should have been more discreet."

"Aye; but there is truth in his words," said the first speaker, sinking his voice. "I know many things myself, which, if told, would make a pretty scandal."

"The truth should not always be spoken," replied the other. "Even a lie is useful at times." And the man laughed loudly, with a knowing leer at his companion.

"Did they seize the fellow who was so ready with his sword?" said another.

Peter shrank back a little from the light, and wished himself safely outside. Before anyone had a chance to answer the question, the portress sauntered leisurely up to the fire. Her eye at once fell upon Peter; and she said loudly: "Art not thou also one of this man Jesus' disciples?"

Every one turned hastily. Peter sprang to his feet, shaking with fear. "Woman!" he stammered out, "I know him not; I know not what thou meanest!"

Then assuming an air of indifference, he sauntered leisurely out into the passage leading to the street, intending to slip away at the first good opportunity. As he sank down on one of the benches there, to try and collect his scattered thoughts, he heard the distant crowing of a cock.

"'Tis near morning," he thought to himself.

Presently he was startled by a voice: "This fellow was also with Jesus of Nazareth. Marta told me that he came in with the other; and we all know that he is a disciple."

Peter sprang up with a smothered oath. "What meanest thou, woman! I do not know the man."

Then he wandered uneasily back into the

courtyard again, though he knew not why he lingered. "I may as well go back to Capernaum," he said to himself sullenly. "The dream is ended."

As he leaned against one of the pillars, thinking, thus gloomily within himself, a man came up before him, and flashed the light of a torch which he was holding full in his face.

"Who art thou?" he asked curiously; then getting no answer to his question, he bethought himself that he had seen that face before, and lately. "Did I not see thee in the garden with the Nazarene?" he continued.

"Thou didst not!" answered Peter stoutly.

"Surely thou art one of them!" insisted the man, who was of kin to Malchus. "For thou art a Galilean; thy speech betrayeth it."

Stung to frenzy by these words, and a horrible inward consciousness of his perfidy, the wretched man burst out into a torrent of oaths and curses. "I tell thee I know not this man of whom ye speak!" And the second time, he heard the crowing of the cock.

He looked wildly about him that he might escape his tormentors; suddenly he saw that they were bringing his Master, bound and helpless, into the courtyard—his Master, whom he had vowed to love and to follow, even to prison and to death!

And Jesus turned and looked upon him; that look sank deep into the soul of Peter. He remembered the word of the Lord, how he had said unto him: "Before the cock crow twice, thou shalt deny me thrice." And he went out and wept bitterly.

CHAPTER XXVII.

ELL us now of thy disciples, and of thy doctrines which thou h a s t been teaching the people. Thou mayst as well make full confession; it will assuredly imperil thy cause to keep back anything from us at this time."

The Sanhedrim was already in solemn session, though it was scarcely dawn. In the midst of the semicircle sat Caiaphas in the full dignity of his priestly robes. On his right was Annas, on his left

Jochanan, and the others in the order of their official rank. Before them, his hands bound behind his back, and closely guarded on either side by the temple police, stood Jesus.

"Answer me, fellow!" said Caiaphas sternly.

The prisoner raised his eyes, and looked full at the high priest.

"I have spoken openly to the world," he said calmly. "I taught ever in the synagogue, and in the temple, whither the Jews always resort, and in secret have I said nothing. Why askest thou me? Ask them which heard me, what I have said unto them; behold, they know what I said."

"Answerest thou the high priest so?" said one of the men who stood by him. And as he spoke the words, he struck him upon the mouth.

For a moment the prisoner was silent. Then he said calmly, as before, with no sign of passion at the foul insult: "If I have spoken evil, bear witness of the evil; but if well, why smitest thou me?"

"He asketh for witnesses," said Annas with a sneer. "Let them be brought."

There was a little stir, as one of the temple officials entered, followed by a small, wizened old man.

"Dost thou know the prisoner?" asked Caiaphas.

"I do, reverend lord," answered the man in a high, quavering voice. "He is a Galilean carpenter, name Jesus. He is a brawler, and is always surrounded by crowds."

"What knowest thou of his teachings?" said Annas with a gratified smile.

"He saith pernicious things, my lord! I, myself, heard him say to the multitude, Beware of the Scribes, and especially of the high priests, for they care for nothing so much as to go about in long robes, and have the best of everything. They make long prayers for a show, and at the same time devour the widows and fatherless. They are hypocrites and fools, and shall be thrust into hell, with all that follow their words. What say ye to that, my good lords? Those be his teachings!"

A fierce murmur ran about the circle.

"'Tis true! I heard something like it myself!" came from one and another.

The old man was elated by the sensation which he had made. Turning his rheumy eyes upon the prisoner, he pointed at him a skinny, shaking finger. "Ha, fellow! thou didst heal me, three years ago, of the palsy, which had withered my limbs; and in so doing took away my living, for my begging no longer brought me money. They told me to work! Yes, work!—an old man like me! Now is not that a shame, my good lords? I led a gay life, at ease on my bed; but now I must needs work, or starve, for thou madest me—an old man—as strong as an ox."

"Take him away!" commanded Caiaphas. And he was led out, still gesticulating, and talking in his high, shrill voice.

After that followed in rapid succession a number of other witnesses, who were examined at some length by Caiaphas, but without eliciting anything of importance.

At last, when Annas and the others were beginning to despair of an acceptable pretext to put the prisoner to death, two witnesses were brought in.

"We were together when this man spoke in the temple," said one of them, "and we heard him say, I will destroy this temple that is built with hands, and within three days I will build another made without hands."

"Nay!" said the other, "thou art wrong! He said, If ye destroy this temple which ye were forty and three years in building, I will restore it in three days."

"Well, is not that the same thing?" exclaimed the first contemptuously.

"Not at all!" cried the other, with heat. "Thou hast the ears of an ass!"

"Is this the place for your disputings?" said Caiaphas, angrily. "Officer, remove these witnesses!"

Then he rose to his feet, and fixing his eyes upon Jesus, who still stood calmly and quietly in his place, he said sternly: "Answerest thou nothing? What is it that these witness against thee?"

But he seemed not to have heard the question. From his eyes shone a strange brightness, a holy calm. Was he thinking that the hour was at hand for the fulfillment of his words?

The high priest looked at him steadily, and said in a loud and solemn voice: "I adjure thee by the living God, that thou tell us whether thou be the Christ, the Son of God."

Then the prisoner, the despised Nazarene, his hands bound, his garments torn and defiled with violence, the mark of the insulting blow still visible on his white face, made him answer: "I am the Christ, the Son of God. And I say unto you, that hereafter ye shall see the Son of man sitting on the right hand of power, and coming in the clouds of heaven."

Then did the high priest rend his garments, and he cried aloud saying: "He hath spoken blasphemy! What further need have we of witnesses? Behold, now ye have heard his blasphemy; what think ye?"

And they all answered, as with one voice: "He is guilty! Let him die!"

Then they led him away to a room underneath in the palace; and there did the servants, and the hirelings of the temple, gather themselves together, that they might look upon him who was condemned to die. And they struck him with the palms of their hands, and spit upon him, crying out: "This is he that shall sit in the clouds of heaven! Behold him! The Christ—the Messiah!"

Then did one of them cast a garment over his head, so that it covered his face; and they began to buffet him, calling out: "Prophesy unto us, thou prophet of Galilee! Who smote thee?"

And these things they did until they were weary.

Now when Caiaphas passed out of the council chamber, he went into an inner room of the palace, that he might eat and refresh himself before going with the prisoner to Pilate. And there Anna, his wife, found him.

"What hast thou done to the Nazarene?" she asked; and her face was white, and her eyes had a strange fire in them.

"We have found him guilty, even as I knew. He shall shortly be delivered into the hand of the governor," said Caiaphas. "I am weary," he continued irritably, "and care not to speak of the thing with thee. Thou art a woman, and knowest naught of affairs of state. Leave me!"

"Nay, I will not leave thee, till I have said what I will," answered Anna. "The man is a prophet; and curses will come upon this house, if thou dost persist in persecuting him."

"Woman!" cried Caiaphas, starting to his feet, "the man is a blasphemer! But lately in my presence he solemnly affirmed that he was the Christ, the Son of God, and would hereafter sit on the right hand of power!"

"Oh, Joseph, my husband!" cried Anna, shuddering, "what if it be so! Release him, I beseech of thee: and let him go into his own country."

"Thou art a woman, and therefore a fool!"

said Caiaphas, with bitter emphasis. "Again I tell thee to leave me!"

"Speakest thou so to the daughter of Annas!" cried his wife, with flashing eyes. "I will leave thee! But thou shalt yet remember my warning, and weep tears of blood that thou hast trodden it under foot." And turning, she swept from the chamber.

It was still early in the morning when an imposing deputation, with Jesus, bound and doubly guarded, in their midst, waited upon Pilate the governor.

"It is not lawful for us to enter into the palace, lest we be defiled," said Caiaphas, "therefore bid Pilate come forth unto us."

And Pilate, knowing full well the temper of the people with whom he had to deal, complied at once. It was, moreover, in accordance with the Roman custom to hold courts of justice in the open air; so that there was in front of the palace, for this purpose, a raised tribunal, known as the Pavement, since it was laid with a mosaic of many-colored marbles. Here, then, Pilate caused them to place his curule chair of wrought ivory—the seat of state, and the sign of his office—and here he sat himself down.

And they brought Jesus, and set him before the governor, his accusers ranging themselves on either side; while a great multitude, which momently increased as the tidings of the arrest flew from mouth to mouth, surged uneasily up to the very edges of the tribunal, where they were kept at bay by a detachment of Roman troops.

Now Pilate was not altogether ignorant concerning Jesus. Always fearful of insurrections among the people, he had, by means of spies, kept close watch of his movements. He knew that his teachings had nothing of political significance in them, and that he had studiously avoided all popular excitement. He was, therefore, disposed to befriend the prisoner, more especially as he saw through the shallow pretense of the Jewish dignitaries, to the real source of their hatred of the man. So that it was with some acerbity that he put his first question to the high priest, who headed the deputation from the Sanhedrim:

"What accusation bring ye against this man?"

"If he were not a malefactor," answered Caiaphas, haughtily, "we would not have delivered him up unto thee."

"I know something of this Jesus, and I can understand your motives in bringing him to me," said Pilate, with a covert sneer. "But it hardly seemeth a case for my interference. Take ye him and judge him according to your law."

"The charge which we bring against this man is not so trifling as thou seemest to think," answered Caiaphas, his voice shaking with anger. "He is worthy of death on a criminal charge. We have so found him. But it is not lawful for us to put any man to death."

"What then hath he done?" asked Pilate in a tone of polite endurance.

"He hath striven to lead away the nation after him, forbidding to pay tribute to Cæsar, and declaring that he, himself, is Christ—the rightful king," said Caiaphas, an evil light in his eyes.

To this accusation all the Jewish authorities assented with loud cries. They looked to see Pilate roused from his apathy by this charge—the most damning of all in the ears of a Roman governor—and ready to make quick work of the hated Nazarene. But they were disappointed. With no perceptible change in his face, he arose deliberately from his seat, and ordering the guard to bring the prisoner, strode into the judgment hall.

When he had sat himself down, he said to Jesus: "Art thou the king of the Jews?"

"Sayest thou this thing of thyself?" answered the prisoner, "or did others tell it thee of me?"

"Am I a Jew?" said Pilate scornfully. "Thine own nation and the chief priests have delivered thee unto me. What hast thou done?"

And Jesus, looking full into his face, made answer: "My kingdom is not of this world; if my kingdom were of this world, then would my servants fight, that I should not be delivered to the Jews. But now is my kingdom not from hence."

"Art thou a king, then?" said Pilate, staring at him curiously.

"Thou sayest it; I am a king," he answered. "To this end was I born, and for this cause came I into the world, that I should bear witness unto the truth."

"Truth!" said Pilate, with a light, ironical laugh. "What is truth?"

'Twas a mere word, an empty sound, to this Roman voluptuary.

Then he arose from his seat without further question or comment, and went out again to the tribunal, where the Jewish dignitaries were awaiting him in a state of anger which bordered on frenzy.

Pilate looked at them scornfully; he thoroughly despised them, but it would not do for them to see that too plainly. He sat himself down, and waited a moment for the fierce murmuring to cease, then he declared in a loud, firm voice:

"I find in him no fault at all."

It was an acquittal! Must all their carefully prepared schemes fall to the ground? Must they see the man escape out of their very clutches? Never! After the first wave of indignant rage had spent itself, one after another of the chief priests and elders arose to speak, each vying with the other in the variety and virulence of the charges which they heaped upon the prisoner, who had been brought back from the judgment hall, and was again standing in the midst.

"Dost thou hear how many things these witness against thee?" said Pilate, addressing him. "Why dost thou not defend thyself? Thou hast my permission."

But Jesus was silent.

Pilate shook his head. "He is a strange man," he thought to himself. "Now is the time and the place for some of his eloquence, of which I have heard so much. He is a fool not to put these fellows down. In truth I would assist him gladly."

Jochanan was speaking, though Pilate was giving him but scant attention. But now a sentence caught his ear.

"He stirreth up the people throughout all Jewry, beginning from Galilee to this place."

"Galilee!" exclaimed Pilate. An idea had struck him. "Didst thou say that he is a Galilean?"

"He is, your Excellency," replied Jochanan.

"Very well, then. I shall send him to Herod. He is even now in the city, and it were most fitting that he should judge a man from his own province."

He arose from his seat, and gave the necessary orders, then retired to his palace, feeling well pleased with himself for this master-stroke of diplomacy. "By this means," he thought complacently, "I shall rid myself of all further trouble in this matter. Moreover, it will flatter Herod, and I shall thus be able to appease his wrath for that little affair in the temple." And he commanded his slaves to bring him refreshments.

"Didst thou say that Pilate had sent me the Nazarene for judgment?" asked Herod, starting up from the purple cushions where he was lolling, sick with ennui, in the Asmonean Palace. "Nay, but that is good news! I have always wished to see the fellow! He shall perform a miracle for me, such as I have heard of. He shall make me some choice wine from water, heal this sore on my limb, and—well, I shall think of other things afterward. Bring him into our presence at once. And, stay!—call the court together; 'twere meet to provide some amusement to relieve the deadly tedium of this place. So that is the man!"—as they brought in Jesus and set him in the royal presence, the high priests and elders, regardless now of defilement, crowding in after him. "And who are these?"

"The chiefs of the Jewish nation," one made answer.

"Let them stand back out of my way! I wish to talk to the man, myself," said Herod impatiently.

He had no idea of conducting a trial, but only of amusing himself and the throng of whispering, tittering courtiers who were gathered about him. So he began to ask questions of the prisoner. "What was his name?"—though he knew well enough. "Could he really work miracles, as people said? and if he could, would he not work one now?"

But the prisoner was silent.

Herod was at first rather flattered by this. "He feareth us," he said patronizingly. "Nay, fellow, I will do thee no harm; I only wish to see thee perform. Do not fear to speak. Thou shalt have wine if thou wilt. Give him some."

But he refused, with a gesture, the proffered cup, and remained silent as before.

Then did his accusers, one and all, break forth into angry denunciations.

"He saith that he is a king, doth he?" quoth Herod, languidly interrupting them. "Well, he doth not look much like it. If he will not perform for us, we will even make some sport out of him. What is the royal color of the Jews? For, truth to tell, I have forgotten it."

The Jews were angrily silent; but one of the courtiers volunteered the information: "'Tis white, your Highness."

"White, is it? Then let a white robe be brought, and put it on him. 'Tis not meet that a king should be so poorly attired."

Then they fetched a white robe, and threw it over his humble Jewish dress.

"Now, good sirs," said Herod, turning his eyes wickedly upon the members of the Sanhedrim, "doth he not look majestic? A king indeed! Let all do him homage."

And the courtiers and soldiers pressed forward in mock adulation.

But Herod, watching from his chair of state, saw something in the aspect of the prisoner which made him feel uncomfortable. "He hath a look which I like not," he muttered, "nor yet this silence; 'tis unnatural. Suppose he should do some awful thing now; they say that he hath unlimited powers."

With an imperative gesture, he summoned one of his officers. "Take the fellow away!" he said. "Take him back to Pilate."

"Shall we take off the robe, your Highness?" asked the attendant.

"No, no!" answered Herod, hastily. "Take him just as he is—and quickly. Clear the room of all these,"—indicating the Jews with a sweeping gesture.

So it happened that Pilate was once again called forth into the judgment seat, and confronted with Jesus.

CHAPTER XXVIII.

IT was with a frowning brow that the governor again seated himself in his ivory chair of state. "Ye have brought this man unto me," he said, "as one that perverteth the people; and, behold, I, having examined him before you, have found no fault in him touching those things whereof ye accuse him. No, nor yet Herod; for I sent you to him with the prisoner; and, lo! he hath sent him back to me uncondemned. I will therefore scourge him and let him go."

He said this, hoping that the scourging, a terrible punishment in itself, might appease the wrath of the Jews.

The multitude, which now numbered thousands—and, as Pilate saw, of the lowest and most debased portion of the population—gave a savage, inarticulate cry, like that of a wild beast.

"What do they say?" asked Pilate, speaking to the Roman official who stood beside him.

"Release! Release unto us a prisoner!" replied the man.

"They are right!" said Pilate, bethinking himself joyfully of the time-honored custom of releasing a prisoner to the people at feast time. And he arose and cried aloud: "Will ye that I release unto you the king of the Jews?"

Now it happened that the chief priests knew of the condemnation of Barabbas, how he lay bound in the dungeons of Antonia, sentenced to suffer crucifixion on that very day, which was the fifteenth of Nisan.

So Jochanan, and other wise ones of their number, mixing with the multitude, craftily brought to their remembrance how Barabbas was about to suffer for his loyalty to the nation. And when the multitude heard their words, they began, with one accord, to yell: "Barabbas! Barabbas!" till the whole city was aroused, and thousands more came running to the palace to see what had happened. And all joined in the cry.

Then Pilate said unto them: "What shall I do then with Jesus, who is called Christ?"

The chief priests answered: "Let him be crucified!"

And the mob, mad with excitement, and thirsting for blood, echoed with a cry which has rung adown the ages: "Crucify him! crucify him! Away with him!"

At this moment one of the officials handed to Pilate an ivory tablet with something written thereon. And he read this warning message from his wife:

"Have thou nothing to do with that just man; for I have suffered many things this day in a dream because of him.   CLAUDIA."

Then, more anxious than ever to save him, he said unto them for the third time: "Why, what evil hath he done? I have found no cause of death in him; I will therefore chastise him and let him go."

But the chief priests saw that he feared the people; and again they raised the cry: "Crucify him! Crucify him!" And again the multitude echoed the words.

Pilate looked out from his throne over that threatening mob, and his heart was as wax within him. "I cannot save the man!" he muttered. "'Tis too late. And what matters it after all—one Jew less in Jerusalem!"

"Bring me water in a basin!" he commanded.

And when it was brought, he stood up and washed his hands in sight of them all, saying solemnly, "I am innocent of the blood of this just person. See ye to it."

And all the people answered him with

the awful words: "His blood be upon us, and upon our children!"

Then he released unto them Barabbas, and commanded that Jesus should be scourged and afterward crucified.

Barabbas came forth out of the prison; and when he heard what had been done, he said scornfully to his fellows: "Said I not that the man was a coward!"

Now Pilate, the trial being ended, went into his palace with a heavy heart. And as he was seeking to withdraw himself into an inner room, he came upon his wife, Claudia.

"Didst thou receive the warning I sent thee?" she asked.

"I received it; but it was too late," said Pilate, faltering.

"Too late!" said Claudia. "What meanest thou? Is the man dead?"

"No. He still lives, but—well—I—I have sentenced him to the cross. They are even now scourging him. I could not help it! Thou shouldst have seen the mob—it was frightful! And those cries—they ring in my ears still!" And the wretched man pressed his hands to his head wildly.

Claudia looked at him with wide, glassy eyes. "Thou hast condemned him?" she whispered hoarsely, "and to the cross! Then may the gods help us! We are undone!" And she wildly fled, leaving Pilate alone.

Then the soldiers took Jesus, and when they had stripped him of his upper garments, they bound him to a low pillar, so that his back was bowed. And they took scourges, made of heavy thongs of leather, weighted at the ends with jagged pieces of iron, and they beat him upon his naked back until they were weary. Then they lifted him up, and putting on him again the white robe with which Herod had mocked him, they dragged him into the judgment hall. And the whole band came together to look at him there.

"Let us worship him!" cried one, "even as did Herod."

The saying pleased them. Stripping off the white robe which Herod had put on him —white no longer, for it was crimsoned with his blood—they clothed him with an old scarlet mantle, which belonged to one of them. Then one brought in branches of the thorn tree, and they made of the branches a crown, and drove it down about his temples; and they put a reed in his hand for a sceptre. Then they laughed aloud, as they looked upon him, till the hall echoed with the horrid sound; and bowing the knee, they cried, "Hail! King of the Jews!" Snatching the sceptre from his pinioned hands, they smote him on the head with it. And they spit in his face.

In the midst of this their brutal sport, Pilate came upon them.

"Bring him forth!" he commanded savagely. And he went out again to the judgment seat, being minded yet to save the man, for the sake of his wife Claudia, and because he, himself, feared—he knew not what.

He stood up before the multitude, which had grown so great that he could see nothing but one mighty sea of faces. And he pointed to Jesus standing beside him, wearing the scarlet cloak and the crown of thorns, his face stained with blood and befouled with insult, his eyes dim with agony, yet withal transfigured into something so divine that Pilate cried with genuine pity and reverence in his tones, "Behold the man!"

It was as if he would have said: See him so agonized and yet so innocent! Hath he not suffered enough? Will ye not pity him and save him?

But the chief priests and officers of the temple were mad for his blood; they had waited for over three hours in the blazing sun, for him to be brought forth unto them. Pilate's appeal, and the piteous look of the prisoner, only added fresh fuel to the flame which was devouring them.

"Crucify him!" they yelled hoarsely. And again and again, "Crucify him!"

Then said Pilate in a rage: "Take ye him and crucify him; for I find no fault in him."

But the Jews, willing to justify themselves in the sight of the multitude, answered: "We have a law, and by our law he ought to die; because he made himself the Son of God."

When Pilate heard that saying he feared exceedingly; and again he remembered the ghastly face of Claudia, as she said: "We are undone." He turned and strode once more into the judgment hall, commanding the guard to bring the prisoner.

"Whence art thou?" he demanded of Jesus.

But the prisoner made him no answer. What use to answer this man who was too cowardly a creature to free him whom he had thrice acquitted!

"Speakest thou not unto me?" said Pilate fiercely, glad of an excuse for anger. "Knowest thou not that I have power to crucify thee, and have power to release thee?"

And Jesus, seeing the dark tumult in his breast, pitied him. "Thou couldst have no power at all against me," he said, breaking the silence of many bitter hours. "Therefore he that delivered me to thee, hath the greater sin."

And Pilate trembled before him.

Then went he forth, yet again, to the people, and spake to them as best he knew how, for the release of the man whom he had thrice acquitted, and twice condemned.

And they despised him and his words, and cried out, saying: "If thou let this man go, thou art not Cæsar's friend."

When Pilate heard the name Cæsar, his soul was shaken within him, for he remembered many things with fear. And he commanded them to bring Jesus forth before the judgment seat; and he said unto them, "Behold your king!"

But they cried out, "Away with him! Away with him! Crucify him!"

"What!" cried Pilate. "Shall I crucify your king?"

The chief priests answered, "We have no king but Cæsar!"

And with that word of power, they beat down the last feeble barrier of his will.

"Take him!" he cried hoarsely. "Take him and crucify him. His blood be upon you!"

And they took Jesus and led him away.

When the multitude saw that he was delivered up to be crucified, they gave a mighty and fierce cry. And the sound of it rang throughout the city, and the women and children shook with fear when they heard it; it echoed in dismal reverberations in the courts of the shining temple, and rolled away—away—upward—upward, till its dying sound reached even the throne of God, and the angels which stand ever before the throne hid their faces.

Now a man who wore the semblance of a wild beast had been hanging about the outskirts of the multitude for hours. Ever and anon he tore his hair, and his garments—which hung in shreds about him; and he raved, and cursed, and cut himself with stones. But the people heeded him not. "He hath a devil," they said. "He seeketh the Nazarene, mayhap; but he must needs help himself now."

And when the man heard that word, he shook the matted hair from out his eyes. "What will they do with him?" they asked. And they answered, "They are taking him even now to be crucified."

At that, the man gave a great cry, and thrusting his fingers into his ears, ran swiftly away. And when he came to the temple he went in, still running, nor could anyone stop him; so that he came even to the place where were certain of the chief priests and elders, who had gathered together that they might rejoice over the murder which they had accomplished.

And the man cast down before them thirty pieces of silver, and shrieked out in a woeful voice: "I have sinned, in that I have betrayed innocent blood!"

And the chief priests and elders feared, when they looked upon the man. But Annas answered: "What is that to us? See thou to that!"

And he fled away from the temple, and going out of the city to the garden which is called Gethsemane, he hung himself there; that he might die in the place where he had betrayed the Son of God with a kiss.

"And the chief priests took the silver pieces and said, It is not lawful to put them into the treasury, because it is the price of blood. And they took counsel, and bought with them the potter's field, to bury strangers in. Wherefore that field was called The field of blood, unto this day."

CHAPTER XXIX.

TITUS awoke on the morning of the fifteenth of Nisan with a dull consciousness of impending horror. This was the day!

He stared with wide, unseeing eyes at the wall of his dungeon, and muttered again and again, "This is the day! This is the day! This is the day!"

Presently he heard a sound. Were they coming even now to take him! He started to his feet, and crouched shuddering in the furthest corner of his dungeon. No, 'twas only the bread and water, thrust in by the rough hand of his jailer. He drank greedily of the water; but the sight of the food sickened him.

Then he gave himself up to the agony of listening. The untended wound in his head had festered, and his veins ran hot with fever. He half forgot for what he was listening, as the hours dragged slowly on; and when, at last, the great bolts turned in their sockets, and the door opened, he started up with crimson cheeks and a light, blood-curdling laugh.

"Thou hast come at last!" he said airily. The centurion stared at him. "Bring him out quickly!" he commanded, "and bind upon him the cross."

"What!" said one of the soldiers. "Shall we not first scourge him?"

"Nay," said his superior. "'Twas not so ordered. Besides, we must hasten; they must all be dead by the going down of the sun; and it is already near the sixth hour."

Quickly they bound upon his back the transverse pieces of the cross, and hurried him out from the prison gate. As the fresh air smote him, his dazed senses cleared a little. He saw that Dumachus, also bearing the ominous pieces of wood, and similarly guarded by four soldiers, was waiting in the courtyard. He had been scourged, as his blood-stained garments witnessed, and he was blubbering and blaspheming under his breath.

"Ha, Jew!" he yelled hoarsely, as he caught sight of Titus. "Now, indeed, lookest thou the son of the high priest!"

But the centurion smote him on the mouth, and bade him be silent.

Under the escort of a strong detachment of legionaries, the two cross-bearers were marched rapidly forward. Not far from the prison they came to a halt.

"Why did they not bring him to Antonia?" said one of the soldiers in a low voice.

"He hath but just been condemned; there was no time. They will join us here," said another. "Hark! They are coming now. Dost hear the roaring of the mob?"

Then came the slow, measured tramping of soldiers: a few sharp, quick orders; and again they moved forward.

They had reached the city gate, and were about to pass through, when again came the order to halt.

"What is it?" asked one of the soldiers who guarded Titus.

"The fellow hath fallen under his cross," answered a man who was perched aloft. "They have caught a stout countryman, who but just came in, and have bound it upon him. Thou shouldst see his face!" And he burst into a great laugh.

Outside the gate a seething mass of humanity! On either side of the road the people stood packed in serried ranks; they clustered in dense masses on roofs, and walls, and trees. Titus looked, and his brain reeled. Had all these come out to see the torture of three wretched thieves?—for so read the accusation which was bound in staring letters on his breast.

Amid the savage, unceasing roar of the multitude he could hear the shrill wailing of women. And now another sound caught his ear; 'twas a voice which he had thought never to hear again: "Father! Titus! Jesus!" shrieked the voice. He caught a glimpse of a white face as it fell back into the crowd.

For the first time he struggled fiercely with his bonds. "Let me go!" he screamed. "Hold thy peace, thief!" said the centurion savagely. "Save thy shrieks for thy cross!" And he smote him on the head with the flat of his sword.

After weeks of fruitless search and forlorn wandering, Stephen had reached Jerusalem. He had determined to go to Caiaphas and give into his hand the embroidered tunic, and tell him all that he knew of Titus. Ragged, hungry and footsore, he had knocked at the great gate of the palace, and been refused entrance by the portress.

"See the high priest, indeed!" she had said scornfully. "Go thy way, beggar!"

"But indeed," persisted Stephen, "I must see him. 'Tis a matter of the sorest need."

"Well, thou shalt not come in, for all of that. Thy urgent business can wait!" And with a loud laugh of derision she had slammed the heavy door in his face.

Then he had wandered away to the temple, with the vague hope of seeing the man he sought.

"Where is the high priest?" he inquired innocently of one of the temple police.

"The high priest, beggar! What dost thou want of him?" said the man.

"I must speak with him; and I cannot gain admittance at his house."

"Canst thou not!" said the man derisively. "'Tis a wonder! They should have urged thee to come in, and given thee the best room!"

Stephen looked steadily at the man, while a slight flush rose to his cheek. "I am not a beggar," he said. "Though 'tis like enough that I look one. But I must see the high priest; I would tell him of his son."

"His son!" answered the man. "Thou art mad! He hath no son. Go thy way. Thou canst not see the high priest. 'Tis a notable day with Caiaphas, and indeed with all of us, for to-night we eat the Passover; and to-day we shall see a great sight—the Nazarene is to be crucified."

"The Nazarene!" said Stephen wildly. "Crucified! Oh, it cannot—cannot be!"

"But it can be, my impudent young beggar! All the city will be there to see it. I myself—"

But Stephen had gone. He was running wildly, though he knew not why, nor whither. Presently he found himself in the midst of a great throng, all hurrying like himself.

"Let us stop here!" shouted a man to his fellows. "We shall see it all finely here!" Stephen looked at him beseechingly. "Is it true?" he gasped.

But the man did not answer. "I shall climb up here!" he shouted again, scrambling, as he spoke, into a stunted tree, which grew by the roadside.

The crowd still poured out from the city gate in countless thousands, and Stephen, carried along by its resistless tide, found himself near the verge of a little hillock not far from the highway. Here the people were kept back by a triple cordon of soldiers.

"Tell me," said Stephen again, this time to a sad-faced woman who stood next him in the press, "what doth this mean? Is it true that—" and his voice broke in a sob—"that they are going to put the Nazarene to death?"

"Alas, yes!" she answered, "'tis true. Ah, the pity of it!—and the shame! 'Tis the high priests; they have always hated him. 'Twas only last night that they took him in the garden of Gethsemane. Early this morning they delivered him to Pilate, and now—" And the woman hid her face in her long veil.

"In Gethsemane?" said Stephen eagerly. "Is it an olive orchard yonder?"

"Yes," answered the woman, her throat quivering. "He went there often—for quiet and prayer." And again she stopped, struggling with her tears.

"I was there," said Stephen. "I heard the noise—but I knew not what it meant. I had been sleeping."

"Hark!" said the woman. "They are coming."

Above the roar of the multitude arose the sound of the regular tread of soldiers, and presently the vanguard of the procession, a detachment of Roman troops, came into view. They were marching stolidly along, their shields glittering in the bright sunshine. Then the three cross-bearers, guarded each by a quaternion of soldiers, and bearing each upon his breast a whitened board with the accusation for which he was to suffer, blazoned thereon in large black letters. That of the Nazarene bore the strange words: "Jesus of Nazareth, the King of the Jews."

Stephen gave one look, and there burst from his lips that frenzied cry: "Father! Titus! Jesus!" Then he sank back like one dead.

The woman ceased her low wailing, and knelt at his side. "Stand back a little, good people!" she cried. "The lad hath fainted; he must have air."

"He is nothing but a beggar!" said a man contemptuously, giving him a push with his foot as he spoke. "Let him be; thou wilt lose it all. They are going to take the Nazarene first."

The woman hastily sprinkled some water from a small gurglet, which she carried at her girdle, on the face of the unconscious boy. Then, as if impelled by a resistless force, she stood up and fixed her eyes upon the awful scene before her.

The soldiers were working swiftly. The Nazarene, already stripped of his garments, was laid upon the cross, which was lying on the ground. Now a few dull, heavy blows of the mallet and the great nails were driven through the palms of his outstretched hands; then through his feet, slightly drawn up and laid the one over the other.

And now they were lifting the cross, with its burden of agony; dragging it roughly along, a dozen strong arms raised it up and with a shout dropped it into the hole previously dug to receive it.

The body of Jesus settled forward with a sickening shock. What was it that he was saying?—"Father, forgive them; for they know not what they do."

Now followed the thieves; they had drunken deeply of the drugged wine, which the Nazarene had refused. The older man fought savagely with the soldiers, when his turn came, but was quickly overpowered and thrown down, and amid a torrent of horrid oaths and screams, his cross was raised to a place on the left of the Nazarene.

Then the young man—" A mere lad!" said the woman, her lips livid with horror. He was silent, even as the Nazarene, save for his piteous groans.

But now the form at her feet stirred. She looked down, then stooped, and raising his head, gave him to drink from her water-bottle.

"God!" he gasped as he beheld the three crosses. "My Jesus! My brother! My father!"

He seemed about to fall back again, but suddenly he leaped up, a fierce light burning in his eyes. "Where is the high priest?" he said wildly. "The young man is his son; he might yet be saved!"

"Hush!" said the woman pitifully. "Thy trouble hath crazed thee. Nothing could save him now."

The lad sank back again weakly. He had eaten nothing for hours; his brain reeled, and things looked dim and strange.

"I must be mad!" he said aloud. Then he was silent. He heard vaguely the voices of the mob, as they reviled the man on the middle cross: "Thou that destroyest the temple, and buildest it in three days, save thyself! If thou be the Son of God, come down from the cross!"

And he saw a group of men gorgeously robed, who stood near the cross, stretching out their arms with mocking gestures. "He saved others; himself he cannot save. If he be the king of Israel, let him now come down from the cross, and we will believe him! He trusted in God; let him deliver him now, if he will have him; for he said, I am the Son of God."

"Those be the chief priests," said the woman to Stephen.

But he made no answer.

The sun was nearly overhead now, and beating down with noontide fierceness, but gradually the brilliant light paled; there was a strange hush in the air. The people, frantic with excitement, did not note the change at first; then one and another began to look uneasily upward. There was no cloud, no sign of storm, but the light was momently fading. Now it was a ghastly yellow; and now it gloomed into a lurid twilight.

The people looked at one another with white faces. "What is it?" they whispered. Then they gazed fearfully at the man on the

middle cross. He was hanging motionless, his head sunken upon his breast.

The man on the cross at the left was groaning and blaspheming horribly; in the frightened hush his words could be distinctly heard. He was cursing the man at his side. "If thou be the Christ," he shrieked, with an awful imprecation, "save thyself and us!"

He who hung on the other side of the Nazarene had been silent till now, save for his piteous sighing; but now he spoke—the fierce agony had cleared his brain at last.

"Wilt thou not hold thy peace!" he cried in his clear young voice; and Stephen listened breathlessly. "Dost thou not fear God, seeing thou art in the same condemnation? And we indeed justly; for we receive the due reward of our deeds. But he is innocent."

Then he turned his dying eyes on Jesus, and said tremulously, beseechingly: "Lord, remember me when thou comest into thy kingdom."

And into the face of Jesus, blood-stained, befouled, and ghastly with the pallor of approaching death, there flashed a look of joy so divine that Stephen's heart leapt.

"Verily I say unto thee,"—and his voice was clear, beautiful and far-reaching as of old—" to-day shalt thou be with me in paradise."

Titus smiled radiantly. What cared he now for the pain, the shame, the dying! "To-day—with him—in paradise!"

Stephen started forward with a great cry of longing: "Oh, take me too!"

Suddenly he became aware that not far from him stood Mary, the mother of Jesus, and with her two other women, and John, the beloved disciple. He could see them all quite plainly in the lurid half-darkness, for the crowd, in fear, had drawn away from the neighborhood of the crosses, leaving them almost alone save for the Roman guard. He crept timidly nearer, till he could have touched the hem of Mary's robe; but he did not speak to her. He dared not.

"My son! My son!" she wailed; and again the dim eyes of the dying man brightened.

He looked at his mother with an infinite tenderness. "Woman!" he said faintly, "behold thy son!" Then turning his eyes upon John, who was supporting her half-swooning form, he said, "Behold thy mother!"

The hours crept heavily onward. The darkness was that of night now—a starless night. The thousands who had come forth in holiday attire, full of insolent triumph, to witness the agony of the crucifixion, were waiting, full of terror, for the end. They dared not move in that ghastly darkness. Save for the groans of the dying man, the silence was almost unbroken.

About the ninth hour, Jesus cried in a voice of agony: "Eli, Eli, lama sabachthani!"

It was the simple Galilean speech of his childhood, and signified those saddest of all words: "My God, my God, why hast thou forsaken me?"

But someone who was watching, hearing only the first words, and understanding them not, said: "This man calleth for Elias."

Then Jesus spoke again, this time faintly: "I thirst."

Now there was, standing near, a vessel full of the common sour wine which the soldiers had brought to refresh themselves with; and one of them, smitten with remorse, hastened to fill a sponge with wine, and putting it upon the stem of a hyssop plant which grew near, lifted it to the parched lips of the sufferer.

"Let be!" shouted another. "Let us see whether Elias will come to save him."

Another silence, broken only by the gasping breath of the crucified one, then in a moment all was over. A look of supreme joy and triumph flashed into the face of the dying man. "It is finished!" he cried. A last low prayer—"Father, into thy hands I commend my spirit!"—and with a great cry of mortal agony, his head fell forward on his breast. He was dead.

Then followed a sound of crashing and grinding rocks, as the earth shook with wave after wave of earthquake. The people shrieked aloud, and prayed wildly in a frenzy of terror.

"We are undone!" they wailed; and they rent their garments and smote upon their breasts.

The Roman centurion, also, and the soldiers that were with him, trembled with fear. "Truly," they said, "this was the Son of God!"

Then the darkness vanished as suddenly as it had come; the sun shone out gloriously, and the multitudes returned into the city, still wailing and beating upon their breasts. They remembered the words which they had spoken: "His blood be upon us, and upon our children."

CHAPTER XXX.

 HOUGH he who hung upon the middle cross was dead, the others who were crucified with him, still lived. The younger of the twain was apparently unconscious, for his head hung forward upon his breast, and he made neither sign nor motion. But the other rolled his great head from side to side, and talked wildly.

"Send me now the high priest!" he cried. "I am a dying man; I must tell him of something before I go hence."

The words caught the ear of Malchus, the high priest's servant, who had stood near the crosses since morning. "What wouldst thou with the high priest?" he asked.

"Give me to drink," groaned the man, "for I am tormented with thirst."

Malchus dipped the sponge into the wine, and gave it to the miserable wretch once and again.

"Where is the high priest?" he repeated, huskily.

"He hath returned to the city," answered Malchus. "Tell me what thou wouldst say to him. I am his trusted servant; I will bear him word."

"I will tell thee—since I cannot tell him, and the time is short." Here he paused to groan, then went on with a visible effort. "The young man on the further cross is the son of Caiaphas, the high priest."

"Thief, thou liest!" cried Malchus, starting back in undisguised horror.

"I lie not," replied Dumachus. "I am a dying man. I stole him with his nurse, Prisca. The girl I loved; the boy I took to avenge myself of a scourging at the hands of Caiaphas, which I deserved not, and which helped make me the devil that I am."

When Malchus heard the name Prisca, he shook with fear. "Where is the woman?" he asked.

"I know not," answered the thief, speaking with difficulty. "She was in Capernaum. I have a son, also, Stephen by name; I know not where he is. But swear to me that thou wilt tell Caiaphas! He will remember the scourging—and the boy!" And the man ground his teeth.

Malchus now ran to the other cross, and

looked keenly upon the face of him who hung thereon; and as he looked, the conviction forced itself upon him that the man had spoken the truth.

He reached up and laid his hand over the heart of the lad; it was beating still, but so faintly that he could scarcely detect the pulsations. "He is almost gone, happily," he thought. Then the words which the Nazarene had spoken flashed back into his mind. "He is near paradise—wherever that may be!" he murmured with a heart-breaking sigh, as he turned away.

Calling one of the soldiers who kept guard, he slipped a piece of gold into his hand. "I must have the body of this young man, when all is over," he whispered. "Manage it for me, and thou shalt have thrice as much again."

The man nodded. "Where dost thou want it?" he said.

"Here. I will come to fetch him away. Do not let them take him down, till I return."

"I will see to it," said the man, looking at the coin in his hand.

Then Malchus sped swiftly away. When he reached the palace he went straight to the private apartment of his master.

Caiaphas was alone. He was sitting motionless in his great chair, his eyes fixed and staring.

"Master!" said Malchus, trembling before that terrible, stony face, "I must tell thee something—something which hath to do with thy son." And he cast vainly about in his mind for a merciful way of telling his frightful tidings.

But Caiaphas did not answer; he seemed not to have heard.

"I have found thy son!" cried Malchus, drawing nearer and stooping over the chair. "I have found thy son; and he is dying, or even now dead."

Caiaphas stirred, and turned his eyes slowly till that terrible, unwinking gaze rested on the face of his servant. "Thou hast found my son? My son is dead! What is it that thou art saying?"

Then did Malchus, in his desperation, pour forth the whole awful story.

Caiaphas did not move. "He is crucified, thou sayest,"—still in the same dull tone—"with the Nazarene. My son and the Son of God! Crucified together!"

Then a frightful change came over his aspect. He sprang up, his eyes flaming, "Thou liest!" he shrieked. "Thou art try-

ing to make me afraid for what I have done! But I am not afraid. I am glad—glad! Dost thou hear? Get thee away out of my presence, and never dare to enter it again! Get thee away or I kill thee!" And with the howl of a demoniac, he rushed forward.

But Malchus was gone. When he had reached the street, he sank down for a moment on the stones, and pressing his trembling hands together, groaned out: "My God! My Master! Help him, I beseech of thee. And forgive, if it be possible!"

Then he arose, and went swiftly away towards Calvary, stopping only to purchase supplies of fine linen and spices.

As he turned the corner of a narrow street he met two men; one of them called him by name. He paused for an instant to look, and saw that it was John, the follower of the Nazarene.

"I have with me a lad," said John under his breath, "who hath a woeful errand with thy master. He knoweth the whereabouts of his son, lost so long ago. I was bringing him to the palace; he cannot gain admittance alone."

"Hath he tried before?" asked Malchus eagerly.

"Yes," said the lad, speaking for himself, "many times yesterday."

Malchus groaned aloud. "I know all that thou wouldst tell my master," he said. "But it will avail nothing to see him now. And as for his mother—let her remain in ignorance of the thing for a time. She hath enough to bear." And he told them briefly of what had passed between himself and Caiaphas.

"I am going to see to the burial of my young master," he said, in conclusion. "'Tis all that I can do for him now, for whom I would have given my heart's best blood."

"I love him too," said Stephen simply. "But I am glad for him; for he hath gone to a better place than this—to be with the Master."

Then all three went sadly on, till they came to the place where the crosses were.

The body of Jesus was being taken reverently down from the cross, as they approached, a number of persons assisting, among whom Malchus recognized two members of the Sanhedrim, Joseph of Arimathea, and Nicodemus.

"They believe on him at last," said John sadly.

"They have long believed on him, but have not dared to confess it openly," replied

Malchus; "even as I, myself," he added humbly.

The soldier to whom he had given the coin, now approached him. "The lad is dead," he said in a low voice, "and the other also. Wilt thou that we help thee? We must, at all events, take the bodies away—and soon, for it is near sunset."

"Yes, help me. Here is gold," said Malchus huskily.

And so it was that as the sun sank behind the horizon, all three rested in the peace of death—Jesus in the new tomb of Joseph of Arimathea, in a fair garden near to the place where he died, and the others not far away. For Stephen had besought Malchus with tears, that the body of his father might not be left to the brutal hands of the soldiers.

As they went away in the twilight, Malchus said to Stephen, "Where now wilt thou go?"

"I know not," answered the boy forlornly. "There is no one, now, to whom I can go; and no place!" and he sobbed aloud.

"Thou shalt abide with me," said Malchus warmly.

But John, who had joined them, drew the lad to his side. "Wilt thou come with me?" he said. "His mother, now mine, shall be thine also; and thou shalt be my brother."

Stephen looked up into the face of the disciple whom Jesus loved, and his heart went out to him; and he was comforted in his sorrow.

Then they went away into Bethany to wait till the Sabbath should be past.

CHAPTER XXXI.

 WAS the solemn hour before the dawn. In the pallid, uncertain light of the waning moon, a solitary woman hastened along the road which led to the garden wherein had been laid the crucified one. It was Mary of Magdala, bearing spices for the beloved dead. Timidly she entered the enclosure, and with many a tremulous pause, made her way through the thick shrubbery. It was very dark, and so silent that she could almost hear the beating of her heart. Presently she stopped altogether to listen; then was the stillness broken by a sound as of soft, mysterious rustling. It was but the morning breeze as it swept through the branches; but she fancied it to be the stirring of angelic wings. The breath of the lilies filled the place with sweetness, like to the holy atmosphere of heaven. She stood for a long time motionless, hardly daring to breathe, still listening—listening.

Suddenly a faint beam of rosy light penetrated the darkness, and high above burst forth the melodious thanksgiving of the lark.

She started forward with a little cry. Behold, the stone had been rolled away from the door of the sepulchre! She gave one frightened glance within, then turned and fled toward Bethany.

The tomb was empty!

"Who will roll away the stone from the door of the tomb?"

The women stopped and looked at one another in consternation. There were four of them—Mary the mother of James, the wife of Clopas, Joanna, and Salome. They too were on the way to the sacred garden in the dim light of early morning.

"It is certain that we shall not be able to move it for ourselves, for it is very great," continued Salome.

"But will not the disciples be also at the sepulchre? Our purpose was known unto them," said Joanna. "Let us go on," she added. "I myself am very strong."

The dawn was brightening momently now. Light wreaths of snowy mist which had lain softly on the bosom of the fields all night were flitting away, leaving a rain of sparkling jewels behind them. Almond trees, just bursting into bloom, showed white and rosy-red against the tender green of the young leaves. Birds in an ecstasy of song, swung joyously upon the blossoming sprays or flitted athwart the glowing sky. All nature was in the great secret of the heavens, on that ever-to-be-remembered morning!

But nothing of the triumphant joy of the new day found its way into the hearts of the women. Mary, indeed, raised her eyes, heavy with weeping, and said half bitterly:

"How can the birds—which he loved— sing, and the flowers bloom, when he—" And her voice broke in a sob.

The others were silent. With bowed heads they hurried forward, blinded with their tears.

And now they were come to the garden. They entered in, threading their way swiftly through the serried ranks of lilies and blossoming trees. And drawing near to the tomb, they saw that the great stone had been rolled away, and lay at one s. of the open door.

Timidly they entered into the sepulchre, then looked at one another in sorrowful amaze. The niche wherein had lain the body of Jesus was empty. Suddenly they perceived sitting on the right side the figure of a young man, from whose garments there streamed forth a mysterious radiance, which lighted all the gloomy place wherein they were standing. And the angel said unto them:

"Fear not; for I know that ye seek Jesus, which hath been crucified. Why seek ye the living among the dead? He is not here; he is risen: behold the place where they laid him. But go, tell his disciples and Peter, that he goeth before you into Galilee; there shall ye see him, as he said unto you. Remember how he spake unto you, when he was yet in Galilee; saying that the Son of man must be delivered up into the hands of sinful men, and be crucified, and the third day rise again."

And they went out and fled from the tomb, trembling. And for a time they said nothing to any one; for they were afraid.

"What mean these strange tidings, thinkest thou? Who could have taken away his body? Mayhap his enemies who murdered him. Have they not done enough, that they must needs disturb him in his last sleep?"

"Let us make haste. The woman may have been mistaken," answered John. "She is crazed with grief."

Then a strange thought—a remembrance of words long since spoken, and oftentimes repeated—flashed into his mind. "The third day!" he murmured.

Then he broke into a run, Peter following; and still running he came to the garden and to the tomb. The stone was rolled away, even as the woman had said, and stooping down, he looked in and saw the linen wrappings which had swathed the body. While he looked in amaze, not daring to enter, Peter also approached, and, seeing the open door, he went into the tomb and beheld the linen cerements, folded together, and the napkin which had lain upon the face of the dead, rolled up in a place by itself.

Then did John also come into the tomb, and there the mighty truth burst upon him. "He is not here. He is risen!" he said aloud—in the very words of the angel.

But Peter was sorrowfully silent. Then the two went away again unto their own home.

"Woman, why weepest thou?"

Now Mary of Magdala had followed them afar off, weeping. And when the disciples were gone away, she came alone to the tomb and stood at the door. "And as she wept, she stooped and looked into the tomb; and she beheld two angels in white sitting, one at the head, and one at the feet, where the body of Jesus had lain. And they said unto her, 'Woman, why weepest thou? Whom seekest thou?' She said unto them, ' Because they have taken away my Lord, and I know not where they have laid him.' "

Then she turned herself about, and saw, through the blinding mist of her tears, the figure of a man standing near. And he spake unto her; and his words were those of the angels who were in the tomb: " Woman, why weepest thou? Whom seekest thou?"

And she thought within herself: " This man is the gardener. Surely he can tell me." Clasping her hands, she said beseechingly:

" Sir, if thou hast borne him hence, tell me where thou hast laid him; and I will take him away."

Jesus—for it was he that had spoken—said unto her:

" Mary!"

And she knew his voice. In an ecstasy of joy she cried, " Rabboni!" and would have laid hold on him, as if to make sure that her sorrow-dazed senses were not deceiving her.

But he said unto her: " Lay not hold on me; for I am not yet ascended unto my Father; but go to my brethren, and say unto them, I ascend unto my Father, and your Father; and to my God, and your God." And he passed from out her sight.

And she came in great haste and joy, and made known these things unto the disciples, saying to them: " I have seen the Lord!"

" Now, behold, two of them went that same day to a village called Emmaus, which was from Jerusalem about threescore furlongs. And they talked together of all these things which had happened. And it came to pass, that, while they communed together and reasoned, Jesus himself drew near, and went with them. But their eyes were holden, that they should not know him.

" And he said unto them, ' What manner of communications are these that ye have one with another, as ye walk, and are sad?'

" And one of them, whose name was Cleopas, answering said unto him, ' Art thou only a stranger in Jerusalem, and hast not known the things which are come to pass there in these days?'

" And he said unto them, ' What things?'

" And they answered him, ' Concerning Jesus of Nazareth, which was a prophet mighty in deed and word before God and all the people; and how the chief priests and our rulers delivered him to be condemned to death, and have crucified him. But we trusted that it had been he which should have redeemed Israel: and beside all this, to-day is the third day since these things were done. Yea, and certain women also of our company made us astonished, which were early at the sepulchre; and when they found not his body, they came, saying that they had also seen a vision of angels, which said that he was alive. And certain of them which were with us went to the sepulchre, and found it even so as the women had said. But him they saw not.'

" Then he said unto them, ' O foolish ones, and slow of heart to believe all that the prophets have spoken! Ought not Christ to have suffered these things, and to enter into his glory?'

" And beginning from Moses and from the prophets, he interpreted to them in all the Scriptures the things concerning himself.

" And they drew nigh unto the village whither they went; and he made as though he would have gone further. But they constrained him, saying: ' Abide with us; for it is toward evening, and the day is far spent.'

" And he went in to tarry with them. And it came to pass, when he had sat down with them to meat, he took the bread, and blessed it, and brake, and gave to them. And their eyes were opened, and they knew him; and he vanished out of their sight.

" And they said one to another, ' Did not our hearts burn within us, while he talked with us by the way, and while he opened to us the Scriptures?'

" And they rose up that very hour, and returned to Jerusalem, and found the eleven gathered together, and them that were with them, saying, ' The Lord is risen indeed, and hath appeared unto Simon.'

" And they told what things were done in the way, and how he was known of them in the breaking of bread."

And while they were talking together of all that had happened, some of them as yet hardly daring to believe, so great was their joy and wonder, Jesus himself stood in the midst of them and said:

" Peace be unto you!"

But they were terrified; for they knew that the doors were shut, and they thought that they beheld a spirit.

And he said unto them, " Why are ye troubled? And why do thoughts arise in your hearts? Behold my hands and my feet, that it is I myself: handle me, and see; for a spirit hath not flesh and bones, as ye see me have."

And he saw their faces full of a great joy indeed, yet mingled with fear. He knew their hearts, that they loved him, yet, being in the flesh, the mystery of his resurrection was too great for them.

Looking at them with a love unutterable, he said gently, " Have ye here any meat?"-- being minded to show them that he was yet their own—not removed to an infinite and unapproachable distance, but the very Jesus who had loved them and cared for them and died for them.

And with trembling and great joy they brought broiled fish and a piece of honey- comb—their own homely and familiar food which he had shared with them so often. And he did eat before them.

Then did they crowd about him, and weep out their joy at his feet. And he talked with them a long time, and made all things as clear as might be to their human under- standing.

And he said unto them, " Thus it is writ- ten, and thus it behoved Christ to suffer, and to rise from the dead the third day; and that repentance and forgiveness of sins should be preached in his name among all nations, beginning at Jerusalem. And ye are witnesses of these things."

CHAPTER XXXII.

ARY the mother of Jesus was sitting motionless at the window of her chamber, her dark eyes fixed on the distant horizon. The look on her face was that of one who had suffered beyond the limit of human endurance, and to whom had come some heavenly panacea. Its peace was the peace of heaven.

As she sat thus musing within herself, some one entered the room and softly ap- proached. It was Stephen. Kneeling lightly at her side, he lifted the waxen fingers which lay idly in her lap, and pressed them to his lips.

" Mother of my Jesus!" he said, " thou knowest how I came to Jerusalem that I might search for Titus—and how that he hath entered into paradise, where he shall abide for evermore with him whom we love. Yet his mother knoweth not where he is."

Then he told her all that had happened, and how Malchus had said, " Let his mother remain in ignorance of the thing; she hath enough to bear."

And Mary turned the solemn radiance of her eyes upon him, as he knelt beside her, awaiting her answer.

" She must no longer remain in ignor- ance," she said at length. " Thou must tell her, and no other. Go, my son." And she rested her hand for a moment on his bowed head in silent blessing.

In the room overlooking the terrace in the house of Caiaphas, the sunshine flickered as cheerily as of yore, the fountain plashed, the birds sang joyously, and the odor of lilies was wafted in on every passing breeze. Yet was the face of its mistress sad; the work had slipped from her idle fingers; her eyes were heavy with unshed tears. She looked up as one of her maidens entered and made obeisance before her.

" What wilt thou, Reba?" she said wearily.

" Most noble lady," replied the maid, " there is a lad waiting in the court of the household. He would see thee and speak with thee. I told him that it could not be; but he was importunate and refused to go away until he had seen thee."

" Thou shouldst not have told him that it could not be, until thou hadst consulted my pleasure," said Anna. " Bring the lad into my presence."

The maiden bowed humbly and went away. Presently she returned.

" Here is the lad, most noble lady," she said; then obeying a motion of her mistress' hand, she went away, leaving the two alone.

Stephen regarded the lady before him with awe. The mother of his Titus! How should he tell her! How should he begin!

Anna saw his embarrassment; her heart went out toward the lad. The earnest and loving regard in his eyes stirred her strangely.

" What wilt thou?" she said very gently, with one of her rare smiles.

Stephen knew that smile—it was the smile of Titus himself! Drawing nearer, he said in a low tone which trembled with the depth of his feeling:

" Thou art the mother of my Titus. I am come to tell thee of him. He is no longer on earth. He is in paradise."

" Nay, I know not what thou meanest," said Anna. Yet she too trembled. " Who is thy Titus?"

" He is thy son. His name was David."

When the mother heard that name, she gave a sharp cry.

"Tell me!" she gasped. "Tell me all."

And Stephen in his own simple fashion told her all the short, sad story of Titus.

"Nay, mother of my Titus, weep not," he said beseechingly, when he had finished. "For is it not well with him? Had he not the promise of the Master, which hath never failed? Is he not safe? Is he not blessed—in paradise—"

"In paradise—yes," moaned the mother. "But I—I am on earth. And I know not whether I shall ever be with him."

"Thou shalt be with him one day, if thou dost believe in Jesus, who died and hath risen from the dead," said Stephen solemnly.

Upon hearing this, Anna raised her head. "What meanest thou?" she whispered.

"That Jesus hath come forth from the tomb, where they laid him cold and dead, after that he was crucified," said Stephen in joyous triumph. "That he is alive! With mine own eyes I have seen him, and I have heard his voice. And if he liveth, we shall live also; moreover he hath said that it is his will that we should be with him where he is. Thou shalt see thy son again. The Father is merciful."

Anna made no reply. She arose, and hastily wrapping herself in a mantle and veil which lay upon the divan near at hand, said tremulously:

"I must see the mother of Jesus. Take me to her."

And the two passed out into the street, the haughty lady following humbly after Stephen all the way till they reached the abode of Mary.

Then came they into the place where Mary was; and when the mother of Titus saw her, she gave a great and bitter cry and fell upon her neck weeping.

Stephen went softly away and left the two women together.

After a time they called for him, and he came into their presence trembling. He saw the face of Anna, that it shone through her tears with joy, even as the sun sendeth forth its beams through the clouds heavy with storm; and his heart grew light in his bosom.

"Come hither, my son," said Mary gently. And he drew near, and the mother of Titus gazed upon him long and earnestly.

"Thou wert nearest and dearest to him while he was upon the earth," she said at length. "I would that thou couldst be ever with me. Yet that may not be." And she turned to Mary with a tender smile. "I would not take thee from her—yet thou must be a son to me also, for thou wert his brother." And rising, she drew the lad to her side and kissed him solemnly upon his forehead.

And so it happened that Stephen found yet another friend—one that loved him all the days of his life. But full of triumph and joy and usefulness as was that life upon earth, it was not long. The world was not worthy of him; and God took him to himself after that he had revealed to him his glory while he was yet in the flesh.

CHAPTER XXXIII.

F I could but see him once more as of old!" said Peter longingly.

He was walking with John in his own garden in Capernaum, and certain others of the disciples were sitting on the wall at the water's edge, talking in low tones. They had come into Galilee according to the word of the Lord, and had gathered together a multitude of the disciples and had told them how that the Lord was risen from the dead. And on this peaceful evening of early summer they had been speaking of his mysterious appearance upon the mountain, where he was seen of over five hundred of the disciples.

"Thou wert not of them which doubted?" questioned John gravely.

"Nay, I doubted not. 'Twould ill beseem me—of all men—to question his mercy. But "—and he lowered his voice—" thou knowest that it was like a vision from heaven. And there were so many to see. If only I could speak with him once again face to face, and know that he hath forgiven me for my dastardly cowardice!" And he dashed the bright drops from his eyes.

Suddenly he turned, and looking out over the placid waters of the lake, now glowing with the thousand shifting tints of sunset, he exclaimed with something of his old energy: "I would fain go fishing to-night."

John looked somewhat surprised, but he only said: "Wilt thou that the others go also?"

"Assuredly," answered Peter. "Do thou speak with them. I will put the boat to rights and bring the nets."

So presently they all set forth, amid the deepening shadows of evening, just as they used to do. And as the boat glided gently along, floating, as it were, between two heavens, John looked forth over the mystic glory of the water as it reflected in its bosom the radiant sky, and murmured: " A sea of glass mingled with fire!"

They toiled all the night, yet caught nothing. When the morning was come, they made for the land, weary and faint.

And as they drew nigh unto the shore they beheld standing upon the water's edge the figure of a man, seen but dimly through the morning mist.

And he called to them and said: " Children, have ye any meat?"

And they answered him: " No."

And he said: " Cast the net on the right side of the ship, and ye shall find."

And they did as they were bidden; for they thought that he might have seen that look on the surface of the water which shows to one skilled in such things the presence of fish. And having cast the net, they were now not able to drag it for the multitude of the fishes.

Then did John, the disciple whom Jesus loved, stand up in the bow of the boat and gaze long and earnestly upon the man who stood upon the shore; and he knew him, and cried out with joy: " It is the Lord!"

And when Peter heard that it was the Lord, he girt his fisher's coat about him and, leaping into the water, swam ashore, and fell at the feet of the Master whom he had denied.

Now the other disciples, dragging the net full of fishes, came also to the shore; and they saw a fire of coals burning, and fish broiling thereon, and bread, just as of yore.

And their hearts were full as they gazed upon their risen Lord, and thought that even in his glory he remembered that they were hungry and must eat.

" And Jesus said unto them, ' Bring of the fish which ye have now caught.'

" Peter went and drew the net to land full of great fishes, an hundred and fifty and three; and for all there were so many, yet was not the net broken."

Then said Jesus unto them: " Come, and break your fast."

And he himself took of the fish, and gave to them: and also of the bread. And they ate and were satisfied.

After that they had eaten, Jesus fixed his eyes upon Peter and said to him: " Simon, son of John, dost thou love me more than these?"

And Peter answered eagerly: " Yea, Lord; thou knowest that I love thee."

" Feed my lambs," said the Master solemnly.

Then he asked him a second time: " Simon, son of John, dost thou love me?"

And again Peter made answer: " Yea, Lord; thou knowest that I love thee."

And Jesus said unto him solemnly as before: " Tend my sheep."

Then said he the third time: " Simon, son of John, dost thou love me?"

Peter was grieved when he said unto him the third time, " Dost thou love me?" Yet in his heart he knew the meaning of it all; had he not thrice denied, and was it not meet that he should thrice confess?

He fell on his knees before Jesus, and with tears cried out: " Lord, thou knowest all things; thou knowest that I love thee."

Jesus looked upon him with a deep tenderness in his eyes, so that the heart of Peter was satisfied. He knew that he was forgiven.

And again he said unto him: " Feed my sheep."

Then after a little silence he added: " Verily, verily, I say unto thee, when thou wast young, thou girdedst thyself, and walkedst whither thou wouldest: but when thou art old thou shalt stretch forth thine hands, and another shall gird thee and carry thee whither thou wouldest not."

And many years afterward, when the enemies of Christ bound Peter and bore him away to a martyr's death, these words were fulfilled. Yet was he triumphant unto the end through the love of his Lord and Master.

Not many days after this, the disciples went back to Jerusalem, according to the word of Jesus, that they might tarry there till the promise of the Father should be fulfilled. And Jesus met them there, and again talked with them; and they asked him: " Lord, dost thou at this time restore the kingdom to Israel?"

And he said to them: " It is not for you to know times or seasons, which the Father hath set within his own authority. But ye shall receive power when the Holy Spirit is come upon you: and ye shall be my witnesses, both in Jerusalem, and in all Judea, and in Samaria, and unto the uttermost parts of the earth. Go ye therefore, and make disciples of all the nations, baptizing them into the name of the Father, and of the Son, and of the Holy Ghost: teaching them to observe all things whatsoever I have commanded you: and lo, I am with you alway, even unto the end of the world." "And he led them out until they were over against Bethany: and he lifted up his hands, and blessed them. And it came to pass, while he blessed them, he parted from them, and a cloud received him out of their sight. And while they were looking steadfastly into heaven as he went, behold, two men stood by them in white apparel; and they said, 'Ye men of Galilee, why stand ye looking into heaven? This Jesus, which was received up from you into heaven, shall so come in like manner as ye beheld him going into heaven.'"

And they returned into Jerusalem with exceeding great joy, and were continually in the temple, praising and blessing God. And most of all did they rejoice in the word which he spake unto them: "Lo, I am with you alway, even unto the end of the world."

And he is with us to-day; for "he inhabiteth eternity." "He is the same yesterday, to-day, and forever,"—not a far-away Jesus in some remote and inaccessible glory:

"But warm, sweet, tender, even yet
A present help is he;
And faith has yet its Olivet,
And love its Galilee.

"The healing of the seamless dress
Is by our beds of pain;
We touch him in life's throng and press,
And we are whole again."

At this moment he is standing by thy side; wilt thou not fall at his feet and cry out, "Lord, thou knowest all things; thou knowest that I love thee!" Then will he lift thee at once from all thy weakness and sin; and thou shalt triumph gloriously through the power of his love.

And so at last we too shall one day be with him in paradise; and there "we shall be like him; for we shall see him as he is."

God grant that every one of us shall be numbered with that exceeding great multitude who shall stand before the throne, and before the Lamb, crying, "Worthy is the Lamb that was slain!"

"For they shall hunger no more, neither thirst any more; neither shall the sun light on them, nor any heat. For the Lamb which is in the midst of the throne shall feed them, and lead them unto fountains of living waters. And God shall wipe away all tears from their eyes."

APPENDIX.

To the readers of "Titus," I would say a word in regard to the book. Its purpose will, I hope, be evident to all. It is to present the life of Jesus upon earth in such a way as to give a fresh interest to the "old, old story;" to bring the Jesus of nearly nineteen centuries ago into our lives to-day—a real, a living Jesus, as tender, as loving, as thoughtful of his children who are upon earth now, as he was with the dwellers in Palestine.

In writing the story I have consulted many books on the subject by other authors, among which I would mention, as having been especially useful to me, "The Life and Words of Christ," by Dr. Geikie; also works by Edersheim, Stalker, Farrar, Hanna, Beecher, and others; as well as numerous Commentaries and Harmonies, together with Smith's Bible Dictionary—a host in itself; and leading books of travel in the Orient.

I found that tradition has handed down three groups of names for the thieves who were crucified with the Savior; Dysmas, or Demas, for the penitent thief, and Gestas for the impenitent, being the most generally accepted. A second tradition gives Titus for the penitent

and Dumachus for the impenitent thief. These names I chose for the characters in my book, for they seemed to me to be the most fitting. Other traditional names were Matha and Joca. It will be noticed that I used the names Gestas and Joca for certain of the robber band who were associated with Dumachus; it having occurred to me that the possible reason for the number of traditional names lay in the existence of just such a predatory band as I have described in my story.

In quoting the words of Christ throughout the story, as well as in the description of certain scenes, I have harmonized the words given us in the different Gospels. I have also used the Revised Version of the New Testament, as well as the Authorized Version, and in some cases have gone back to the original Greek, that there might be the greatest possible clearness and completeness of the narrative.

My prayer for this book is that it may go out into the world and preach the Gospel of Jesus.

And so farewell.

FLORENCE MORSE KINGSLEY.

West New Brighton, Staten Island, N. Y.